I0588949

SUCKERS

Book 3

Killing A Vampire

Jacky Dahlhaus

Folla Fiction Publishing

First published in February 2018

ISBN 978-0-9956719-2-8

jackydahlhaus.com

This book is a work of fiction. All characters and
events in this publication, other than those clearly in
the public domain, are fictitious and any resemblance
to real persons, living or dead, is purely coincidental.

Books written by Jacky Dahlhaus:

Releasing A Vampire

Living Like A Vampire

Raising A Vampire

Killing A Vampire

Short Shockers

jackydahlhaus.com

Contents

Interview

My decision to go on national television meant all my hopes and dreams for a quiet suburban life would be forever lost. Yet here I was, my hands sweaty and my breathing deliberate. It hadn't been an easy decision as there were more consequences. There had always been protesters, sucker-haters, but this time they had shown up in great numbers at the entrance of the studio, trying to prevent me from going in. The guards had to protect me and get me safely from the cab to the entrance. It would only get worse after the show. It would also trigger more interview requests, more paparazzi, more work. Something Charlie didn't agree with.

I picked up Sonny to distract myself from the anticipation, and while cuddling him, I waited for the signal.

"Ladies and gentlemen, please welcome Kate Clarke!" I heard the woman's voice say.

The man with the headphones and clipboard pointed at me. He mouthed, 'You're on,' and my adrenaline level peaked.

"Let's go, Mommy," Sonny said, a broad smile on his face.

I stepped onto the stage, sincerely hoping I wouldn't

trip with my son in my arms. The bright stage lights shone in my eyes and their warmth hit me with equal surprise. Emma, the show host, waited for me at the white couches. I put Sonny down before shaking her hand. Instead of giving Sonny a handshake, she ruffled his hair. The three of us sat down on the comfy two-seaters; Emma on one, Sonny and me on the other. I had expected Sonny to cuddle up with me, but he decided to occupy the other half of the couch, his legs just not reaching the end of the seating cushion.

Please don't let his shoes make any marks on the white fabric.

He bumped his feet together, never sitting completely still. When he caught my eye, he smiled at me.

"So glad you could make it, Kate," Emma said. "I see you brought your son, Sonny. Hi, Sonny." She beamed an extra broad smile at him. I presumed to make him feel at ease.

"Hi, Emma," he said to her. Sonny wasn't a shy boy at all.

"Sonny, why don't you give Emma the drawing you made for her?"

Sonny eagerly moved off the couch, took the drawing he had made out of his back pocket, and handed it to Emma.

"You're not going to bite me when I take it from you, are you?" Emma said to Sonny. He hesitated to answer, turning to me for help. "Just kidding, kiddo." Emma took the paper from Sonny's hand and with her other hand ruffled his hair again. "Aw, thank you, sweetie. That's so cute. It's me holding hands with Kate and Sonny." She showed the drawing to the audience. One of the cameramen ran up to take a close-up shot of the stick-figure drawing which instantly appeared on the big screen behind us. The audience 'aw'd' with Emma.

I patted the couch where Sonny had sat a moment ago. He climbed back onto the couch but cuddled up to me this time.

"You call him Sonny because he's your son. And of course, it's a good shortening of his full name, Nelson. Nellie would sound a bit strange." The audience laughed. "He isn't the son of your partner though, is he?"

"No, Sonny was conceived as a cruel experiment in the sucker internment camp."

"That must have been a terrible experience for you. Good things have come from it though. One of them is sitting right next to you." Emma smiled at Sonny again. "Isn't he adorable, ladies and gentlemen?" The audience agreed. I hugged Sonny as I completely agreed with Emma. "Another result of your predicament was that you became the head figure of SAMM, the Suckers Acceptance Movement in Maine. Can you tell us a bit more about what SAMM does?"

I shrugged as I let go of Sonny and leaned forward.

"SAMM tries to help integrate suckers into everyday life. When the *Succedaneum* virus plagued the world during Black October thirteen years ago, a lot of lives were lost. People blamed suckers for it, but it was actually the government who was the cause of the sucker pandemic as they made the virus and failed to contain it. People infected with it had no choice but to act upon their bloodlust. They aren't to blame. The vaccine they created eradicated most suckers from the planet, but there were cases in which it didn't work, when vaccination was too late to have any effect. These people will always be suckers, even though they didn't ask for it. Most children conceived during Black October ended up in an internment camp, but some parents were able to keep their sucker children out of the hands of the government. They kept them in hiding from the public out of fear of retribution. These children deserve to have a normal life as well. Sucker children should be able to grow up, have friends, and have a happy future like any other child. SAMM tries to help people accept suckers into their communities and to not be fearful of them. They are normal people with a disease, a manageable disease. Suckers aren't a threat to society anymore."

"That's so true," Emma said, "and you, of all people, know this first hand because you have two sucker children, don't you? Sonny, who is here with us today, and Sue, your older daughter. How old is Sue now?"

"Officially, Sue's twelve years old, but because sucker children grow twice as fast, she's already a fully grown adult. Sonny looks like he's ready to go to Kindergarten, but he's only two years old."

"And they don't display any of the aggressive behavior suckers did during Black October?" Emma asked. "Because that's what it's all about, isn't it; people fearing we'll have another Black October on our hands if we let suckers loose into the world."

"Absolutely not. Sucker children need a strict upbringing, I don't deny that. They need to be taught to be gentle as they are a lot stronger than other children. Otherwise, they are as playful, strong-willed, and cuddly as any other child. They still need to be loved."

"What about the older suckers? The ones for which vaccination came too late? Are they a threat to us? I mean, I don't want to walk next to one, and he suddenly 'fancies a snack.'" The audience laughed at Emma's comment. I didn't find it funny at all.

"There are still some suckers that have lived underground since Black October and haven't changed their attitude. SAMM is there for these people as well. Once these individuals are discovered, SAMM will guide and counsel them. With the help of the Army, we rehabilitate them, so they can live in our society once more. As you know, there is a mandate for every sucker to register and requiring them to give a DNA sample, so that if a biting incident happens, authorities will be able to tell which sucker has been the perpetrator. This system for suckers is similar to the fingerprint-system used by the justice department for virus-free humans."

"That's so comforting to hear. Now, I can't keep my eyes off your son as he's so adorable. He must be very special to you."

"He sure is, Emma."

Sonny just sat there, taking it all in his stride. It always amazed me how 'grown up' he was. As if he was an old soul.

"He's actually very special in a broader sense, isn't he? What time is it now? Early afternoon?" Emma made a show of looking at her watch. "And you both came here by cab. No under-cover-of-darkness stuff."

"That's right. Sonny's extra special because he's a daywalker."

"And not only a daywalker but also a half-blood which means he doesn't drink blood but eats meat, or so I'm told. Is this correct?"

"Yes, it's true. As a daywalker, he isn't affected by sunlight, and because he's a half-blood, his diet isn't limited to blood alone. He can also eat meat, but only raw meats."

"So, wouldn't it be handy if all suckers become meat-eating daywalkers? Problem solved?"

"I wish it were that easy, Emma, but there's only a

small window during the incubation of the virus when suckers can become daywalkers. Unless their mother was a daywalker, children are born true suckers and photo-phobic for life. It lessens over time, but they will always be affected and move slower in daylight. There also aren't many half-bloods around. Only a few special individuals appear to be immune to the aversion to mate with 'the others,' so to speak, and create a half-blood. I'm extremely lucky that both my children have come from such a union. They are both able to eat meat."

"I can't imagine what that would do to your grocery bill," Emma replied, and of course the audience laughed again. "It's better than getting blood from heaven knows where, though. Tell me, where do suckers get their blood from?"

"The virus changes the body, so, just like cats can't be vegetarians, suckers need to drink blood to survive. Fortunately, suckers can survive on animal blood which has been a huge waste product from slaughterhouses, and until recently, only a part of it was used to make fertilizer and food additives for animal feed. Most of it was dumped in sewers or landfill. Now it fills a gap in the market. It's treated to prevent the spread of diseases like mad cow disease, and bagged blood is currently available for human consumption in supermarkets, next to the blood sausages. It's one of the major triumphs of SAMM's efforts."

"I don't know if you know this, but I'm actually a vegan, and I'll tell you, my stomach content is churning with all this talk about consuming blood. I think it's time we end this conversation. It's been so nice talking to you and hearing about all the good work you've been doing with SAMM for suckers. I wish you all the best."

"Thanks, Emma. Thank you so much for having us on the show."

Emma rose from her seat, and so did Sonny and I.

"Ladies and gentlemen, Kate Clarke and her son Sonny!"

I waved at the audience as they applauded. Sonny copied me. We followed the instruction we had received earlier to leave the stage on the opposite side of where we had come from. Once backstage, a woman took off my microphone and guided us to the room downstairs where our belongings were. I took off the make-up they had put on and donned my jacket. I then put Sonny in his jacket and gave him a kiss.

"Time for us to leave, Little Man. Let's see if we still have a home to go to."

Missing

The flight from California back to the Portland airport in Maine was about six hours long. The total trip back home took over eight hours, and I was exhausted by the time the cab pulled up on our drive. Sonny had fallen asleep hours ago and continued sleeping when I lifted him out of the cab. No light shone from the house, and I assumed Charlie had gone to bed already. Normally, he would leave one light on for me to find my way, but not this time. Maybe he forgot. Maybe it was deliberate.

I had tried to call him from the airport, before we got onto the plane to LA, but couldn't get a hold of him. His cell had gone straight to voicemail. I had assumed he was busy with something at the time, making it impossible for him to answer, and expected a message from him by the time we had landed. I had been so disappointed when there wasn't. As a taxi brought us to the studio, I had tried to call him again but still couldn't get through to him. Either the battery of his cell was dead, or he was still pissed off because of what I had said to him before I left.

Once inside, I left my travel case in the living room and continued upstairs. I carefully lowered Sonny onto his bed. As I undressed him, he stirred a little but put his arm around his teddy bear and slept on. After I pulled the duvet over him, I kissed his cheek. He was such an easy child, just like Sue had been. Time flew by so fast with them growing up at double speed. Sometimes I was jealous of parents having normal children and able to enjoy their kids twice as long. I sighed and reminded myself I was blessed with both my children being healthy.

Well, physically speaking.

Sue's mental health worried me. I sort of expected her having nightmares after watching two men die violently when we escaped the sucker internment camp, but after three years, she still suffered them. Thank heavens we had a good friend who was a general practitioner, and Harry was able to diagnose her with PTSD pretty soon. He had prescribed drugs and cognitive behavioral therapy. The drugs made a difference, made her sleep without nightmares, but I didn't like her being reliant on them. It was only a treatment of the symptoms, not taking the cause away.

In the beginning, Sue and I argued about her thinking she was to blame for the deaths until Sue had made it very clear she didn't want to talk about it with me anymore. Her therapist, Dr. Strang, had instructed me not to push her, so I had stopped bringing up the subject. Unfortunately, Dr. Strang didn't seem to make any progress with her either.

Sonny was still untroubled by the world's events and

the happiest kid you could imagine. I turned off the light in his room and sighed, hoping my son would stay happy for a long time. As quietly as I could, I closed Sonny's bedroom door.

Taking a few steps down the stairs to get my travel case, I changed my mind and went back up to the landing. I decided to see Charlie first as we desperately needed to talk. I tiptoed into our dark bedroom and slipped my hands under the duvet, searching for Charlie's shape. Moving further and further, causing the duvet to be pushed in my face, my hands reached the other side of the bed.

What the...?

Now lying across our empty bed, I threw the duvet out of my way and turned on the bedside lamp. I squinted at the sudden, bright light. By the time my eyes had adjusted, I knew I wasn't mistaken. Charlie wasn't in the room.

Strange.

I checked my cell phone. It still didn't show any messages from him. Noting the time, I realized it was way too late to call anyone. A yawn escaped me, and I decided to wait and see. I figured Charlie would surely show up in the morning.

Lying in bed, alone, there was a niggle in the back of my mind that something wasn't quite right.

***

The continuous beeping of the alarm clock woke me up.

Why doesn't he turn the damn thing off?

I rubbed my eyes and opened them. The bed was empty next to me. I strained to listen over the sound of the alarm but didn't hear the shower running. Then I remembered yesterday. I reached out and turned the maniacal sound off.

Where can Charlie be?

I took my cell from the charger and pressed Charlie's speed dial button. Again, the phone immediately went to voicemail. I then called Sue. It didn't take her long to answer.

"Morning, Mom," she said. Her voice sounded like she'd been up a while.

"Morning, Little Smudge. How are you today? Did you sleep well?" I was certain my voice betrayed I had just woken up.

"Sure did. Good to hear you're back. How did the interview with Emma go? Is she really that crazy?"

Kitchen noises sounded in the background. Marlon must have come home for an early morning coffee. Farmhands never got to sleep in.

"Yeah, it was fun." I sat up against the headboard, pulling the duvet with me. "I don't know what she's like in real life. I only saw her on stage. Hey, is Dad with you?" I plucked at some pilling on the duvet cover.0

You need to throw these old rags out and buy a new one, girl.

"No. Why would he be? Isn't he home with you?"

Crap.

My hand stopped plucking. "No. No, he's not. Your father wasn't here when I got home last night. Do you have any idea where he could be? Did he mention he was going out at all?"

"No, not to me. Marlon?" The sound became muted as she put her hand over the speaker. "Have you heard from my Dad? Any idea where he could be at the moment?" Muffled murmurs didn't sound optimistic. "No? Okay. Nope, Mom. Marlon hasn't heard from him either. Maybe he's with Uncle Harry. Why don't you try him?"

"Yeah, I'll give him a call. He's probably there. I'll be dropping Sonny off shortly, so I'll see you soon." We said our goodbyes, and I ended the call.

Where the hell can that man be?

A sound came from the hallway. It startled me. Was it Charlie? I jumped out of bed. A hint of disappointment washed over me as I found out the sound was made by Sonny, shuffling sleepily through the hallway on his way to use the bathroom. I kissed him good morning after which he continued his mission. My mission to find Charlie took me into Sonny's bedroom. Alas, it was as empty as my own. I hurried to check downstairs, but everything there was still dark. Back upstairs, I put Sonny under the shower before I had one myself. By the time we sat down for breakfast, I finally had the nerve to text Harry.

Please, Smudge, be at Harry's.

I checked the time on my cell before I contacted Harry. His surgery would already be in full swing, so I didn't expect him to pick up the phone. I asked him in a text if Charlie had stayed the night with him and Rhona. Five minutes later, Harry called me back.

He must have a cancelation.

"Hi, Harry."

"Hi, Kate. What's up? Why are you asking if Charlie stayed with us?" he asked. "He never does."

"I know, but Charlie didn't come home last night. He still isn't home. I'm worried. Have you heard from him since yesterday?"

"No, we haven't seen him since last Friday. Have you tried Sue?" he asked.

"Yeah, I have, but they haven't heard from him either. I'd hoped he was with you guys."

"I'm sorry, but I'm afraid I can't help you, Kate," Harry said.

A silence followed. I suddenly realized Sonny was following the entire conversation. I gave him a quick smile, but he didn't return it.

"It's very out of character for Charlie not to come home," Harry said. "I don't want to worry you, but have you tried the police? It's probably nothing, but I think you should check." His voice now had the same worried edge as mine.

We're fooling each other. What fun.

"I know. I'm probably worried about nothing." I put on a brave face, to take the edge off for Sonny. "He'll probably turn up with a silly reason for not coming home. I'll give them a call."

"Let me know if I can help in any way. See you tomorrow?" Harry said.

"Tomorrow?"

"Remember, my party." I didn't react. "To celebrate me becoming an associate in the practice. Don't tell me you've forgotten, Kate."

I pressed my fist against my forehead.

"Ah, that party. No, I haven't forgotten, not at all. But... I don't know, Harry. I've got to find Charlie first."

"Kate, I'm sure he'll have turned up before then. You'll see."

"Let's hope so."

"Gotta go. Don't forget, tomorrow at seven." Harry hung up, no doubt already late for his next patient.

"Where could Charlie be, Mommy?" Sonny said as soon as I put my cell phone away.

Sonny calling Charlie by his first name hurt me now more than ever, but Charlie had insisted on Sonny not calling him Dad from the beginning, and that's the way it was. I could see Charlie's point of view, but to me, it was a constant reminder of my one-time indiscretion.

"I don't know where he is, Little Man. That's what I'm trying to find out." I stroked his cheek and kissed his forehead. I then cleared the table, and when I had put the dishes in the dishwasher, I said, "Let's go to the farm, shall we?"

"Okidoki." Sonny slid off the chair to go and put his shoes on.

Check, Check, Double Check

When Sonny and I arrived at Julie's farm, I parked at Sue and Marlon's place, set back from the other buildings. It had come as a surprise to Charlie and me over a year ago when Sue told us she wanted to move out of our home and go live with Marlon. Ever since Marlon's participation in our rescue from the suckers internment camp, Sue had been in love with him. He loved Sue back and was very good to her. Charlie and I had agreed only reluctantly after Julie had offered to build them a small bungalow on her farmland. I was happy for Sue to live near her auntie and not too far from me, glad she and Marlon hadn't decided to live in Portland. I would've been devastated if Sue had have moved so far away from me.

As I got Sonny's bag out of the car, Marlon came down the steps. Sonny flew into his arms upon which he lifted my boy up above his head with ease. Marlon's long, black hair flew out as he whirled Sonny around like a plane. Sonny screamed with delight. Marlon's love for Sue's little brother added to my affection for him. I wasn't sure if it was his Penobscot heritage or the fact he was a sucker child which made him a pleasure to behold as well. Whichever the case, I could see why Sue

17

had fallen for him.

"Hi Marlon, good to see you."

"Morning, Kate." He put Sonny back on the ground. "Go and see Sue inside, Little Man." Sonny didn't need to be told twice and ran as fast as he could to find his big sister.

"How did she sleep?" I asked as I walked up to Marlon.

"As I recall, she told you already, and I've informed you a week ago her new medication works well." He folded his arms in front of him and stuck out his chin in a playful manner.

"I know, I know. I just keep hoping she won't need them one day. You know my point of view. When's she seeing Dr. Strange again?"

"She's seeing Dr. *Strang* next Thursday."

"Just kidding. Let me know how it went once she's back."

"Will do. Hey, what's this about Charlie missing?" Marlon stuck both his hands into his front pockets. I held out the bag with Sonny's stuff in it until he took it from me with a cheeky grin. He shouldered the bag, and together we walked toward the front door.

"When I arrived home late last night, he wasn't there. There were no signs of him having been home from work at all. No dishes in the sink, no empty beer cans, nothing. He's not at Harry's place either. I checked. I have no idea where he could be."

"Very odd. It's not like Charlie at all to take off unannounced. What can we do to help?" Marlon said as he held the front door open for me.

"Nothing that I can think of at the moment, but I'll let you know when I do." I stepped inside.

Their bungalow's modern, open-plan design let me see immediately that Sue had given Sonny another bowl of minced meat in the kitchen.

"My god, child," I said, "you'll grow to be a giant, I'm sure of it." Sonny looked up at me while he continued to stuff his face, his eyes not hiding his mischievousness. "And you shouldn't feed him, Sue. I know you don't have the income to match his hunger." I pulled out my wallet. "Here's some cash. Also, could you take your brother to daycare for me today? I need to go find your father."

"Thanks, Mom. And don't be too hard on Dad when you find him."

"Of course not." I 'accidentally' showed the crossed fingers behind my back, and Sue slapped my arm playfully.

"I've got to go. I'll pick your brother up later this afternoon." I hugged Sue and gave Marlon a peck on the cheek. "Give me a hug, Little Man."

Sonny stood on his chair, jumped off, making the chair fall over, and flew into my open arms. The force of his jump made me take a step back.

"Careful there, Little Man. Don't break your sister's

furniture," I chuckled.

"Sorry," Sonny said to Sue, who had already picked up the chair.

"Don't worry, little brother," she said with affection.

"Now," I said, "have fun at daycare. And be extra nice if there are any new children."

"I will, Mommy. Find Daddy, please."

His words made a lump well up in my throat.

"I will, sweetie," I whispered as I gave him another hug before I handed him over to Sue and hastened to my car, blinking as frequently as I could without seeming to have something in my eye. Sue followed me outside with Sonny in her arms. I waved a quick goodbye without making eye contact and drove off.

Deep down in my gut, I knew there was something very, very wrong. Not sure if it had something to do with Sonny calling Charlie 'Daddy' or with something else entirely, but whatever it was, it made me break the speed limit to get to the Bullsbrook police station.

***

After I parked the car, I didn't get out.

Did you check all options before making a fool of yourself, Kate?

I took out my cell and phoned Julie. My sudden urge to go to the police station had made me completely forget to visit her at the farm to discuss the day's schedule for SAMM. But that wasn't why I called her.

"Hi sis, where are you? Aren't you coming in today? Should I be worried?"

Julie was always worried about something. She had the farm to think of, but also the school. When we started SAMM together, the first thing we had done was set up classes for sucker children at Bullsbrook High. Those that had been kept in hiding since birth hadn't had a proper education, and we wanted to make sure they received one. There hadn't been much of a problem organizing classes since they happened at night and didn't clash with normal daytime lessons. Although it was I who predominantly managed the sucker school, Julie kept an eye on issues when I was busy with council meetings and interviews. She did an amazing job, and I always wondered how she managed to keep her sanity. It probably made a difference she was single and had no kids.

"Hi, Jules. No, I'm not coming in today." I didn't tell her I was at Sue's place fifteen minutes ago.

"How did the interview go? How was Emma? Was it fun?"

"Yeah, it was fun. A bit on the short side for such a long trip, but I got to say what I wanted to say. Great promo for SAMM."

"But what was Emma like? Tell me all about it," Julie insisted.

"Sorry, Jules, I'll tell you another time. I need to

know if you've heard anything from Charlie. Did he call you at all yesterday?"

"No. Why? What's up, sis? You sound weird."

Thanks, Jules. You know how to make a girl feel better. Not.

"Charlie didn't come home yesterday, didn't come home last night. I can't reach him, Jules. His cell goes to voicemail. I have no idea where he is."

"That's weird. Do you think something might have happened to him? Do you think he may have had an accident? Did you check with Harry?"

"Of course I checked, and with Sue too. Neither of them has heard from him. I don't know what to do."

"Did you check with the school? Maybe he went to work, fell ill, and a friend from school took him home? That's a possibility."

I suppressed huffing at her. Julie knew Charlie didn't have any close friends at school, so mentioning this option was far-fetched. Still, it was possible Charlie went home with another teacher for whatever reason.

"No, I haven't checked with the school yet. I'll give them a call. Maybe he's there already."

"I'm sure there's a bizarre reason for him not coming home last night," Julie said.

It's possible the reason isn't that bizarre.

"I'm sure you're right."

"Okay, sis. Gotta go. I've got a second call coming through. Probably another interview request for you,

I'll let you know. Keep me up to date about Charlie's whereabouts. Love you."

"Love you too."

I dialed the school number, hoping they could tell me if Charlie had been injured during one of his woodwork classes or had suddenly come down with a bug and was taken to the Portland hospital. Mary, the receptionist, told me she was glad I called as she had been trying to reach me all morning but got an engaged dial tone every time. After I explained the situation to her, she told me Charlie had taught his art classes as normal yesterday. He was, however, missing in action this morning. That's why she had been trying to call me.

She also told me she wasn't happy she had to arrange for a substitute to come in, and that she had to deal with the class herself until he arrived which caused disruption to her morning routine. She went on and on about how teachers were supposed to tell the school well in advance of any absences.

Well, I'm sorry he has caused you such an inconvenience, but Charlie could be lying dead in a ditch for all I know.

Mary's admonition irritated the hell out of me. It wasn't as if I had misplaced my keys or something trivial like that. Listening to her whining, I pretended to strangle the girl through the phone. After I hung up, I closed my eyes and took a few deep breaths to calm myself down. When I opened my eyes again, I expected to feel better but couldn't stop thinking negative thoughts.

I got out of the car and hurried into the police station.

Police Report

It was quiet inside the red brick building. I heard a fluorescent tube buzz. Someone was using a photocopier in a backroom. The occasional person walked through the office, but I was alone in the lobby.

Bullsbrook, the safest country town in Maine.

I approached the wooden counter. There was a young man in uniform behind the window, sitting perpendicular to the counter, frantically typing away on a computer. I tried to see what was on the screen but couldn't. My glance drifted back to the face of the young man. It was so devoid of hair that he looked as if he should still be in school.

"Excuse me," I said as close as I could to the holes in the Perspex barrier.

He scared me half to death when he jumped in his chair and clicked away on his mouse as if relaying a Morse code. Had I caught him watching porn?

On a police computer? I think not. He was probably emailing his girlfriend or his mother in the boss's time.

Once he realized it was only me, he got up and straightened himself, the blush disappearing from his face.

"So sorry, Ma'am. I didn't hear you come in. What

can I do for you?" He now sported a big smile.

I looked over my left and right shoulder before answering.

How can he not have heard? The place is dead quiet.

"I'd like to report a missing person."

"A... a missing person," the boy repeated.

I could almost imagine what went through his mind.

The leap of joy at the presentation of a 'real' case. The anticipation of doing the very thing why he'd joined the force and finally be able to help innocent people fight the monsters. The relief of boredom from domestic abuse and stolen goods. Some real detective work for a change.

"Gimme a minute, and I'll find the form you need to fill in." He sat down and vigorously typed away on his computer.

Or maybe he was just trying to remember what form goes with that.

I turned around and leaned with my back against the counter as I waited for baby boy blue here to find the correct form. I noticed a board on the wall. Pinned on it, pamphlets with headshots caught my eye. I strolled over to have a closer look. Missing; a young girl of seventeen, gone missing after attending a party. Missing; an adult man, last seen eight months ago. Missing; another teenager, last seen 3 years ago. There were many more. So many people appeared to be missing. My hand grabbed my throat in an attempt to stop the bile rising, and my eyes sought a bin, in case I was going to be sick.

"Excuse me, Ma'am. I've got the form," the young man behind the desk called out to me.

Glad of the distraction, I inhaled deeply and returned to the counter. I stuck my hand out to receive the form through the slit at the bottom of the Perspex barrier, but the boy didn't give it to me. Instead he pressed a button, and I heard a click to the side of the counter. A door opened.

"Please come through," the young officer said.

I followed him into a room to the side of the open plan office. It was empty except for a table and a few chairs. "Please fill in the form and the detective will be with you shortly." He laid the form and a pen on the table.

"Thanks," I said and sat down.

The young man left and shut the door behind him.

The form was printed on dull, gray paper. I picked up the pen and began reading. First, they wanted to know the victim's details.

I don't know if he's a victim of anything yet. I only know he's missing.

I filled in Charlie's name, address, and description. I left the vehicle details blank. Then, they wanted to know the circumstances of the missing person's disappearance. I wrote, 'Didn't come home after work.' The next section was titled 'the complainant's details.'

'Complainant'... Hmm, wrong word choice. 'Worrier' is more like it.

I resisted the urge to put a line through the word 'complainant' and filled in the section. When I was certain there was nothing else for me to fill in, I waited. I racked my brain if I had seen a coffee machine en route to this room as I was dying for some caffeine. Without another distraction available, I began the nasty habit of biting my nails.

After what seemed like an eternity, the door finally opened, and a tall man stepped through. He wasn't in uniform, so I guessed he had to be the detective. His heavy, dark eyebrows and a fair bit of gray in his hair immediately gave him a stern appearance.

"I'm Detective Grayson. I'll be asking you some questions," he said as he sat down opposite me. His voice had a nice, low timbre, matching the warmth in his light-brown eyes which I could now see.

The man didn't do with handshakes, probably because his hands were filled with two plastic cups. He put them on the table and carefully pushed one in my direction. He slid his now free hand over his styled hair, making sure his locks were still in place.

"I hope you like your coffee black. We're out of sugar, and I don't trust the milk."

I embraced the cup as if it was my savior. "Black is fine," I said and took a sip. As soon as the liquid touched my taste buds, my face scrunched up.

I didn't know they could mistreat coffee this bad.

Grayson didn't see my face contort as he had picked up the form and was reading my answers.

"So…" he said as he rasped his fingers over the stubble on his jaw, "Charlie… didn't come home last night."

"Yes. I mean no, he didn't. I'm worried."

"Has Charlie stayed out all night before?"

"No."

"Never?"

"Never. Well, not since we've been together and from that moment onward, not without my knowledge of where he was. We've been together for thirteen years, so I kinda know what he's like."

"Hmm. What was the last conversation you had with him like? Did you argue about anything?"

Crap.

"Look, it was nothing. We argued over the work I was doing for SAMM yesterday morning—"

"Sorry, who's Sam?" Grayson cut in.

I stared at the man. All the work, all the advertising, all the publicity I had organized over the last three years, and he told me he had never heard of SAMM.

"SAMM is a 'what,' not a 'who.' It stands for the Suckers Acceptance Movement in Maine. We help integrate suckers into society, especially the children."

Grayson nodded. "Okay. Yes, I've heard of them. I do recognize you now."

Thank you.

"Go on. So what was your argument about?" he said.

I sighed as I recalled the last words I had exchanged with Charlie.

"Well, as you know, I am a spokesperson for SAMM which means I am out a lot, often taking Sonny with me." Grayson raised his eyebrows. "Sonny's our son, he's two. Charlie doesn't want me to take him along to these meetings. He prefers him to have a more settled upbringing. We actually argued quite a lot about this lately." I plucked at a loose piece of plastic on the side of the table.

"What were your exact last words to each other?" Grayson asked.

The man appeared to have a cunning ability to spot trouble. Tears welled up in my eyes and my chest constricted.

"I... I told Charlie to shut up as Sonny wasn't his to worry about."

It had been, of course, the most stupid thing to say. Apart from not being his biological father and Charlie's refusal to have Sonny call him Dad, Charlie was Sonny's father in every other aspect.

It was, of course, also the most stupid thing to say to the detective right then.

"Okay. Harsh words." Grayson pouted his lips. "Did Charlie know your son isn't his?" He folded his hands together in front of him, his face devoid of any judgment.

"Yes, he knew even before Sonny was born. Listen, Charlie and I have a great relationship. He's my sun and moon. Yes, we argued, but doesn't every other couple once in a while? The argument wasn't that big a deal for him to walk out on us." My eyes fixed on Grayson's. I had to convince him that Charlie would never leave us.

Would he?

The Relief Teacher

Grayson shrugged and didn't continue his questioning. He already got out of me how I really felt about Charlie.

"I don't want to alarm you," he said, "but I checked the Bullsbrook medical center and the Portland hospital before I came in. Just in case he got involved in a car crash or a fight. There's no record of anybody being brought in unconscious or seriously injured in the last twenty-four hours."

I gave the detective a quick smile. Harry would have called me if Charlie had been brought to the medical center, and I'm sure he'd checked the Portland hospital by now as well. Nevertheless, hearing from the detective that Charlie wasn't lying somewhere unconscious in a hospital bed eased my mind.

"Charlie getting involved in a car crash is very unlikely. He doesn't drive."

"He doesn't drive?" Grayson repeated.

"No. We live near the school, so Charlie can walk to work. He prefers me to use the car to go shopping and such, not wanting to adapt our car every time we switched being drivers." Grayson's brow creased into a frown. "Charlie's a dwarf," I said.

Grayson checked the form again, his eyes following

my words of Charlie's description all the way to the end.

Maybe you should have mentioned it first, Kate.

"Oh, I see. And he went to work as normal yesterday, you say?"

"Yes, he's been at school, I checked, but there's no evidence he came home."

"This means something must have happened to him on his way home from work. Right, let's go for a drive." Grayson stood up and took both our cups as well as the form from the table before he held the door open for me. I saw him chuck the cups into a bin which contained more half-filled cups than empty ones. He then gave the form to the young man at the reception desk and held the door to the lobby open for me.

"George, I'm going out," Grayson said to the boy. "Please log the details of the form into the system. Call my cell if you need me."

"Will do, sir," the rookie answered.

Grayson led me to his dark blue sedan. Again, he held the door open for me like a true gentleman. Charlie never opened the car door for me. Not that he wasn't a gentleman. It was just because I was always the driver, and the situation didn't call for it. I didn't mind.

The exterior of the car was dented and faded, unlike the interior which was well maintained and tidy. Grayson put his body into the driver's seat with grace. Guessing the man's age was difficult as the amount of gray in his hair confused me. It made him look over fifty, but there were hardly any lines around his eyes which suggested a far younger age. I grinned when I realized Grayson resembled his car like dog owners resembled their pets.

"Let's start at the school," he said as he put his key into the ignition.

***

Our country town wasn't that big a place, so within minutes we arrived at Bullsbrook High. Like the police station, the school was extremely quiet. The first period had begun half an hour ago, and all students sat in classrooms.

Grayson and I got out of the car. We obtained visitors passes at the reception from Mary. She tried to get more information about what was going on from us, but Grayson was tight-lipped.

"Show me the classroom where Charlie normally teaches," Grayson said to me.

I walked him to the auxiliary building that housed the arts department, and in there lead the way to Charlie's room. Charlie had been teaching at Bullsbrook High for thirteen years now and had sort of laid claim to the room. As soon as I opened the classroom door, I saw the relief teacher. My heart stopped as did my body, abruptly, and Grayson bumped into me.

"Oops, sorry. Didn't mean to do that," he muttered even though it wasn't his fault.

I didn't react to his words. My hand remained frozen on the door handle while my eyes were locked with my rapist.

No. Attempted rapist, remember.

Grayson walked around me. He followed my gaze at John, whose stare was locked on me, and back at me again.

"Why don't you stay in the hallway," Grayson said. "I'll take it from here." He pried my hand from the door handle and gently pushed me out of the classroom, closing the door behind me.

Once alone, I inhaled deeply and closed my eyes.

It's in the past. He can't hurt you now.

When I opened my eyes, I slumped against the door, letting my breath escape, and my hands became fists.

I thought you'd be able to deal with it by now, Kate.

All my muscles tensed again, reminding me of the lean, mean fighting machine I was after three years of training martial arts with Marlon, and that I had no reason to be afraid of John.

Son-of-a-bitch.

I hit the wall with the back of my fist. Three years ago, John had initiated a chain reaction, causing pain and misery to my family. Emma's words rang in my ears, reminding me that a lot of good had come of it too.

Besides, John hadn't actually gotten what he wanted. He hadn't gotten to third base with me.

But he's teaching Charlie's class now. Isn't that what he actually wanted?

My jaw dropped, and I clamped my hand over my mouth.

Would he have something to do with Charlie's disappearance?

I turned around and peeked through the narrow glass panel of the door. The children were all sitting at their desks, working individually on a drawing of some sort. Grayson stood bent over Charlie's desk, rummaging through a drawer. John stood near the windows, his long arms folded in front of his skinny body. He must have noticed my movement, and our eyes locked once again. Automatically I shut mine. I immediately forced them open and stared back. This time, I wasn't letting him get the better of me.

I opened the door and made my way to him with a purposeful step. Grayson noticed me but didn't say anything. He did change his position to an eye on us. I stood next to John, facing the class. The children had looked up when I had walked in, but, as nothing happened, they continued working silently on their drawing project, the design of a garden tool. It was one of Charlie's standard projects for ninth graders. John looked at me from the corner of his eye.

"So, you're teaching Charlie's class," I whispered.

"You finally got what you wanted after all these years?"

"No, I didn't get what I wanted," he whispered back. "Your fuckin' daughter interfered, remember?" He turned his head to me to make sure I saw his smile.

He damned well knew I meant Charlie's job. It was so like him to twist my words and remind me of the time he'd had control over me.

"You bring Charlie back, or I'll make sure she finishes the job, you hear me," I hissed at him.

"So, that's what this is all about," he said, his glance flinching toward Grayson. "Charlie finally realized what a bitch you are and took off, didn't he?"

My moves were fast. The kick to the back of his knee made him lose balance, and my backward arm swing easily pushed him over. John was lying on his back before he knew it. The children jumped out of their seats. Grayson dashed over and held onto my arm, preventing me from making the follow-up hit to John's face. Grayson yelled at the kids to sit down and dragged me out of the classroom.

Halfway down the hallway, I tried to yank myself free from his grip.

"You can let go of me now. I'm not going to run back to that moron."

Grayson eyed me with suspicion but let go of my arm.

"Would you mind telling me what that was all about?" he said as we continued to walk to his car.

"John Smith is a vindictive, brainless rapist. He forced himself upon me three years ago. He's always been jealous of Charlie getting the job he wanted while he had to make do with the janitor position."

Grayson had his hand on the handle of the car door. I waited for him to open it. When he didn't, I looked up, finding him staring at me.

"So he would have a motive to get rid of Charlie?" he said.

The Lunchbox

I didn't reply Grayson immediately.

"Yes, he would, but no, I don't think he did it. I told John to bring Charlie back just then, and his response was one of surprise. He didn't know why you were there. I don't think he's got anything to do with this."

"Pity," Grayson said. He hit the fob button after which we got in.

We drove slowly as Grayson followed my directions. We were trailing Charlie's walking route from school to home. Grayson had told me he had found nothing suspicious in Charlie's desk, and that this was the next step. I had no idea what we were looking for. Grayson had said he didn't know either but insisted we do it anyway.

It was drizzling, and the streets were deserted apart from those folks who obviously had no choice but to be out in the rain. A crow cawed carelessly in the distance. October was normally a pretty time of the year, but so far, it had only been wet and cold.

"Those were some impressive moves back there," Grayson said. "Where did you learn them?"

"Thanks. For the last three years I've been training martial arts with Marlon, my daughter's partner. He's a sucker child, daywalker. After John had attacked me, I vowed to make sure I was able to take care of myself in the future. I could've done a lot more damage to John if you'd let me."

"I bet you could have. I bet you could," Grayson said as he scanned the street and drummed his thumbs on the steering wheel, "but if you had, I'm afraid I would've had to arrest you." He threw me a quick sideway glance. "He may press charges for assault, you know."

"He deserves a good kick in the nuts," I said, keeping my chin up.

Grayson began a speech on hate crime and violence, and how it wasn't worth it. I knew he was right, but I wasn't in the mood for a lesson on morals right now. I didn't interrupt him, but let the memories of when I had kicked Caleb in the nuts overtake my thoughts. How I wanted it had been John both those times instead. Caleb had not deserved to get so cruelly hurt by me.

An ache surged through me. It hurt still every time I thought about how Sonny would never know his father. I sighed. Focusing on the street, trying to divert my thoughts, I heard Grayson now talking about the statistics of crime. Then I spotted it.

"Stop the car," I yelled.

Grayson hit the brake. I jumped out and ran toward the little, yellow, plastic box lying in the mud. I didn't pick it up. Grayson parked the car and joined me.

"Is it his?" he asked.

"I'm not sure. Can I touch it?"

"No, it's better to be safe than sorry. Your fingerprints will very likely be on it already if it is his, but we don't want to smudge any that shouldn't belong there."

Upon hearing his words, my throat closed up, and I squeezed my eyes shut, trying to swallow the lump away.

"It doesn't mean anything, you know," Grayson said as he put his hand on my arm. "He could've just dropped it while he tried to catch the bus." I looked up to find him pointing at the bus stop sign not too far away. I smiled weakly at Grayson. His face was kind and reminded me of my father. There wasn't a single feature on his face that has any resemblance to my Dad, though. It was the look in his eyes, the caring, fatherly look. But my father had died during Black October, and I didn't want Grayson to take his place.

I averted my eyes and waved my free arm vaguely in the air. "It's not that. You said 'smudge.' That's my nickname for Charlie."

"Oh, sorry. I didn't know. Strange nickname." Grayson let go of my arm.

"It's a long story."

I took a packet of paper tissues out of my pocket to blow my nose. The rain wet the tissue and made it almost fall apart when I used it. I returned the soggy clump of paper filled with watery snot back into my pocket.

Grayson waited for me to explain my comment, but when I remained silent, he walked over to his car and returned with surgical gloves and a plastic zip-lock bag. He took a photo of the yellow box lying on the ground with his cell phone, and, after putting on the gloves, put the box into the zip-lock bag.

"I'm sure it's Charlie's now," I said. "See, it's got his name on it."

Grayson turned the lunchbox the right way up. It had been lying upside down in the dirt, and I hadn't been sure. The name of Charlie branded in the lid of the box took all doubt away. Stickers Sue had put on when she had given the box to Charlie as a birthday present so many years ago, now half-washed off and faded, surrounded his name.

Grayson wrote some details on the bag with a permanent marker. We looked around the area where we found the lunchbox and found Charlie's cell phone not far off. Grayson checked if it still worked, but the batteries were dead. He secured it in a zip-lock bag as well. We couldn't find anything else lying around that belonged to Charlie.

"Well, that's it. I'll drive you back to the police station," Grayson said and turned to go back to the car.

"Hang on. Shouldn't we call in a forensics team or something?"

"No, the rain has washed away any footprints or any other traces." The drizzle had indeed developed into a good shower by now. "Besides, there's still no evidence of a crime. Maybe he just doesn't want to be found."

My stomach knotted itself into a ball, and that annoying crow cawed in the distance again.

"Charlie's missing, Grayson. He didn't come home. Something must have happened to him. He would never throw away his cell or his lunchbox. He wouldn't just up and leave and not tell us about it." I resisted the urge to stamp my foot.

"He wouldn't be the first to go out for a packet of cigarettes and not come back," Grayson said before he got into his car.

Charlie doesn't smoke.

He leaned over, opening the passenger door from the inside for me, but desperation and frustration rooted me to the spot. I held my fists tightly to my sides.

"Get in," he said.

"No, thanks. I think I'll walk." I jammed my fists into my pockets, regretting it immediately. I pushed the soggy tissue away from my cold hand as I stomped off in the direction of the police station where my car was.

"Suit yourself," I heard Grayson say, and he shut the car door.

I expected him to drive off, but he followed me at a snail's pace. Thunder rolled, and the shower became a downpour, drenching me. When I arrived at the intersection, Grayson caught up with me and opened the passenger door's window a slither.

"Get in," he yelled over the cacophony of the rain on the tarmac. "You're getting drenched."

My eyes refused to make contact with his. Raindrops blurred my vision and cold water trickled steadily down my neck and over my back, wetting my top. I cursed myself for forgetting to put on a scarf in my hurry to leave the house this morning. Resentfully, I gave in and got into Grayson's car. He was wise enough to keep quiet. In silence, we drove to the station.

After Grayson parked the car, he turned to face me.

"Look, I believe there's something fishy going on," he said. "The way you react... it doesn't seem fake. But you've got to agree with me; there's still no evidence whatsoever there's been any foul play."

"What are you suggesting?" I stared ahead of me, not focused on anything in particular.

"I'm not suggesting anything. Go home and wait. Maybe he'll call. Maybe he'll show up. Who knows? In the meantime, I'll have the lunchbox checked for fingerprints, and the cell phone recharged and checked for phone calls on the day. I'll also dig up all I can about this John Smith character. At the moment, he's all we've got."

I finally turned to face Grayson. He was looking at me with that expressionless face.

How often have you said words like these to all those people who have pinned the pictures of missing persons on the board?

Do you practice this look in your bathroom mirror?

Maybe I was paranoid. Maybe Charlie had met an old friend and got sidetracked. Maybe one of the kids at school had given him a new lunchbox and cell phone because Charlie's looked so tattered.

And he couldn't find a bin to put the old ones in.

I unbuckled my seatbelt.

"Call me as soon as you know something," I said as I got out.

"I will. You too, Kate."

I ran to my car even though I was already soaked. Grayson's car had been warm, but outside it was cold and it made the wetness even more uncomfortable. Inside my car, I couldn't be bothered to put on the heater as I'd be home before it would kick in. Besides, no matter what I did, the cold seemed to have plans to stick with me for a while anyway.

The Dream

Once home, I went into the kitchen and put the kettle on. I then took my wet jacket off and threw it over a kitchen chair. As I waited for the kettle to boil, I looked out the window and saw the puddles in the garden. I had a déjà vu.

Why does it always rain on miserable days?

I took out my cell phone and checked for messages. There were four. None of them from Charlie, of course. Sue, Julie, Harry, and Rhona all wanted to know if I had heard something from Charlie yet. With a hot cup of coffee in hand, I moved into the living room and curled up on the couch. I replied to each of them we had found his lunchbox and cell phone. Immediately the questions followed. Who were 'we'? What did it mean? Were there signs of a struggle? What were the police going to do?

By the time most information had been exchanged, a bone-felt tiredness pulled me into the couch. The activity accompanying the third anniversary of SAMM was taking its toll. On top of that, the episode with John had drained me emotionally, but the last drop of energy was spent when I had been frustrated with Grayson.

I put my empty cup on the coffee table and slipped into a more comfortable position on the couch. The coffee had warmed me a little from the inside, making me feel slightly better. When I closed my eyes, sleep came almost instantly.

The dream began with me standing on a beach. The sun warmed my face, and the sand was packed with sunbathing people. I carried Sonny on my left hip, and Sue held my right hand. Even though she had the body of a toddler, her face was her adult one. Julie was there, as were the girls from the farm and their kids. I knew we were there with Charlie, but I couldn't see him. He had been there a minute ago. I was sure of it. I scanned the faces of the people surrounding me. There were so many of them, suddenly all milling about. They made it hard to see far.

Now desperate to find Charlie, I walked around looking for him, dragging Sue behind me. As I called Charlie's name, I searched left and right for his face. There were a lot of faces, most of them unknown to me. One familiar one kept reappearing. It was Harry's face, yet it wasn't. I couldn't put my finger on it. Maybe it was because it had a blue hue, as if he was freezing. Sue began to cry, and Sonny became heavier and heavier to carry. A dread crept over me as I pushed through the ever-thickening crowd. Not making any progress made me panic.

Suddenly, I stood at the water's edge. All the people

had disappeared, including Sue and Sonny. I was alone. The sun's warm rays disappeared behind a cloud, and I shivered. It became darker and darker. When I looked up, I realized it wasn't a cloud blocking the sun but a massive tidal wave. Up and up it went, higher and higher. There were faces appearing and disappearing behind the water's surface. I tried to make out whose faces they were. Momentarily, I thought one of them was Caleb's, but the face disappeared as soon as I tried to focus on it. The surge of what I now believed was blood instead of water towered over me. Then it came crashing down.

I woke up breathing hard and covered in sweat. I sat up to catch my breath. Or was it to make sure I didn't fall back asleep into the same dream?

Welcome back.

Nightmares about tidal waves had plagued me before, but they had stopped thirteen years ago when they had made way for those of Caleb's dying eyes. I hadn't dreamed about tidal waves in years. What did it mean? Why did I think I saw Caleb's face? It didn't make any sense.

You're going cuckoo, Kate.

Reaching into my back pocket, I retrieved my cell and checked for messages again. There were none. I sighed. What to do now?

The cold emptiness of the living room stared back at me, the white cabinets a dull gray as rain clouds blocked the sun. A few of Sonny's toys which I hadn't put away yet lay in a corner. A few magazines lay on the coffee table, next to my coffee cup. Even though the house looked as it always did, it didn't feel the same. It felt empty, no longer like a home. It was a shell that gave me shelter, a place to sleep, and warmth. Nothing more.

I put my empty coffee mug in the dishwasher, grabbed my jacket, and left for the farm.

Talking to Julie

During the drive to the farm, I began to feel guilty. Grayson had told me to stay at home, to wait for Charlie, and I had disobeyed him. For a moment I contemplated turning the car around, but before I could act upon it, the feeling why I had left the house re-surged so much stronger than the size of my guilt. I would just say hi to Sue and Sonny, see if I could help Julie, and then go back. It wouldn't make a difference if I was home or not. Somehow, I knew Charlie wasn't going to show up.

Keep thinking positive, Kate.

The window wipers were going like mad. I wished they could wipe away my fears. Unfortunately, they had as much effect on them as they did on the rain. I hated driving when it rained. It gave me tunnel vision, making cars jump in front of me as if out of nowhere. It also stopped me from driving the maximum speed, and all I wanted right now was to be at my destination, anywhere but at home or in this cold car.

I parked at the main farm building and went to the Kindergarten room where the farm girls had raised their own kids before SAMM. The daycare center for the new generation of suckers they had set up added good business to that of the farm.

Before I went in, I looked through the window and watched the kids play. They all seemed so care-free. Sonny talked to one child and then walked over to another. He was an exceptional boy, always making sure the people around him were happy. He would step in when other children had a fight over a toy or when one didn't let another child play along. The staff, Ellie and Sandy at the moment, had gained quite some experience raising their own sucker children, yet they were very happy having Sonny in their class as it made their job a lot easier.

Sonny noticed me standing at the window and waved. I waved back. When I entered the room, he almost flew into my arms. His jumps were serious competition for an adult athlete. Through SAMM, we had already asked the Olympic Committee about setting up an event for suckers as they would be no match for uninfected people. Thinking my son might one day be an Olympic champion made me smile, and I gave Sonny a big hug.

"Did you miss me already, Little Man?" I nuzzled his nose.

"Did you find Charlie, Mommy?"

"No, I didn't yet, but there's a police officer looking very hard for him now."

"That's good." Sonny put his index finger on his bottom lip before he spoke again. "Is he good at finding people?"

The pamphlets of missing persons on the pinboard at the police station flashed before my eyes. Instead of answering, I put Sonny down. "Why don't you and I go say hi to Auntie Julie?"

"Yay!" Sonny clapped his hands. He knew there were always cookies in Julie's office.

I told Ellie where we were going and, holding hands with Sonny, the two of us skipped down the hall to my sister's office. I could never be unhappy with Sonny at my side.

Julie was on the phone when we entered.

"Yes, this afternoon three p.m. would be great. See you then." She hung up.

"What's going to happen at 3three p.m.?" I asked.

"Another insemination, never-ending story. This time it's my prize cow though, so I want to be there."

Again, I couldn't figure out how she kept on top of it all. Without her, the place would fall apart.

"Did you hear anything about Charlie yet?" she asked as she took the large cookie jar in the shape of a honeypot from a filing cabinet and offered its contents to Sonny. He immediately put his arm in.

I sat in one of the chairs opposite Julie's desk.

"Sonny, why don't you take the jar and give everyone in Kindy a cookie?"

Julie frowned but handed Sonny the jar. He was more than happy to be the bringer of good tidings.

I waited until Sonny was out of earshot.

"No, no news from Charlie yet, and I don't think we're going to hear anything either. The detective, Grayson, isn't treating it as a priority. He seems to think Charlie did a runner. I told Grayson we had been arguing before I left for California. And now..." I sighed and put my head in my hands.

"What did you say to Charlie?" Julie asked.

I glanced at her through my fingers.

Gossip whore.

"I better tell you, I guess. Otherwise you're going to bug me about it all day, aren't you?"

Julie replied with a wicked smile.

Her cell phone rang. She picked it up, looked at the screen, then swiped the call away.

I'm glad you have your priorities in order.

"Charlie was nagging me again about how he didn't want me to take Sonny to California. Going on and on about how it was better for Sonny to have a more stable upbringing. So I told him Sonny wasn't his to worry about."

Julie gasped.

"You didn't?"

"I did. And don't tell me how wrong it was. I knew it was a stupid thing to say as soon as the words left my mouth." I got up and paced the little space available in the office. Julie's eyes followed me as she bit her lip. I had no doubt she had a hard time not saying anything.

"I knew I had hurt him big time as soon as I said it. It's just…" I stopped pacing and exhaled. "I was so tired and fed up with him moaning about it all the time. He couldn't let it go. I had told him over and over again about the good effect Sonny has on people, yet he kept on saying it wasn't good for Sonny. But Sonny doesn't mind. He's a very easy-going kid. He likes being out and about with me. I've been cooped up for nearly ten years. I enjoy talking to people."

I clutched the back of the chair I had sat on, preventing my hands from strangling myself for my stupidity. Had I gone too far? Had I really driven Charlie away from me? From Sonny? I loved him. I never wanted to hurt him. If I could take back my words… if I could have Charlie back… I'd give my soul for that.

When I looked up at Julie, she was about to say something, but my cell phone rang. I looked at it and pressed the answer button.

"Where the hell are you?" Grayson's voice was harsh.

"I'm at the farm, my sister's farm. Why? Did you find a fingerprint?"

"I told you to go home. You need to follow instructions." He sighed audibly. "And no, no fingerprints yet. It's way too early for that. We did find something else though, and I need to talk to you about that."

"Okay, I'll come to the station."

"No, you stay put. I'll come to the farm. It'll give me an opportunity to meet your family, get an idea of the situation. Give me the address, and I'll be over right away. Don't go anywhere else in the meantime, though. This is the last time I'm running around after you."

I gave him the address. When he had hung up, I sat down. Julie's face was a big question mark.

"He's found something. Not a fingerprint."

"What is it then?" Julie asked.

"How the hell should I know?" I snapped.

Julie's phone rang again. This time she did pick it up, turning her body away from me as she answered the call. I rolled my eyes, got up, and walked past Julie's desk to the window, my back to her back, like a couple having a row.

She had a nice view of the farm grounds from here. Pity it was still raining. I followed a raindrop rolling down the window, merging with others on its way. When it arrived at the bottom of the glass pane, my eyes picked a new one at the top and followed that one. Watching the raindrops merge on their way down made me feel less lonely but also more anxious. Whatever was going to happen, I hoped I didn't drag anybody down with me this time.

What about Charlie? Isn't he already down?

Julie finished her phone call, and we chatted about my interview with Emma. It had been the first time I was asked to go on national television and it was all very exciting for SAMM. After about a quarter of an hour, one of the girls showed Grayson into the office.

A Clue

I acknowledged the girl with the ugly scar on her neck. Black October had left her more than physical scarring, and she was never one for talking much after what had happened to her.

"Thanks, Alex," Julie said.

Alex nodded back to us and disappeared into the hallway.

"Grayson, this is Julie, my younger sister. Julie, Detective Grayson."

They shook hands over the desk and exchanged pleasantries. When their hands let go, Julie's hand moved up in a fluent motion to tuck a strand of her blonde hair behind her ear.

Oh, for fuck's sake, Julie, not now. He's a detective, probably with a wife and kids.

"You wanted to talk to me?"

Grayson shrugged and gave Julie another quick look before directing his full attention to me.

"Yes, alone, if that's possible."

"You can say anything you want in front of my sister. She knows everything about me."

Grayson's head turned back toward Julie for a moment, who smiled her sweetest smile at him.

Your drooling will stain the carpet, my dear sister.

"Are you sure?" He frowned, worry in his eyes.

"Have a seat." I indicated one of the two chairs in front of Julie's desk as I sat in the other. "What did you find?" I was on the edge of the chair, my body leaning forward, eager to hear what Grayson had to say.

"Is it possible Charlie had an affair?" He said it with his emotionless face.

An awkward silence followed until Julie began laughing out loud. I sat back, blinking at Grayson.

"You're kidding?"

He didn't have a chance to answer my question.

"Charlie? Having an affair? Don't make me laugh." Julie wiped away tears from laughing.

Too late.

"Are you serious?" Julie said. "Charlie loves Kate like Anthony loved Cleopatra, like Napoleon loved Josephine. She's his world, the center of his universe. What you're suggesting is ridiculous."

Grayson tucked in his chin. I felt sorry for him.

Don't worry, Grayson, the first impression has already been made.

"Why do you ask?" I said.

Grayson cleared his throat before answering.

"Before I sent the lunchbox off to latent prints, where they look for fingerprints, I carefully opened the box, just to check if there was anything inside that could be of interest. There was a bundle of black hair stuck with sticky tape to the inside of the lid. It was tied with a small, elastic hair tie, the kind little kids often wear. You know the kind?" I nodded and motioned with my hand for him to continue. "Well, as you don't have black hair, I'm asking you. Does Charlie know anybody with black hair?"

Apart from Marlon and his mother Molly, only one of the farm girls had black hair. May Ling, however, was a very quiet girl. I couldn't remember Charlie mentioning her once over the years. Julie confirmed my thoughts.

"Molly, who is a Native American, doesn't have any interest in men anymore. May Ling is Asian," she said, "but I'm sure she has no feelings for Charlie. She's in a relationship with Alex. Alexandra."

Julie and I exchanged glances, but neither of us mentioned Marlon as we both knew he couldn't be involved with Charlie like that.

"I'm afraid that doesn't mean anything nowadays," Grayson said, "but I'll take your word for now. Anyone at the school where Charlie works, possibly?"

I racked my brain, trying to remember Charlie's colleagues.

"I don't think so. But I must admit I haven't been to any school meetings for years."

"Did Charlie ever come home late? Did he ever have excuses for doing any after-hours work, perhaps?"

"No, not that I can remember. Apart from parent

evenings, of course. He has those on a regular basis. Otherwise, he always comes home right after school. Unless I've asked him to bring something from the shop on his way home, but that never takes too long."

"Okay, let's move on to the next question then. What about your... um..." He glanced at Julie for a split second before looking at me through narrowed eyes.

"Are you sure you don't want to have this conversation in private?"

"It's fine," I said as I waved the suggestion off the table.

"Spill it out, man," Julie said.

"Okay. What about your sex life? Did you guys do any fancy dress-ups or anything?" Grayson kept his eyes on me, studying my reaction.

I bit the inside of my bottom lip as I imagined Charlie in a black leather outfit with straps and chains. I struggled not to laugh out loud as Julie had done before. Once my initial reaction had passed, I said, "What on earth does that have to do with anything?"

"Well," Grayson said. "I'm pretty sure the hairs are synthetic, as if from a black wig."

My smile dropped, and I felt the blood drain from my head.

An Old Acquaintance

It was as if my insides had been sucked into a black hole and the rest of my body was about to follow. Grayson grabbed my arm. His grip barely kept me upright.

"What is it? You've gone as white as a ghost. As a matter of fact, you both have."

When I was sure I wasn't going to pass out, my eyes met Julie's. She was indeed looking rather pale. Her lips not as red and full as they had been when she was flirting with Grayson moments ago, and her cheeks somehow looked more hollow than normal. I guessed I didn't look any better.

"What do you know? You need to tell me," Grayson said, shaking me a little to bring my attention back to him.

"It's... it's Sasha. Sasha's taken Charlie."

"Who's Sasha? Is she one of the girls here?" he asked Julie the last question.

"She most certainly is not," Julie answered, her voice as cold as ice.

It appeared Black October continued to haunt me. The stench of singed flesh hit my memory as I relived setting Sasha's black wig on fire. After melting away the synthetic hairs, the flames had fed on her face. She had knocked herself unconscious on the supermarket floor in an attempt to flee my attack with a make-do flame-thrower, and I had to pour a can of pumpkin soup over her face to douse the fire. From that day on, I had refused to eat pumpkin soup. The smell always reminded me of her burned flesh.

"Kate, you need to tell me." Grayson had raised his voice, but I couldn't answer him, afraid my breakfast would come out if I opened my mouth. "Julie, who is Sasha?"

Julie wrapped her arms tightly around her body. "She's the most despicable, cruel bitch you'll ever meet."

Grayson turned to me again, and his expression made it clear he was in dire need of a more substantial answer.

I inhaled deeply a few times and was relieved when the bile stopped coming up. My stomach was still in a knot, but I could now tell Grayson about Sasha.

"During Black October, there was a pack of suckers run by Duncan, an army guy, very strict. He had a partner, Sasha. Together they run the pack like evil dictators, killing those who wanted to leave. They had taken Julie hostage to make me tell them how to become a daywalker. It's a long story I won't bother you with. There was a fight in which Charlie and I overtook them and freed Julie. In the process, Charlie shot her in the knee, and I set her wig on fire. A black wig."

Grayson rubbed the stubble on his jaw.

"Ah, yes. I can see why you think this Sasha has taken Charlie. She definitely has a motive for harmful intent. This ups the stakes." He took out a notepad and pen from his coat. "Can you give me her surname? Would you perhaps know where she is? Where she lives?"

We don't have coffee together every week if that's what you're asking.

"I haven't seen her since the trials after Black October. I only know her surname is Morozov, and that she was convicted for crimes committed against humanity during Black October. She and Duncan went to prison, not a sucker internment camp. That's what I don't get. She should be in jail. How could she possibly have taken Charlie?"

The things she could do to Charlie.

"Are you okay? You've gone pale again," Grayson said.

For a moment, I couldn't make myself reply or focus on anything for that matter.

"I'll try to find out everything I can about this Sasha Morozov. Could there be anyone else who would want to hurt Charlie, or hurt you?"

I looked up at Grayson, his words barely registering.

"What about the haters?" Julie said.

"Haters?" Grayson asked with raised eyebrows.

"There's always the sucker-haters," I said. "People

who can't forget Black October. They were there when I went on the Emma show. Tried to stop me from entering."

"Did they ever threaten you?" Grayson asked.

"No, not really. I mean, they've always been there when I go to Council meetings and interviews and the likes, shouting abuses at me. But they don't know where I live. I've never received any letters with death threats or anything."

Grayson rose from his chair.

"Okay. I'll see what I can find out. I'll get back to you as soon as I know more."

I nodded and Grayson left.

After I heard the door shut, Julie came around her desk and gave me a hug. It made me feel safe, a stark contrast to Charlie's predicament should he really be in Sasha's hands. I grabbed a tissue from the box on her desk and blew my nose. Julie sat back in the chair where Grayson sat a minute ago.

"It may not be Sasha," she said.

"And pigs can fly."

"Yeah, you're right. It's far more likely Sasha has Charlie than Charlie having an affair and doing kinky stuff."

There was an awkward silence and when our eyes met, we both couldn't help but giggle. It was just nerves.

Imagining Charlie in a black, leather outfit wielding a whip is funny, though.

"Why? Why would she do this? Why now?" I sighed and raised my eyes to the ceiling as if I could find an answer there.

"Who knows? She's one crazy bitch," Julie said. "She scared the hell out of me during Black October. She manipulative, cruel, and sneaky. She can make people think it was their idea, as if she had nothing to do with it, getting away with murder. Literally. The fact that she left that bundle of hairs in Charlie's lunchbox is pure and only because she wants you to know it's her."

"Why did she take Charlie? Why didn't she take me? I was the one Caleb fell in love with. I took him away from her. And I was the one that shot him."

As I said it, a horrible thought popped up in my mind.

"Oh my god, Jules. Sasha doesn't know Caleb didn't die that day. She may still think I killed him. Do you think she'll kill Charlie?" A wash of adrenaline surged through my veins, but I had no use for it. I couldn't do anything. I was useless. It was a terrible feeling, like when I had seen my friend get killed by a mob of suckers while I was at a safe distance. I began to hyperventilate.

Julie grabbed my hand, and the rush ebbed away. As did the confidence I was going to get Charlie back alive. The thought of never seeing him again paralyzed me. Now I couldn't breathe from fear. Julie pinching the skin between my fingers. It hurt but made me focus on her.

"Kate, look at me. He'll be okay. Charlie will be okay. Grayson will find Sasha, and we'll get Charlie back. We'll put that bitch back where she belongs, you hear? She'll have her comeuppance. We'll make sure of that, won't we?"

I nodded. She rubbed my arm, and I smiled at her. Yet somehow, I didn't think it was going to be as easy as she made it sound.

Party Invitation

Julie gave me another quick hug, not letting go of me until I said I was okay. She got up and moved back behind her desk.

"I'm so sorry, sis, but I've got work to do. Let me know immediately when you hear from Grayson again."

I stood up, making ready to leave.

"Yeah, about Grayson..." I said.

Julie looked up at me with a wicked grin on her face.

"What about Grayson?" she said as innocently as she could.

"You don't fool me, girl. I saw how you looked at him. What on earth do you see in him? He reminds me of Dad. And I know you never said so... but I always thought you liked girls..."

I didn't want to break down this door at this particular moment, but it was the best opportunity I'd had to raise the question since Black October. Patiently, I waited for her to answer. She was either going tell me to get lost or confirm my suspicion. Julie swiveled her chair toward the window. I was almost out of the room when I heard her turn back. It surprised me she looked confused.

"I actually also thought so for years. Duncan was the last drop. I'd had enough of men. I really found my place with the girls here at the farm, but I never found that special person I was looking for. There never was that spark, not until I met Grayson. I'm as shocked as you are. I know he's a fair bit older than I am, but so was Duncan. Maybe that's just my thing."

I smiled at my sister.

"Whatever your thing is, I'm happy for you to finally find it. You deserve to be loved. But you better make sure your 'thing' isn't married."

Julie grinned. "I already checked if he was wearing a wedding ring. He isn't. You've got to find out more for me, sis." She smiled as sweet as candy as she leaned forward.

"Don't worry, I will. I don't want you to burn yourself on this one."

I nearly had the door shut when I popped my head back into the room. "The Emma interview is airing tonight, by the way. Don't forget to watch."

"Thanks, sis. I wasn't going to miss it for the gold in the world," Julie said and turned her attention back to her computer.

Back in the Kindy room, I told Sonny I'd pick him up later that afternoon.

I found Sue in the barn. Julie and I had decided to let her work with the young animals as it wouldn't give her too much stress. Feeding the calves was a fun job.

"Hi, Little Smudge. How's it going?"

Sue looked up from feeding a calf a bottle. Fortunately, there were only a few calves who had lost the care of their mothers.

"This one's so hungry. She's going to be another great addition to Julie's prize stock." The calf finished the bottle, and I walked with Sue to the kitchen to prepare the next one. The noise of her rubber boots sounded as if they were too big for her. "Did you hear anything about Dad yet?"

I brought her up to speed with Grayson's visit.

"Sasha?" she said. "The one from Black October?"

"The very one."

"But you don't know for sure. It could be anybody's black wig. The hairs may even not be from a wig. You said so yourself Grayson only thought the hairs were synthetic. They may not be. You're over-thinking things, Mom." She shook the bottle with the formula and warm milk in one hand as she wiped her other hand on her overall.

"Let's hope so, Sue. I hope it's something less sinister."

I walked with her back to the calf pen and she picked another one to drink from the bottle.

"So, what now?" she asked as she resisted the force from the thirsty calf.

"I don't know. I suppose we've got to wait if the box shows any fingerprints. There's not much else we can do."

The calf lost the teat of the bottle and Sue struggled to get it back into its mouth with the other calves trying to get some as well.

"I'll let you get on with the feeding. I'll talk to you soon."

She gave me a smile, and I left Sue to the feeding.

***

Parking the car on my drive, I remained seated and took in the house that Charlie and I had made our home. I recalled the time Charlie had put a new coat of paint on the porch a few weeks ago and came inside covered in paint. I remembered how he, last spring, had put a hose into a drain pipe to unblock it and completely soaked my shoes when it had suddenly unblocked. We had laughed so hard. I smiled as I looked up at the windows of the top floor. Charlie always washed the outside of them for me, insisting he stood on the rickety ladder we had found in the shed after we bought the place, not me. Charlie was always going out of his way to make my life easier. He spoiled me rotten. And now he was gone.

I had no proof, but I knew he wasn't in a good place. Whatever it was, he didn't deserve this happening to him.

Once inside, I didn't know what to do with myself. The house still gave me the same eerie feeling that had made me leave this morning. I decided to get over it and distracted my mind with some good old-fashioned cleaning. The bathroom was first in line. Next, the toilet. Last but not least, the kitchen floor received a good scrub. I was mopping it when my cell phone rang.

"Hi, Rhona."

Our friendship hadn't been as close as before our spat during our time locked up in the sucker internment camp. We were working hard on accepting the choices we had made then but weren't contacting each other on a daily basis yet. Certainly not twice daily. I wondered why she called.

"Hey girl, how're you holding up?" she asked with her typical nasal voice.

"I'm okay. It's a waiting game at the moment."

"I heard Sasha may be behind Charlie's disappearance." From the tone of her voice I wasn't sure if it was a question or a statement.

You work fast, Julie.

"Yeah, it's a possibility. There isn't any evidence yet to know for sure." My gut told me it was true, though, which was enough evidence to me.

"I hope they're wrong, I sure do. The cunt's as crazy as a whore dying for some crack." Rhona's choice of words never ceased to amaze me. It was the one thing I hadn't really missed during the year of silence between us.

"Um, I hope they're wrong too."

And thanks for making me feel better about it. Not.

"Listen," she said, "remember the party for Harry tomorrow evening? I hope you're still coming? It'll take your mind off things."

I had again completely forgotten the party. I hadn't bought anything for Harry yet. Not even a card.

So it's you who called Julie.

"I'll be there, don't worry. I know it's a big thing for him."

"Great, see you tomorrow at seven." She hung up.

Leaning on the stick of the mop, I contemplated calling her back and canceling. Surely, I couldn't go partying while Charlie was being held a prisoner by Sasha?

You still don't know that for sure, Kate.

I shook my head and decided against it. It would mean a lot to Harry if I was there. He was a good friend, and I didn't want to let him down. Besides, like Rhona said, the party would take my thoughts off the situation for a moment. There wasn't much else I could do. There wasn't a lot more cleaning to do in this house either, and it would beat sitting on my couch thinking of all the things Sasha could do to Charlie. To avert my thoughts moving into dark places, I resumed mopping the floor with increased vigor.

Confirmation

Grayson didn't contact me until the next morning. He asked me to come into the office at around lunchtime. I was there before noon, and George the Rookie buzzed me through the door. Grayson, fortunately, didn't let me wait and immediately joined me in the interrogation room. I got up as soon as he entered.

"What did you find? Is it Sasha?"

"Sit down, Kate," he said and took the chair opposite me. He put a folder on the table. When he opened it, I could see a photo stuck with a paper clip to the inside of the cover. Sasha still had that face that could belong to a man or a woman, but I knew it was her because her face was marked with ugly scar-tissue. It almost reached her right eye and covered over half of her scalp. Some patches still had hair sticking out, but it was cut short.

Grayson had taken a paper from the folder and began reading out loud from it.

"Alexandra, also known as Sasha, Morozov, thirty-eight years old," he said. "Born in the Nekrasovka District of Moscow to a single mother, Anna Morozov, who was a sex worker and heroin addict. An Italian fashion mogul discovered Sasha when she was sixteen and working in a bar. He took her out of the country and cleaned her up. She entered the fashion industry as a model, eventually traveling with Versace, Christian Dior, and the likes. She was in Portland for a show when Black October happened. Caught by the US Army, she was vaccinated and convicted for life. Due to a bullet wound in her right knee, she has a limp, and her facial disfiguration was caused... well, you know." He gave me a quick glance and cleared his throat before he continued. "In prison, she gave birth to twins, both sucker boys, who were taken away from her and raised in a sucker internment camp. Half a year ago, they released Sasha on parole due to continuous good conduct and changes in the law."

Grayson put the paper down and looked at me without saying anything further.

I stared back at him.

"So, to cut a long story short, you're saying Sasha's out."

"Looks like it."

Fuck.

I took a deep breath, and as I exhaled, I spread both my hands flat on the table. Suddenly conscious of my cloven nails, I withdrew my hands underneath the table, and wiped my sweaty palms on my jeans.

"Now what?" I asked.

"Now we try to find her."

"Sorry, I don't get it. You just said she's on parole.

Shouldn't you guys know where she is?"

Grayson hesitated a moment before answering.

"She disappeared as soon as she was out. There's a warrant for Sasha's arrest for skipping parole, but at the moment, we have no idea where she is."

My stare bored into his eyes. Grayson finally put his hands up and looked away.

"You've got to be kidding me..." My anger began to warm up like a sack of cherry stones in a microwave.

"They say she had connections with the Russian mob," Grayson said. "She's probably gone back to Russia. There's no other way she could've disappeared so quickly and untraceable."

I rose, making the chair scrape over the linoleum floor with a loud, grinding sound. With the tip of my index finger purposefully resting on the table in front of Grayson, I looked him straight in the eye.

"So you're saying that the woman who was set on fire and disfigured by me, who was shot by Charlie, who went to prison for the last twelve-and-a-half years due to my actions, who had her children taken away from her because of her predicament caused by my interference in her affairs, who went missing half a year ago, and who has left a calling card in Charlie's lunchbox, you're saying that you think that woman's gone back home? You really think so? Are you thick or something?" My anger now bubbled like an overheated bowl of pea soup on the edge of explosion.

Grayson just looked at me, apparently lost for words.

"Fuck you, Grayson."

I stomped out of the room. I was seething, clenching my jaws until it became painful, puffing out my cheeks with every breath. How could those idiots be so stupid? How could Grayson be so stupid? Sasha was out for revenge. There wasn't a single hair on my body in doubt of that. I would if I were her. I wouldn't rest until I had my revenge. Why couldn't Grayson see that Sasha wouldn't rest either?

I got to the exit door and tried to open it. It didn't budge.

"George, open the fucking door," I yelled at the poor rookie.

He fumbled but finally hit the buzzer. When I went through, I heard Grayson call out behind me.

"Kate, be reasonable. There still isn't any evidence."

I walked out without replying. I didn't give a shit about evidence. The fact that Sasha was out there and that Charlie had disappeared was evidence enough in my opinion. I slammed my car door shut and with screeching tires sped out of the police station's parking lot.

It took me at least fifteen minutes before I calmed down. I found myself in the middle of the countryside and parked alongside a paddock fence. After I killed the engine, everything went quiet. I couldn't stop the empty feeling sucking away my energy. It was as if I tried to breathe in outer space. A calf in the paddock cried for its mother. The sound was heartbreaking and made me wish I could talk to my own mother right now, ask her for guidance, for support, but she'd been gone since Black October. I leaned my forehead against the steering wheel and cried.

Dark Stranger

When I came home from my meeting with Grayson, I decided to have a bath. Maybe it would help me calm down and distract me. As soon as my large toe told me the hot water was a tolerable temperature, I stepped in and let the warmth envelop me. At first, the heat felt oppressive, and I nearly got out. I persevered, though, and the water began to relax me.

The memory of having a bath together with Charlie popped up. It had been a surprise gift from him on my birthday when Sue was still a baby. I had come home from my cleaning job to find he had strewn rose petals all the way from the front door, into the hallway, up the stairs, and into the bathroom. I found Charlie sitting there, dressed in a bathrobe, surrounded by candles, and a foamy, hot bath waiting. It had been so romantic and perfect. Tears rolled down my cheeks with the memory. I submerged my head to stop feeling them. Only when my lungs felt like they were lined with acid did I come up for air.

I cut my intended long bath time short as it appeared I couldn't find my peace here either.

I organized for one of Julie's girls to babysit Sonny at Sue's place for the evening and for him to have a sleepover there as well. Sonny loved staying on the farm. I then went out to buy Harry a card and a bottle of liquor after which I could focus on getting ready for Harry's party.

Getting ready was harder than I thought it would be as every other second my thoughts drifted off to Charlie. It took forever trying to figure out what to wear. First, I picked out a black dress, but that seemed too doom and gloom for the occasion. I then went for a colorful dress. Too cheerful for my liking. The swapping of outfits continued on and on, but it was always too this or too that. I tried on the whole of my wardrobe content before I settled for bleached jeans and a simple, dark blue shirt. It also took quite some time to get everything back into my wardrobe.

Doing my makeup was the hardest. Every time I stared into the mirror, I imagined I saw Charlie in the background of the mirror image, asking me what shirt to wear or asking whether he should wear a tie or not. I only found an empty space whenever I turned around to look for him. I ended up using far more eye-liner than I normally did, to hide my red-rimmed eyes.

***

Harry and Rhona lived on the other side of town, near the medical center where Harry worked. When I arrived at eight, there were already lots of cars parked in the street. I had to get rid of mine on an empty lot, away from the tarmacked road, and I cursed Rhona's abundance of friends. It seemed she had invited all of them. I did my best to dodge the deep puddles with my open-toed high heels. Thank heavens it wasn't raining at the moment.

I rang the doorbell, and Milly opened the door. The music had already been audible from where I had parked my car, but after the door opened it was like I had entered a movie screening for the hard of hearing; the sound coming from the living room was deafening. Milly let me in gave me a big hug.

"Thanks for coming, Kate. Dad will be so glad you made it."

Milly was always so nice to everybody, unlike her twin Maddy who took after her mother and copied her foul language.

"Thanks, Milly. Where can I find your dad?" I asked as she took my jacket.

"He's in the kitchen, I think."

I made my way to the back of the house, hoping I could get rid of the heavy bottle as soon as I said hello to Harry. When I entered the kitchen, I saw him with his back turned toward me, pouring himself a drink at the breakfast bar. He was wearing all black which was unusual for him and especially on this happy occasion.

"Congratulations, Harry," I said as cheerfully as I could muster and moved to hug him, bottle in one hand, envelope in the other. As soon as he turned around, I realized my mistake. His hair was slightly darker, his face narrower than Harry's, and his eyes an icy blue. "You're not Harry," I said and halted my embrace.

The man grinned and showed off long fangs like Harry's. He leaned in close, his mouth next to my ear. I smelled the alcohol on his breath through his cologne.

"Don't tell anyone. I've been getting some awesome presents."

"Milly said I would find you here. I see you've met my brother." Harry's voice coming from the doorway startled me. He smiled as he approached us and gave me a big hug.

I returned the hug and held on a bit longer than was customary. In it, I expressed my unspoken worry for Charlie's wellbeing, and I had no doubt Harry understood. When he backed away, his smile had changed into a set line. I sighed.

"Tom, this is Kate, a dear friend of mine," Harry said to his brother.

"I've heard much about you. Anyone who's a friend of my brother is a friend of mine," Tom said.

He moved forward and to my surprise, he hugged me in the same fashion as I had Harry, holding on to the hug longer than was necessary. The funny thing was that in his hug, even though he was a stranger to me, I felt safe. He conveyed comfort and care. When he let go of me, I stepped away from him, blinking, confused. How could this man be so much like Harry? I knew they weren't twins. And his stare was definitely different, more piercing.

"Are those for me?" Harry asked, breaking the awkward moment. He indicated the bottle and card I was holding.

"They sure are," I said, throwing a sideway glance at Tom, and handed them to Harry.

"I'm glad I got here in time. I have a feeling a lot of my presents have disappeared into the wrong hands," Harry said, also looking in a sly way at Tom.

"You don't look like you need more alcoholic presents, little brother," Tom said with a bit of a sneer, eying Harry's waistline.

My eyes did a quick comparison of Harry's and Tom's torsos, and it was true. Harry was no longer in possession of the lean six-pack he had sported thirteen years ago when we had met for the first time. His job as a general practitioner didn't leave him much time to exercise. Tom's abdomen, in contrast, looked like he was still exercising. A lot.

I wonder what kind of exercise.

"So be careful, or I'll sit on you," Tom said.

I frowned.

Harry snorted, and Tom laughed.

"Tom used to sit on me whenever we had a fight when we were little," Harry explained. "He was bigger than I was and won every fight that way."

"Only after I conquered you with my fast moves," Tom quipped and took another sip from the amber liquid in his glass.

"Don't believe a word he's saying, Kate. Lies keep pouring out of his mouth like fruit from a cornucopia." With that warning, Harry left us and returned to the living room.

Dancing

I wanted to follow Harry to the rest of the party-goers, but I also didn't want to be rude to Tom and leave him on his own. Not sure what to say, I put my hands in my back-pockets and glanced around the kitchen to find something to talk about.

"So, you're the famous Kate," Tom said, breaking the silence first. Now his brother had left us, his eyes didn't leave mine, his stare still intense and unsettling.

"I'm not famous."

"Sure you are," Tom said. "You were on the Emma show yesterday, so you're famous."

"I didn't take you for someone who'd watch the Emma show." It amused me he watched something as mundane as that program.

He leaned in, like he had done before, and said in low tones, "I didn't say I did."

There was something about his scent. There was the alcohol, obviously, but I smelled something else. A scent I couldn't place, one that I had never smelled before. It was cool and refreshing, like an ocean breeze. It intrigued me.

Kate, you hate the smell of the sea.

I had to stop myself from following Tom's

retreating body.

Before I could say anything, he moved fast and suddenly stood on the other side of the breakfast bar.

"My brother's a bad host. What would you like to drink, my dear?"

"Um, a White Russian would be nice." A wry smile crept across my face.

If only I could drink Sasha's blood right now.

"Coffee mixed with alcohol, my kinda choice. I like you more and more every minute." Tom picked the Kahlua from the liquor bottles displayed on the breakfast bar for the party guests. There were all sorts of glasses available as well, neatly sorted in rows, and Tom chose a tumbler. He added some cream he found in the fridge and vodka from a bottle that looked like it should contain perfume. Before he handed me the drink, he topped up his own, a malt whiskey. He held his glass up, and I copied him. We clinked.

"To a new and interesting friendship," he said.

I gave him a nod and took a sip of the cocktail. It was mixed to perfection. When I met his eyes after my sip, that intense stare was back again. It was so unnerving. I turned toward the living room.

"Come, let's join the other guests," Tom said as he came from behind the breakfast bar, acting as if he owned the place.

As soon as we entered the room and were in the company of others, I relaxed. I was glad of the distractions here and hoped that these would stop Tom's creepy stare. We occupied a spot in the corner where there was just enough space for two to stand comfortably. The room was packed with party-goers. I spotted Julie, Sue, and Marlon at the center of the room, dancing.

"Are you here alone?" I asked Tom, trying to make small talk over the loud music. I had to yell to make myself heard.

"No. I'm here with the Asian chick cooing over the ankle-biters." With the index finger of the hand holding his glass, he pointed in the direction of a beautiful, slender woman in a body-hugging, black, silk dress. She was chatting with some mothers holding their infant offspring.

Tom was already looking in another direction, and my eyes drifted back to the Asian girl.

"She was fun but is now getting past her use-by date..." I said to no one in particular.

"Not only pretty but also witty," Tom said. He clinked my glass again and held his up toward me before taking another sip.

It was then that Sue spotted me. She came over and grabbed my hand.

"Mom, you're here. Come on, come dancing with us," she said as she grabbed my arm.

I resisted her pull. "No, really, I shouldn't," I said.

"It's okay, Mom. We're all on the dance floor." Sue

could be persistent if she wanted to be.

"No, sweetie. I can't leave Tom all on his own now, can I?" I looked at him, my eyes pleading for help.

He gave me a cheeky smile.

"Sure you can. I won't be offended at all. You go, girl."

I threw him an angry look while Sue took the opportunity to drag me onto the dance floor. Reluctantly, I joined the bobbing throng of people. Julie greeted me with a hug and continued dancing to the music. I moved to the beat not to stand out. The music was actually great. At least I recognized the songs. Slowly but surely, the tunes overtook me. I moved my arms a bit more, careful not to spill my drink. It felt good. God, it had been ages since I last danced. Was it back in college?

After a while, I gave in to the music and danced freely like the others. I tried to get rid of my glass, but someone filled it with something that didn't taste too bad, so I kept dancing with the glass in my hand, sipping from it now and again.

The alcohol went to my head sooner rather than later as I had forgotten to have dinner while deciding what to wear. Happily, I continued to dance for what seemed like hours. My family left the dance floor at some point, but not I. They kept filling my glass, and the alcohol within me as well as my spirits reached higher and higher levels. I finally got rid of my glass, but by that time my drunk brain reasoned that if I stopped dancing, I would miss Charlie and would cry. I couldn't let that happen, not in public. So I danced like there was no tomorrow.

Now and again, my gaze fell on the dark stranger in the corner of the room. Every time it did, I met his stare. He just stood there, leaning against the wall, watching me. It kind of felt perverse how he observed me while I danced, watched me when I moved my booty in sensuous circles. It aroused me. The alcohol repressed my inhibition, and I began dancing more and more sensuously, my hips twisting and turning. I enjoyed getting a good workout.

After a slow pirouette, I looked up to get a glimpse of the dark stranger again and found Tom standing right in front of me. He startled me. His body began moving to the beat, and my body followed suit, closely following the movements of his. Feeling the heat radiating from his close proximity gave me renewed energy, and we danced together for a while. It was uncanny how our bodies moved in sync, as if we'd practiced for years. It felt great. At some point, I had the idea that people were staring at us, but I didn't care. Nothing mattered but moving to the beat. I had to keep moving, couldn't stop.

The upbeat songs were suddenly replaced by a slow one. I looked up at Tom, and he smiled.

"You're not going to leave me now, are you?" he said.

I shook my head and put my arms around his neck. As I rested my head against his muscled chest, he put his arms around me and we swayed to the soothing tones of a saxophone.

I could fall asleep right here, right now.

I closed my eyes, and Charlie's image popped up in my mind.

"Don't leave me," I murmured. "Don't leave me. Come back. I love you."

I vaguely felt Tom move me off the dance floor. Familiar faces passed by. Voices talked. I was put into a car and lifted out again. Then the memories of the night stopped.

A Parcel

The next morning, I woke up parched like a mummy, and every time I moved my head, a pounding within my skull followed. Darkness surrounded me. On good faith, I flung my arm out, found a string, and pulled it. Before my eyes had adjusted to the bright light, I knew I was at home, in my own bed.

My head spun around to Charlie's spot, but it was still empty. Disappointed and dizzy, I slowly turned back around to find a bottle of water on my bedside table and a box of aspirin leaning against it. I took out two tablets, washing them down with the water. As I put the bottle back on the night stand, I noticed my cell phone. Groaning, I reached a bit further and grabbed it. A resistance made me realize it was attached to the charger cord. I pulled the cord from the cell, and fell back onto my pillow, closing my eyes for a moment. The painkillers didn't work as fast as I wished. Activating my phone, I saw it was only 5:50 a.m.

Great.

A message icon blinked at the top of the screen. My index finger hit it and the app opened.

'Good morning, Sunshine. I hope you slept as well as you danced. Don't forget to keep drinking water. See you at Harry's. Tom.'

Slowly, the memories of last night came back to me. When the images of me dancing with Tom appeared, I pinched the bridge of my nose.

"Oh, no."

You really made a fool of yourself, Kate.

I stared at the message again. The word 'Sunshine' jumped out at me.

At the moment, I'm as close to looking like a ray of sunshine as a pile of vomit looks like a good meal.

My thumb hovered over the reply button while I focused on keeping bile down. Once I was certain none was coming up any further, my mind went blank regarding what to say to Tom. He would still be asleep, no doubt, so there was little haste, anyway. A yawn escaped me. I put the phone away and snuggled down underneath the warm duvet. Within a few minutes, I was asleep again.

***

When I woke up for a second time, it was light. Birds chirped outside, and I felt a lot better than a few hours ago. After taking a few gulps of water, I snoozed for a bit longer, reliving yesterday evening. I couldn't remember what had happened after I got home. Suddenly, my eyes flew open in alert. With trepidation, I lifted my duvet and saw I was undressed yet still wearing my underwear. Surely Tom wouldn't have had his way with me and then put my underwear back on? I closed my eyes and sighed with relief. I had made the right choice to wear my fancy, black underwear last night. 'Always wear nice underwear,' my Mom used to say, 'you never know what might happen.' I was sure she had been talking about traffic accidents, but it was good advice, nevertheless.

I turned onto my side and moved my hand as if to stroke Charlie's arm, touching nothing but air. My hand flopped onto the bed.

"I'll get you back, Smudge."

Not being able to stay in the lonely bed a minute longer, I threw off the duvet and got up.

A shower refreshed me, and by the time I got downstairs, I was able to keep a coffee down. I dialed Sue's number to find out how Sonny was. It didn't take long before she picked up her phone.

"Morning."

"Hi there, Little Smudge. I hope I didn't wake you."

"Of course you didn't wake me, Mom. Sonny has been up two hours already." Sue sounded like she had been up for a while as well.

"So sorry, girl. I owe you. How is he? Did he have a good time yesterday?"

"He had a great time. Ellie watched some videos with him, and they played a couple of games. She told me she tucked him in at 7 p.m. and that he has behaved like an angel."

"That's great to hear, sweetie. What're you up to today?"

"We're going to take it easy. Nice and relaxed. I'm assuming you'll be picking up Sonny soon?" Her voice didn't betray her eagerness to spend time alone with Marlon.

"Of course, it's playground day. Can you put Sonny on for me?"

"He's right here."

Sue passed the cell to Sonny.

"Hi Mommy, guess what I had for breakfast."

"Um, I bet it was porridge that tasted like cardboard."

"No! Sue made me pancakes! With blueberries!" Hearing his enthusiastic voice made me so happy.

"Did she? Your sister is spoiling you rotten, you hear. I better come and pick you up before you don't want to live with us anymore. And then we'll go to the playground. How about that?"

"Yay!"

Sonny's voice drifted off as he had handed the cell back to his sister and went to tell Marlon where he was going. We went to the playground each and every week, but Sonny was excited about it every single time.

"See you soon, Mom," Sue said.

"Till then, Little Smudge."

She made no comments about my drunken

behavior, so I assumed she and Marlon had left the party before I made a fool of myself. I now felt guilty for letting Sonny have a sleepover at their place last night.

I put on my jacket and opened the front door. My car wasn't in the drive. I face-palmed myself realizing Tom must have driven me home in his car. My car would still be at Harry's and Rhona's place. When I opened my eyes again, I spotted a box lying on the porch.

Did we get mail delivered on Saturdays? I couldn't remember. Maybe letters, but parcels? I picked up the cardboard box and scanned the street. It was empty. I went back inside, taking the box into the kitchen. It looked strange, small. It smelled weird too but couldn't put my finger on it. I turned it over this way and that, but there wasn't an address or sender's details anywhere written on it. It must have been delivered personally by someone, and I must have been too deep asleep to have heard them knocking. With a knife, I cut the tape holding the two top flaps together. After I removed some scrunched-up tissue paper, the content of the box became visible. A wave of nausea overtook me.

On a bed of kitchen towel, lay a finger. It was near white, with dark blood staining the tissue where the finger had been cut off from the hand it had belonged to. On the finger was a ring. A dragon ring. Charlie's ring.

Procedures

I spun around to hang my head over the kitchen sink. My body heaved, but I had nothing to bring up but a dribble of coffee and bile. Perspiration formed on my forehead and upper lip. My clammy hands clenched the edge of the countertop although I knew it wouldn't help should I faint. With deliberate, fast, deep breaths, I managed to stay conscious. When I was sure I wasn't going to pass out, I rinsed my mouth with water and slowly turned back around to behold the cruel gift. It was still there.

Not a figment of my imagination, then.

My hand went to cover my open mouth. I was certain it was Charlie's finger. Through my tears, I recognized the stubbiness, the rough skin, and his ring. I pulled out my cell phone but didn't know Grayson's number by heart, so I pressed Harry's on speed dial. As soon as he answered, I spoke.

"Harry, get over here. She sent me Charlie's finger."

"I'll be right there," was his immediate reply. Harry knew me long enough to know I wouldn't be joking about something like this.

Five minutes later, the three of them found me sitting in the kitchen, staring at the finger in the box.

Harry and Tom walked up to the table and also stared into the box. I wanted to thank Tom for bringing me home and taking care of me last night, but I couldn't get any words to come out of my mouth. When he noticed me watching him, he returned my stare with one of concern. Rhona came around the table and gave me a hug before also turning her attention to Charlie's chopped-off digit.

"Holy fuck," she said when she saw it.

Another silence followed.

"You know what pisses me off?" I said after a while. "Apart from the obvious."

They all threw me a quick glance.

"No, what?" Harry said.

"It's his middle finger. The bitch is flipping me the bird."

The three of them alternated their stare between me and the finger.

"No way," Tom said.

"Yes, way."

"I've heard the stories about her, but this tops them all," Tom said.

"What stories?" I asked.

Tom began to reply, but Harry interrupted.

"How long have you had it for?" he asked.

I frowned at him.

"Why? I've only had it for a few minutes before I called you. I have no idea how long it's been sitting outside on my porch, though."

"Well, you better put it on ice. Just in case they can still reattach it. Did you call the cops?"

A new pounding in my head presented itself. After I had called Harry, I was too mesmerized by Charlie's chopped-off finger and completely forgot to call Grayson. I immediately took out my cell phone, googled the police station's contact details, and called them. An officer, not George, told me Grayson wasn't there, so I left him the message that he needed to get to my place as soon as possible.

On Harry's recommendations, I put the finger on ice in the fridge. I also called Sue to tell her I wasn't going to take Sonny to the playground after all. She was distracted by Sonny and, fortunately, didn't question me about the reason why.

Tom told us he heard Grayson's car arrive and left the kitchen. I thought he was going to let Grayson in, but I noticed him disappear into the hallway off the living room. I presumed he was going to use the toilet, so I got up and headed for the front door. Tom apparently had exceptional hearing as it was indeed Grayson about to knock on the door when I opened it.

"Where is it?" Grayson asked, skipping any pleasantries.

"It's in the fridge, on ice," I said as I led the way through the living room.

"How did you get it?" he asked.

"I found it on my porch as I was about to leave. There's no writing on the parcel, so it wasn't the mailman who brought it. Sasha must have been here." The hairs on my arms stood on end.

"You didn't touch it, I hope?" Grayson said as we entered the kitchen.

"She's not that stupid," Tom's low voice came from behind us. He stood there, leaning his shoulder against the hallway door post, arms folded, watching us. He seemed to like watching people from a little distance.

"You!" Grayson's eyes narrowed.

"Hello to you too," Tom said, "and no, I've nothing to do with this one," he added.

What do you do for a living, dark stranger?

Grayson held Tom's stare for a moment, before returning his attention back to me.

"Show me," he said.

I put on new sterile gloves from the first aid kit and retrieved the box from the fridge. I opened the lid, removed the tissues and ice, and held the box up to Grayson.

Without touching it, he studied the finger minutely.

"You're sure that's his ring?" he asked as he looked up.

"For fuck's sake, man. She's been with the guy for thirteen years," Tom said. He had joined us in the kitchen now. "Surely she knows what his ring looks like. And it doesn't look like he got it from a gumball machine either."

I wondered how the two of them knew each other.

Grayson chose to ignore him and returned to studying the content of the box. Rhona anxiously awaited Grayson's verdict. Harry looked angrily at Tom. Tom squeezed his eyes half-shut while pouting his lips in my direction. For a moment, I didn't know if I should be annoyed with him or laugh. I ended up smiling, either out of nervousness, or because I was flattered by Tom standing up for me. Suddenly, I remembered Grayson had asked me a question.

"Yes, I'm positive it's his ring. He made it himself. There's no other like it."

Grayson straightened himself and took a large zip-lock bag out of his coat pocket. He put all of it, including the box and the ice into the bag. After he had sealed it and written notes on it, he looked at Rhona and Harry.

"You guys haven't touched it?" he asked them.

Tom let out a sound of exasperation while Harry shook his head.

"Of course not, man," Rhona said.

Grayson returned his attention to me. "What time did you get home yesterday?"

"Um, I don't know. Tom?" I felt a blush cover my cheeks.

Grayson refused to look in Tom's direction. In fact, his facial features completely froze. Tom's face, in contrast, began to radiate like a ray of sunshine after a spring rain.

"Let me see," Tom said, "what time would it have been?" He rubbed his chin for dramatic effect. "I think I got you home at about 1 a.m., but what time did I leave?" His hand moved to scratch the back of his head. Rhona's head flicked toward me.

The cheeky bugger. Is it me or is he really trying to irritate everybody?

"I need to establish a time frame for the delivery," Grayson said through gritted teeth.

"One-thirty, I left at 1:30 a.m.," Tom replied.

Grayson was only doing his job, and it wasn't fair he was getting such attitude in return.

"What are you going to do with it?" Harry asked, indicating the box in the bag.

Visibly relieved not to have to deal with Tom for the moment, Grayson replied.

"It'll have to go to latent prints, to let the forensic team do their work. I would've called in a team to look for traces the deliverer of the parcel could have left, but, seeing as you three have been driving over and trudging on any possible tracks, that's out of the question now. Next time, call me first." Grayson spoke the last sentence directly to me. He handed me his business card.

I lowered my eyes as I put the card in the pocket of my jacket. I had stuffed up. They could have possibly found evidence, got us closer to finding Charlie, and I had screwed up.

"How long will it take? What if they don't find any prints?" I said. "Then what?"

"What about keeping it on ice? What if we find Charlie? Could his finger still be attached?" Tom asked before Grayson could reply my question.

I looked at Harry, but it was Grayson who answered the question.

"We'll keep it on ice, during transport and any research. The cut looks clean and we have a window of about four days in which a reattachment could still be successful. It's cold enough at night for the finger not to have deteriorated too much, if it was delivered that long ago. The forensic guys will be able to tell us more on that. What we don't know is what the state of Charlie's hand is. They probably bandaged it, but how sterile... who knows? If there is an infection, chances will be slim reattachment will work.

I tucked my shaking hands away in my armpits, and Rhona put her arm around me.

"So what are you fuckers going to do about it? Wait until the next goddam piece arrives?" she said.

Grayson looked at her with tired eyes.

"Someone must have delivered the box. We'll go through any camera footage in the area we can find. We'll also go door to door to ask if anybody has seen something. When I get back to the office, I'll enter the details into ViCAP, the Violent Criminal Apprehension Program. They'll compare the new data with what they have in their system and look for a pattern that has come up elsewhere, possibly one that matches a crime of which we know who the perpetrator is. That's all we can do for now. In the meantime, Kate, it's a good idea if you have a security system installed, one with cameras covering all the entrances to the house."

I gave Grayson a nod.

"I also need a DNA sample from Charlie, to be able to verify one hundred percent that this is his finger. Do you have a hairbrush with hair or nail clippings from him?"

"Not a problem," I said and ran upstairs. I emptied the waste bin in the bathroom. At the bottom, I found old nail clippings that I knew were Charlie's. I put them in a tissue, threw in some hairs from his hair brush for good measure, and brought them downstairs. "Nail clippings and hair," I said as I gave them to Grayson, who put them in another plastic bag and wrote down the details on it.

"Stay here, in case she calls or comes by again. I'll call you as soon as I know more." When he walked past Tom, he paused to turn around to face me. "And stay away from this one," Grayson said to me as he indicated Tom with his thumb. He then resumed walking out the door.

An Argument

As soon as Grayson had left, I took off the latex gloves and filled the kettle under the tap.

"I could do with a coffee. What about you guys?"

They murmured a unanimous 'yes,' and the three of them sat down at the kitchen table. Everyone looked relieved now Charlie's finger wasn't pointing at us anymore. I busied myself with getting mugs ready.

"I can help you with a security system," Tom said.

"Thanks, Tom. That would be great. When Grayson mentioned getting one of those, I had no idea where to begin looking." I leaned against the countertop as I waited for the water to boil.

"I hope it isn't one of those that have fallen off a truck?" Harry said.

"Of course not, brother. Who do you take me for?"

"My brother," Harry replied.

I didn't miss the slight worry in Tom's eyes as they briefly met mine.

So it probably did fall off a truck. This explains what you do with your time and your relationship with Grayson.

At the moment, I couldn't care less where the security system would come from, only that it was installed as soon as possible.

"I'll pay you whatever it costs, of course." Silently I hoped it wasn't too expensive. Living on only Charlie's wages was a tight budget.

"Forget about it." Tom sat back, his expression sharp like that of a child about to do something naughty. "See it as a thank you gift for making my brother's birthday less boring." The corners of his mouth curled up into a cheeky smile. Was he happy about being able to thank me or about taunting Harry?

"If you don't like our parties, you can always fuck off," Rhona said. "Saves us having to deal with your dumped girlfriends."

"Who asked you to open your mouth?" Tom replied.

My jaw dropped involuntarily from the hostility flying around the room. In all those years, I hadn't seen Tom at Harry's place ever. Harry had hardly ever mentioned his brother in any conversation either. Now I began to see why.

Harry sighed.

"Here we go again. Tom, remember what we discussed?"

"Yeah, yeah, family, blah blah blah." Tom averted his eyes as he said it. Whatever he had discussed with Harry regarding family, it didn't sound like he agreed with the part about Rhona.

"Fucker," Rhona said.

"Bitch," Tom replied.

Harry suddenly slammed his hand on the table. I jumped. He looked like steam would come out of his ears any minute. I had never seen Harry this upset.

"For fuck's sake. Stop it, the both of you. You act like a bunch of toddlers." He said more composed but still frowning, "There's more important stuff to talk about." Harry looked at me as he said the last sentence.

You could say that again, Cecil.

I returned his gaze with a quick smile. The kettle boiled, and I turned away from the awkward situation to make the coffees. When done, I put the mugs on the dining table and sat down next to Rhona.

"Thanks for coming, guys," I said, breaking the silence after a little while. "I realize I should've called Grayson first, but I'm glad you're here."

"What can we do to help?" Harry asked.

"To be honest, I wouldn't have a clue. Grayson has to come up with results from the research first although I doubt they'll actually find something. Sasha would be so stupid as to leave fingerprints. And if they see her delivering the parcel on a video, so what? We still wouldn't know where she could be right now."

"That's not true," Tom said. "If she got here by car, which is most likely, they might be able to get the license plate number from the footage. If they have an image of her face, they can search for her with the help of digital facial recognition programs. There'll be plenty of data from street cameras. They can backtrack where she came from and find out where she's hiding."

I was amazed by the information Tom had.

"Wow, I didn't know they could do that."

"Technology stands for nothing, nowadays," he replied.

"What do we know about this Sasha so far?" Tom asked.

I told them what Grayson had told me the other day, and when they began discussing Sasha, I excused myself to call Julie. She didn't know what had happened yet. I wasn't sure how to bring it to Sue and thought it would be better if I discussed it with my sister first. I dialed her number as soon as I was alone in the hallway. As expected, she was horrified and said she'd be over immediately. When I put my cell away, I heard raised voices in the kitchen. Harry and Tom appeared to be arguing about something. I hurried back.

Now what?

"Don't ever assume you can tell me what to do, little brother," Tom said with a sudden fire in those icy-blue eyes. He stood up with force, and said to me, "I need to talk to you." Before I could ask what about, he grabbed me by my arm and dragged me out the kitchen, through the living room, and out onto the front porch.

"Excuse me! What the hell are you doing?"

He shut the door behind him and let go of my arm. I rubbed it. His grip had been like a vice.

"I didn't mean to hurt you. Sorry about that," he said. He truly looked apologetic.

"So you should be. What the hell happened back there?"

"They don't get it," Tom said. His hand rasped through the short hair on the back of his head, and drifts of a sea-side scent came my way. "Look, I have connections, amongst which a guy called 'Dirty Harry.' I'll ask him to look out for Sasha. Maybe he knows something. I'll be back later this afternoon to install that security system for you."

"Okay... thanks." I wanted to smile but was unsure how I felt about Tom's rough handling. He clearly wanted to help, but he had a strange way of showing it.

"Sorry," Tom said again as he noted I was still rubbing my arm. He stomped off without looking back.

I stayed out on the porch until he was out of sight. Who was this stranger? Why did he care for me? I was taken, obviously, so why the hell did he care?

Hey, my car is back. Fancy that.

Tom must have returned my car on the way over, and I regretted I didn't thank him for it. I went inside and smiled when I found my keys in the dish on the sideboard.

When I returned to the kitchen, Rhona had gotten up and was putting the empty mugs in the dishwasher. She still knew my house inside out from the time she helped me with the housework when I home-schooled her daughters. I sat down opposite Harry.

"What in the world did you say to him?"

Harry leaned forward.

"Kate, don't get involved with Tom."

"Why not? He said he has connections. He may be able to get information about Sasha's whereabouts faster than the police."

"They're the wrong sort of connections, Kate. People you don't want to owe anything. I strongly advise you not to get involved." Harry looked worried for me.

Staring at him with a blank face, I decided I didn't want to take his advice. I wanted Charlie back. Any which way.

Don't tell me what to do indeed.

"By the way, that wasn't what the argument was about," Rhona said.

Harry threw an unfriendly glance at Rhona, who was leaning with one hand on the back of a chair and the other on her hip. She gave him a look of 'why not?'

"What was it about then?" I asked. Of course, I had to know now.

Flyers

His face grim, Harry met my stare as I waited for his answer. He looked away before answering my question.

"He suggested staying over, so you'd feel safe,"

I sat a bit straighter and blinked. That was actually a rather nice gesture of Tom. I must have smiled as Rhona abruptly sat down and put her hand on my wrist. Her expression set to 'don't you fuckin' dare.'

"Cupcake, he's a screwed-up motherfucker."

"Rhona..."

Rhona momentarily exchanged glances with her husband before continuing her speech to me.

"He's got a new chick on his arm every fuckin' month, goes through women like they're disposable cups. Don't become one of his throwaways, doll."

I pulled my arm away and frowned at her.

"Excuse me. I'm a grown woman, and I love Charlie. I can handle myself."

Harry and Rhona both stared at me with raised eyebrows.

"Yeah, okay. I made a mistake in the past. I get it. But I've gotten wiser since. Thanks for the heads up, guys. I do appreciate it. Consider me warned."

Rhona rose and gave me a hug.

"I'm afraid we've got to go. Maddy and Milly will be worried they'll have to do the party cleanup on their own," she said.

"Oh dear, I completely forgot. Do you want me to come over and help?"

"Of course not, silly cow. You've got other things to worry about. You take care. Keep us up to date and let us know as soon as we can do something."

Harry gave me one of his bear hugs and they left.

***

Julie arrived ten minutes later. Her terrain wagon had a specific, low, humming sound which I recognized. I put the kettle on before she came into the kitchen. As Julie entered the house, the smell of cow manure hit my nose. Julie always smelled of the farm. I preferred a horse scent over that of cows, but unfortunately, Julie didn't run a horse stud farm. She walked up to me and gave me a big hug.

"I can't believe what you told me is true," she said. "I feel awful for Charlie. Was the finger really his? Do the police know anything yet? Did Grayson have any news?"

The kettle boiled, and I poured her a coffee. On a whim, I poured myself another one as well. I needed all the caffeine I could get today. We sat down, and I filled Julie in with the information Grayson had given us about the procedure that would follow. She listened attentively.

"So, we'll have to wait until they find something," I concluded. "We must find Charlie in four days though, or he'll definitely loose the finger."

I cradled my mug, warming my cold hands on the warm ceramic.

"What finger was it?" Julie asked.

"You want the gory details, Jules?"

"Do bears crap in the wood?" she said and smiled behind her mug before she took a sip of the hot coffee.

Why did I even ask?

"It's his left middle finger, the one with the dragon ring." I stared at an unspecific spot on the wall behind Julie as I recalled the vision of Charlie's finger. "The flesh was ghostly white, almost as white as the kitchen towel it was on. Where it was cut off, dark, dry blood caked the wound and the towel."

"Eww," Julie said and wrinkled her nose. "Was it a clean cut or, you know... ragged, like it was sewn off with a rusty jigsaw?"

"Goddammit, Jules. Why do you have to make me imagine that?"

"Well, it makes a difference to when they try to reattach it again."

"If you must know, it looked very smooth. She must have used a butcher's knife or something."

"That's good news. If you know what I mean..." Julie

looked guilty for her choice of words.

"I'm glad it's his left-hand finger," I said, changing the subject.

"Yeah, otherwise he may have a problem keeping his job, I suppose," Julie said. She put her hand on my arm and squeezed it.

"Yes, that too. I was actually thinking about the magical things he can do with his right-hand finger."

Julie frowned before her face turned into one of disbelieve. She teasingly slapped my arm.

"How can you think about something like that at a moment like this?"

I giggled. "Well, he does use that finger in a magical way. I'd miss it if he'd lost it."

I knew it was inappropriate, but I forced myself not to go into the downward spiral of the rabbit hole, afraid I wasn't able to climb out of it if I ever got sucked in it.

"Talking about magical things," Julie said, "why didn't you tell me Grayson was coming here? I wouldn't mind seeing him again, but I can hardly go to the police station and ask to meet him without a reason, can I?"

"There were other things on my mind, Jules. I didn't even call Grayson immediately after I discovered..." I swallowed. "You know, Charlie's finger. I called Harry instead. He, Rhona, and Tom came over and ruined all tracks that Sasha may have left. I was so stupid. We may have been able to get a clue about Sasha, and I ruined it."

I sighed and stared into my coffee mug. Where was Charlie now? What was Sasha doing to him? Why did she take him and not me? I had hurt her more than Charlie ever did. He didn't deserve to be treated this way.

"Sis, keep it together," Julie said and pulled me back from going into the rabbit hole. "You need to be strong now, for Charlie, for your kids. You can't let her get to you. That's what she wants."

Julie stared at me until I nodded.

"But what can I do? I feel so useless! Grayson doesn't want me to leave the house, in case she makes contact again. I really want to go look for Charlie even though I have no clue where to start."

"We need to find out if anybody has seen Sasha somewhere," Julie said. "But how?"

An idea popped into mind.

"Not too long ago, one of my neighbors lost their dog Pooky, a Pekinese. They put up flyers with a photo of the dog, asking people if they had seen it. What if we put up flyers with Charlie's face? Do you think that might work?"

The idea lifted my mood. It plummeted right back down again when I thought of the number of flyers pinned on the board in the police station lobby.

"Yeah," Julie said, her face lighting up. "We'll put them up everywhere, on trees, at the shops, and any noticeboard we can find. Wouldn't it be better to put up photos of Sasha as well, though?"

"Why not both?" I said. "We can put Charlie's and Sasha's picture on the flyer with, 'Have you seen these persons?' above it."

Julie nodded in thought.

I got up and ran upstairs. From my travel case, I retrieved my laptop and charger and took them downstairs. I hooked the laptop to the charger.

"What are you doing?" Julie asked.

"We need a photo of Sasha. I've got plenty of Charlie but obviously none of her. She used to be a photo model, so there must be heaps on the internet."

"Good thinking," Julie replied and came to sit next to me.

We scoured the internet for headshots of Sasha. We didn't find any suitable photos when we googled Sasha's name. She may have been using a stage name. We had no idea what company she traveled with either, but Grayson had said she was in Portland when Black October happened. It wasn't hard to find the fashion show in question from that information. From there, we could backtrack the show and tried to find a suitable photo.

"Oh my god, can you ever imagine yourself wearing something like that," Julie said as we scanned through the images. Sasha and the other models wore clothes that were incredibly impractical to wear. "That just doesn't make sense."

"I know. What I can't imagine is that people pay big money to see it or even buy it."

We chuckled at some more outfits the models were wearing. Sometimes it was hard to tell if they were male or female. Sasha, too, could easily have posed for a male. She was extremely flat-chested, looked as tall as the males, and her face was hard to read. I tried to figure out what made a face male or female but gave up when I couldn't.

"There. What about that one?" Julie said as she pointed at a photo that was a close-up of Sasha presenting a ridiculous hat.

"Excellent," I said and saved the image to my laptop. I then cropped the photo, so it didn't show the hat.

"How about you send the photo to my email, and I'll print the flyers from my office," Julie said.

"Thanks, sis. You're my hero."

Julie was about to get up and leave when I remembered what I had wanted to discuss with her initially.

"Jules, I'm worried about Sue."

Julie, who was already half out of her seat, sat down again.

"Why?" she asked.

"She's already in a fragile state with her PTSD and I don't want to make it any worse. Marlon only tells me the good things, not wanting to upset me." I tapped my nails on the kitchen table before popping the question. "I don't know if I should tell her what happened to Charlie." I looked at my sister for an answer. Sue lived and worked on her farm, and I hoped Julie had a better idea of my daughter's state of mind lately.

"I can't tell you that, sis," she said. "You need to ask Dr. Strang. He's her therapist."

"I know, but how's she been lately? How's she doing? Do you think she would be able to handle the stress? She seems okay to me at the moment, but I'm not sure she is. Ever since she's moved out, I feel like I've lost her. She confides in Marlon and that stupid therapist now, not me. I miss her so much. I want to help her, but she won't let me." I took a deep breath and sighed. "I would prefer to keep this news from her, but I don't know how she'll react when she finds out about it from someone else."

"Talk to Dr. Strang," Julie said and got up again.

We hugged.

"Call me when you're seeing Grayson."

"Will do. Don't worry."

Julie left, and I had to make a decision.

Julie meets Tom

Even though I couldn't stand the man, I dialed Dr. Strang's number. He sort of was the competition, and he had won Sue's confidence, leaving me in the dark about my own daughter's wellbeing. Communication with him was always forced. I guessed he knew what my problem was, but as I wasn't his patient, so he didn't care.

"Dr. Strang," his creepy voice said.

"Ah, Dr. Strang, Kate Clarke here, Sue's mom. I have an urgent issue I need to discuss with you."

"Please make an appointment with my secretary."

The hairs on my neck rose and my free hand clenched open and shut.

Keep your cool, Kate.

"I'm afraid this cannot wait. Sue's father is missing. He's been kidnapped. Sue knows this as I have told her. What she doesn't know is that the kidnapper cut off his finger and sent it to me. The police are dealing with it, but I don't know what to do. Do I tell Sue or not?"

I drew a quick breath and held it. Dr. Strang let me simmer a little while before he answered.

"I see. You should tell her, but only the bare minimum, don't go into details. Keep it positive. I'll have my secretary move her appointment forward." He immediately hung up on me.

When my breath left my mouth, so did a few curses. The guy was being paid top wages, and he did bugger all for it.

"The bare minimum," I murmured as I put my cell phone away. "Keep it positive."

Hey Sue, we got Dad back. Okay, just his finger, but look on the bright side; part of him is back!

Positive, my ass. I vowed to beg Sue to search for another therapist as soon as this whole episode was over.

I made myself some sandwiches for lunch but could hardly eat. I sat chewing the bread a million times, wondering if Sasha was starving or feeding Charlie. Would she be cutting off another finger tomorrow? Or maybe a toe? Who would do such a thing? Why? I had never cut off anything of Caleb's. I had killed him. At least, Sasha would most likely think so. We all had thought so. Would she really kill Charlie to get back at me?

The thought made my lunch come up, and I turned around just in time to vomit into the sink.

When I had finished cleaning myself up, there were three hard knocks on the front door. I jumped, nearly dropping the plate I was putting in the dishwasher, and my heart skipped a beat. Could it be another parcel? I took some deep breaths and moved toward the opening between the kitchen and living room, so I could see who was on the porch. Relief washed over me when I saw it was Tom, holding a large box. It had images of cameras and other electrical stuff on it. I hurried over and opened the door.

"Don't tell me you received another parcel?" he asked. "Your pretty blush is completely gone."

I stepped aside and let him in.

"No, thank heavens no. I'm having problems eating," I said.

"I know the feeling," Tom said and walked straight to the kitchen. He put the box on the kitchen table and began opening it. "Four outdoor cameras, four indoor cameras, all with motion sensors, a HD control panel, a Digi-Wifi module, and multiple alarm settings. All in all, a state of the art system," he said as he unpacked the box.

"Wow. That must have cost a fortune. I don't know if I can afford that, Tom."

He looked at me sternly. Harry's eyes were a darker blue, like his father's. Tom must have inherited his icy-blue eyes from his mother. I had never met her, unfortunately. She must have been a nice woman raising such nice sons.

Tom was saying something, and I quickly returned my attention to him. "...told you before, it's a gift. Accept it."

"I'm grateful, but I still hope I can repay you for it

one day, somehow."

He stopped unpacking for a moment.

"Okay, if you insist." His eyes narrowed, but not in an evil way. Right? He still had that grin on his face. I shrugged and looked away.

"We'll talk about it later. I'll start with putting the outdoor cameras up first," he said. "Do you have a toolkit and a ladder?"

"Yeah, we have, in the shed. I'll go and get it." I hurried out of the kitchen and out of his presence.

***

Tom had installed the outdoor camera covering the front of the house and now worked on the one on the back porch when Julie returned. She had what seemed like a whole ream of paper in a box.

"Wow, that must have drained your ink cartridges," I said, flicking through the content of the box.

"Don't you worry, all tax-deductible." Julie smiled.

I took the top flyer out of the box and read it. 'Missing,' it said in big letters at the top. Then 'Have you seen these persons?' underneath. Next were the two photos of Charlie and Sasha, followed by 'Please contact—my cell phone number—if you have any information regarding either of these two persons.'

"Don't you think people will think Sasha's missing as well when they read this?"

"Maybe," Julie said, "but who cares. They've seen her, or they haven't. You want to know if they have."

"Ouch, fuck it," came the muffled sound from Tom outside.

Only then did Julie notice him standing on a ladder on the back porch.

"What's he doing here?" she said.

"I told you. Tom offered to install a security system after Grayson had advised me to get one. He doesn't want me to pay for it, but I insisted I will. Not sure how I'm going to repay him though. The kit looks expensive," I said as I stared at Tom's partially exposed six-pack. He was busy attaching the camera to the ceiling of the porch.

Suddenly, I felt Julie watching me.

"What?" I said.

"You're terrible, you know that?"

"Why? I didn't say I was going to sleep with him. There's nothing wrong with a bit of eye candy now and again. For fuck's sake, you all think I'm going to hit the sack with everybody I look at. I'm just glad I've got something to keep my mind occupied instead of going crazy thinking about Charlie's predicament."

"Alright, I believe you," Julie said. "Don't get your panties in a knot. You wanna go and put these flyers up?"

"Actually, I really want to go and talk to Sue. I talked to Dr. Strange earlier, and he said I should tell her.

According to him, I need to 'tell her the bare minimum' and 'stay positive.'" I mimicked the doctor's voice when I said his words.

Julie snorted. "How in heaven's name are you going to tell her what's happened and stay positive?" she said.

"My thoughts exactly. The guy's such an idiot."

Tom entered the kitchen.

"I sure hope you aren't talking about me," he said.

"Don't worry, plenty of other idiots to talk about."

Tom put the ladder down and squinted at me.

"Other idiots?"

"Crappy word choice, sorry," I said. I felt my cheeks warm with my blush. "I'm very happy with your help. Honestly, I appreciate it."

Tom grinned at Julie. "I love it when women go onto their knees for me."

"I bet you do," Julie said.

Her reply and the way she said it made everybody avoid eye contact for a moment.

"Tom, I'm off to see my kids. I'll be back as soon as I can. Julie, can you stay here while I'm gone? I'll be back as soon as I can."

Tom picked up the ladder, ready to put up the next camera.

"Are you afraid to leave me alone in your home?" he asked.

"Well, I'm not one hundred percent sure my furniture will still be here when I return if I leave you to it."

Tom glanced into the living room.

"You sure you don't want a new couch? You seemed to rather like the one you sat on so comfortably during the Emma show," he said.

"So you did watch the show."

He didn't take the bait. Instead, he walked off with that cheeky smile on his face.

I grinned, gave Julie a hug, and left.

Telling Sue

The trip to Sue's place was only a quarter of an hour. I wished it was three hours, so I had more time to figure out how to break the news to Sue. I had called Marlon before I left and had asked him if he could arrange for one of the girls to take Sonny to the park with the playground. He was too young to hear this horror.

When I arrived at their place, Alex was just leaving with my boy. Sonny broke away from her and ran up to me, jumping into my arms with a mega jump as he always did.

"Good morning, Little Man," I said and kissed him.

"Mommy, Alex is taking me to the playground. Are you coming with us?"

He put his arms around my neck and there was such joy in his eyes. It tore at me to turn him down. I so wanted to be with my boy right now.

"I'm sorry, but Mommy's got something important to discuss with your big sister. I hope you don't mind."

"That's okay. We'll go together another time."

He gave me another hug, and I let him down. He ran up to Alex, who put him in the child seat in her car. As I waved them off, Marlon came to stand next to me.

"More news?" he said, frowning.

I stopped waving.

"Yeah, and it's not good. It'll be hard on her."

Marlon nodded, gave me a hug, and we went inside.

Sue must have heard me arrive as she was in the kitchen making coffees. I had lost count of the number of coffees I'd had today.

"Hi, Mom," she said with a cheerful smile.

I walked up to her and gave her a kiss and a hug. This was the girl I loved. The happy-go-lucky girl that enjoyed life. Hugging, smiling, looking happy. How I hated what I was about to do to her. I knew it was better to do it earlier than later though. She had to be prepared for the worst and doing it gradually would make it easier for her in the long run.

"Morning, Little Smudge. Thanks for taking care of Sonny for me."

"I don't mind, you know that. He's such a funny lad. He makes me laugh."

"Come and sit on the couch with me. I need to tell you something." I sat down and patted the seat next to me.

Her face became one of concern, but she did as I asked and handed me a coffee.

"Did you hear something about Dad?"

Marlon, who stood behind her, gently squeezed her shoulders.

"Just listen, Sweetheart," he said to her.

Sue, still frowning, nodded to him and returned her

attention to me.

"Is Dad okay? Was this the reason you couldn't pick up Sonny?"

They say people suffer the most from the suffering they're fearing. This was certainly true at that very moment, but it wasn't my suffering I feared.

I closed my eyes, Charlie's finger lying in the box popping up in my mind immediately. I took a deep breath and spoke slowly.

"Just as I was about to leave this morning, I found a parcel on the porch. When I opened it, I... I found Dad's finger. They have chopped off his finger and sent it to me."

Sue's facial expression didn't change. It seemed she hadn't been listening to me at all. I took her coffee from her and put both our mugs onto the floor. Taking her hands in mine, I tried again.

"It isn't as bad as it sounds, Little Smudge. It's his left-hand middle finger. He can still work without it, and the detective said it could still be reattached if we find him soon."

Then she shook her head, trying to pull her hands away, her face set in one of horror. I could see the switch being flipped, the light at the end of her tunnel fading, the happy girl following the rabbit down the hole. I needed to bring her back, and fast, before it was too late.

"Sue, listen. It's not the end of the world. We're going to get him back, and Sasha's going to pay for what she's done to Dad."

"No, no, no!" Sue wailed. "I don't want to lose Dad. I can't lose him. She can't kill him," Sue cried. "Sonny needs him. You need him. I need him. He's my Dad."

I pulled my daughter into a hug and held her.

"Nobody said anything about killing, Little Smudge. Nobody's going to die. It's going to be alright. The police will get him back." I tried to convince her everything was going to be okay as much as I could. I stroked her hair while she cried. The crying turned into sobbing, and I expected her to stop after a few minutes, but she didn't. She kept on wailing, telling me she didn't want her father to die. I caught Marlon's eyes as he paced the floor.

"Come, let's get you to bed," I said to Sue. "You better get some rest."

Together, Marlon and I took Sue to the bedroom, she could hardly stand on her own legs, and we tucked her in. She was in a very bad state. With the bedroom door shut, I discussed Sue's situation with Marlon.

"I talked to Dr. Strang this morning. He advised me to tell her what happened. I brought it to her as positive as I could, but she took it so much worse than I had hoped. I shouldn't have listened to that man."

"Yeah, it doesn't look good, does it," Marlon said. "I'll give her one of those sleeping tablets, so she can calm down a bit."

"The doctor said he would have his secretary move

her appointment forward. Make sure she sees him on Monday. I don't want her to go on like this any longer than necessary."

"Okay, I'll do my best." He hesitated for a moment, then said, "Is it true? Does Sasha have Charlie?"

I bit my lip.

"There still isn't any evidence, but I know in my gut it's her. The police weren't doing much about Charlie's disappearance before I got that package. They thought he'd gone for a pack of cigarettes if you know what I mean. I hope they're making a bit more effort to find him now. We only have four days to find him, to have any chance of his finger being reattached successfully."

"That little time? I sure hope we find him, Kate. If there's anything I can do, you know I'm here for you," he said.

"Take care of my daughter, Lon. She needs you now more than ever. And if you don't mind, take care of Sonny for me for the next few days. I don't want him to be there in case anything else turns up."

"No, that's fine. Sonny has a good influence on Sue and may help in her recovery. He can stay as long as he needs to."

Marlon was the best Son-in-Law a mother could wish for. I gave him a big hug.

"Thanks. Much appreciated," I said. "I'll keep you up to date with what's happening. Let me know how Sue is tomorrow. And what the doctor has said after the appointment on Monday."

"I will."

Marlon saw me to my car and waved me off. I watched him get smaller in my rear-view mirror. The poor guy. This hadn't been what he had signed up for; taking care of a PTSD patient and a toddler at the same time. I hoped with all my heart the situation would soon improve.

.

Asking Around

When I arrived home, I found Julie sitting on the couch. The TV was on, but she was looking at her cell. She put it away and clicked off the TV as soon as I came in.

"How's Sue?" she asked.

I threw my keys into the dish on the sideboard and hung my jacket behind the door.

"Not good. She had a total meltdown as soon as I mentioned Charlie's finger."

I rubbed my face with both hands, the way Charlie always did when he was upset.

Funny how you pick up things from the person you live with.

Julie got up and gave me a hug.

"It'll be alright," she said. "We'll all be laughing about this in about a year's time."

I raised my eyebrows at her.

"Okay, maybe ten years," she said.

"Yeah, one day." I sighed. "Where's Tom?"

"Probably going through your knicker drawer," Julie said while her glance moved up to the ceiling.

"Excuse me?"

"He asked me if you'd be okay if he installed a

camera in your bedroom," she said.

"Oh, hell no!"

"That's what I told him. I think he was joking, but I'm not entirely sure. The way he looked at you last night…"

I sat down heavily on the couch.

"Ugh. Please don't remind me of last night," I said. "I made a complete fool of myself."

Julie dropped down next to me.

"Tell me more, sis." Her eyes twinkled with the possibility of hearing gossip.

Julie would always be Julie. She was my sister, and I loved her, but sometimes her nose was a little too big.

"Get out of here," I said and gave her a playful push. "Go and take care of the farm, do something useful instead of wasting your time with your silly sister."

"Okay, okay. I'm going," she said with a wicked smile on her face.

Always jumping to conclusions.

"Hang on, wait," I said as Julie made for the door. I ran back to the kitchen and grabbed a small pile of flyers out of the box. I pushed them into her hands.

"Put them up, you know, anywhere you can think of," I said.

As Julie took them from me, her smile disappeared.

"I will, sis. We're going to get him back, you know." She gave me another hug and left.

As soon as Julie was gone, I went upstairs.

"Hey there, Sunshine," Tom said before he saw me.

He stood on the ladder attaching a camera to the hallway ceiling. Its view would cover the whole landing, so anybody coming in through the bedrooms would get picked up by it as soon as they stepped out.

"How's it going?" I asked. "How many have you put up now?"

Tom tightened a screw. Working above his head must have been taking its toll on his arm muscles, but it didn't seem like he had a problem with it at all.

I bet he's one of those guys that can do all sorts of chin-ups on a pull-up bar.

"This is the last one." He came down the ladder. "There's one on the front porch, one on the back porch, one aimed at the shed and one covering the side of the house. There's a camera covering the living room, one in the kitchen, one in the hallway downstairs, and this one. Anybody makes a move in this house and you'll know it." He folded the ladder away.

"Thanks so much. You have no idea how much this means to me." I stepped aside to let Tom pass me. "You want me to carry something?"

"Just the toolbox would be great. I'll take care of the ladder," he said.

After we packed everything away, he showed me how to work the alarm. There was a control panel by the front door, and he set up the system so the notification of the alarm tripping would go straight to my cell phone. I was so glad he knew how this all worked. It would have taken me ages to figure it out.

"Happy?" Tom asked.

"Very. What can I do to repay you?"

"I told you, it's my repayment for a great night," he said. "But, if you insist, a peck on the cheek would be appreciated."

He had that cheeky smile on his face, and I couldn't tell if he was joking or not. My mind raced to find an answer that wouldn't insult him.

"Or dinner, that would also be nice," he said and winked at me.

"Dinner it is," I said, relieved I didn't have to kiss him. "Hey, I know you've already spent more time here than you probably care for, but would you mind helping me put some flyers up? I can leave the house now the alarm system is working, but I really don't fancy doing this on my own at the moment."

I showed him the box with the papers Julie had printed. Tom studied them and nodded in approval.

"Yeah, sure. I don't mind, seeing as I'm staying for dinner, anyway."

***

Together we walked through the streets. We had already put up three-quarters of the papers. Tom carried the box while I attached flyers to every other lamp post. It was cold. The wind had an icy touch it hadn't had so far. I shivered every time I thought of that single T-shirt underneath Tom's jacket. I would freeze to death wearing that.

"So, what sort of contacts do you have? Harry said they're the wrong sort of contacts." We were strolling along High Street, Bullsbrook's main street.

"Did he now?" Tom replied. "Yeah, I guess he would say that. Harry doesn't approve of my choice of friends. Our father doesn't either. To be honest, they're not really my friends. Just contacts."

I glanced sideways at him.

"Are you saying you don't have any friends?" I said.

"No, I didn't say that. I said my contacts aren't my friends. You really should pay more attention to what I say."

The man of mystery.

I stopped walking.

"Tom, what do you do for a living?"

Tom walked on for a moment, but when he noticed I had stopped, he turned around. There was that grin on his face again. He smiled like this so often, I was beginning to think it was his 'normal' face.

"Wouldn't you like to know," he said.

"That's why I'm asking. Duh."

He squinted while taking me in.

"I'm in the information business," he said after a moment.

I continued walking, and he followed suit.

"You mean IT?"

"No, not really."

He didn't explain it any further, and I understood he didn't want to discuss it. I was dying to know, but I had the idea I wouldn't get it out of him unless he decided to tell me, so I left it at that.

When we ran out of flyers, we headed back home. I dreaded finding another parcel on my doorstep. Fortunately, there wasn't one.

Passing the Time

Leaving Tom at my place, after making him promise me he wasn't going to exchange my three-seater for one that resembled Emma's couch, I ducked out for some groceries as I had run out of milk and the likes and I thought I better get him something decent to eat.

Tom gladly ate the T-Bone steak I cooked for him. I knew I couldn't go wrong with an easy, protein-rich meal to keep those muscles of his in shape. He liked it rare, just like I did. He didn't complain about the rest of my cooking, which I appreciated, even though I was well aware the veggies were undercooked. After we finished dinner, I got up and began clearing the dishes. Tom also got up to help, something I never let Charlie do. I preferred him to entertain Sonny as he missed spending time with him while he was at work.

"No, no, you stay put. You've done enough already," I said to Tom.

"That's okay, Kate. I haven't been doing that much. Besides, I feel awkward sitting here watching you do this on your own."

"Oh, okay. Consider my arm twisted."

Why was this man still single?

Somehow, it didn't feel strange. He asked me where

to put stuff now and again, but mostly he found his way around the kitchen and began cleaning the kitchen table as I cleaned the stove.

"Do you have a girlfriend?" I blurted it out before I could stop myself.

Tom continued wiping the kitchen table. Was that grin back again? When he was done, he turned around and cleaned the cloth under the tap.

"Why do you ask?" he finally said.

"Why do you always come back with a counter question when I ask you something?" I replied.

He half-laughed, half-snorted, but still didn't answer.

"So, do you?" I repeated.

Tom neatly put the cloth away.

"Sometimes," he said.

I picked up the kettle and moved closer to Tom. He stayed put, looking at me with a strange look in his eyes until he figured out I wanted to fill the kettle under the tap. He quickly stepped away from me.

"Nobody special then?" I said as I filled the kettle.

"I haven't been able to find her yet. The good ones are usually taken."

When I looked up at him, that intensive stare had returned, but as soon as my eyes met his, he looked away, blushing.

Oh heck! You've got *to be kidding me.*

I moved to put the kettle on and to get the mugs for

the coffee out of the cupboard.

Now how to get yourself out of this one, Kate?

"Tell me more about those contacts of yours." Changing the subject always worked with toddlers.

Tom sat down at the kitchen table. I'm sure I heard him let out a sigh of relief.

"Well, my biggest hope lies with Dirty Harry," he said. "If anything happens around here, he knows about it."

"Dirty Harry, what a strange name."

"Yeah, a strange name for a strange man, but he is my main source of information. I'm one of the few who can put up with him."

"What do you mean?"

"Never mind, just keep your pretty, little fingers crossed he can help us."

The kettle had boiled, and as I poured the hot water into the cups, I studied my fingers.

They may be little, but they're definitely not pretty. They resemble zombie dinner leftovers.

"I'd keep my legs crossed, too, if that would help," I said as I handed him his coffee.

Tom opened his mouth but closed it again without saying anything.

I joined him at the kitchen table. As I warmed my hands on my mug, I let my gaze wander around the kitchen, trying with all my might to find another subject to talk about. I didn't know if Tom planned to stay the night as Harry had mentioned earlier. He was welcome to do so, on the couch of course, but I didn't know how to bring the subject up. I didn't want to embarrass Tom either, in case he hadn't planned on staying. It was Saturday evening after all, and I assumed he needed to search for Miss Perfect.

"You want to stay and watch a movie?" Again, my brain had no control of what was coming out of my mouth. I looked down to prevent him from seeing my embarrassment.

"Sure, I'd love to," Tom said to my surprise.

I let out my breath. Of course, I had hoped he would as I dreaded being alone at the moment. Thoughts on Charlie's terrible situation would consume me and drive me insane. To have Tom here would at least make me pretend I wasn't going around the bend from anxiety and fear for Charlie's life.

"What sort of movies do you watch?" he asked.

"Oh, all sorts. Let's move to the living room."

With our coffees in hand, we went to sit on the couch. I switched on Netflix and browsed through the menu. I couldn't deal with comedies right now. It was wrong to be laughing considering Charlie's situation. I couldn't deal with love stories either, or horror movies. Action movies didn't do much for me now as they seemed so fake compared to reality. In fact, I found a problem watching any movie as all of them reminded me of Charlie somehow. Tom patiently let me read the blurbs and flick from one movie to the next. In the end, I turned to him.

"Do you mind watching a nature documentary?"

"Not at all. I love nature," he said and leaned back comfortably, hands behind his head, his oceanic scent drifting my way.

I picked a whale documentary. I grabbed us some beer and potato chips after and we watched two more underwater ones. We kept ourselves cool with more beer while watching a documentary on volcanoes after which we followed up with one on Pompeii. During the Pompeii one, I began to yawn. I checked my cell phone. It was after midnight. When the documentary ended, I switched the TV off.

"I don't know what time you normally go to bed, but I'm dog-tired." To make myself clear, I yawned expressively, arms up in the air and all.

Tom finished his can of beer and put it on the coffee table.

"Do you want me to stay?" he said.

Dirty Harry

I stopped mid-yawn, my arms dropping instantly.

"What do you mean?" I honestly didn't know. He had been sending out signals I had no intention of returning.

Tom grinned before he spoke.

"Would you like me to go or stay the night, here, on the couch," he said.

"Oh, um, yes. I'd like that very much. For you to stay. Here. On the couch. Harry said that's what you mentioned earlier. That that's why you argued."

"Don't listen to Harry. He doesn't know what he's talking about." Tom rolled his eyes. "I'd be happy to stay here, on the couch," and he pointed at the seat. "To make sure you're okay. I'd hate to leave you and find you're also missing tomorrow, alarm system or not."

"Thank you, I appreciate that. I also don't want to be missing tomorrow." I smiled, but it was a half-hearted smile as his suggestion was very real. The relaxing effect of binge-watching nature documentaries for the last five hours was erased as soon as we started talking about my safety.

"Let me get you a sleeping bag."

I dug one out from the hallway cupboard upstairs.

When I had Tom set up for the night, he checked how I set the alarm for the outside cameras. He seemed pleased that I had remembered how to work the system correctly. With him sleeping on the couch, Tom advised me against setting any of the downstairs indoor alarms, in case he needed to get a glass of water or use the toilet in the middle of the night, which was to be expected considering the amount of beer he had been drinking.

"But don't worry, I'm a light sleeper," he said. "If Sasha manages to sneak in without being picked up by the outdoor motion sensors, she still has to deal with me before being able to get to you. Okay?"

"Okay, no problem. See you tomorrow then."

"Goodnight, Kate," Tom said and sat down to take his shoes off.

Lying in bed, I felt okay. Not happy, definitely not happy, but I was glad Tom was in the house. I felt safe and was asleep in no time.

***

The next morning, I had a shower and dressed before going downstairs for breakfast as usual, not just because Tom was there. As I entered the living room, I saw that the sleeping bag lay neatly folded on the couch. I found Tom already dressed in the kitchen, making me a coffee.

"Perfect timing. Just the girl I wanted to see," he said cheerfully.

"Good morning. Did you sleep well?"

Tom put a hot cup of coffee in my hands, and we both sat down at the table.

"As well as can be expected. Hey, guess what? I received a call from Dirty Harry. He's got news for us."

Eager to hear more, I moved to the edge of my seat.

"Why didn't you wake me earlier? Tell me all about it."

"And set off the alarm, resulting in both of us being deaf for the next half hour? No, thank you very much. Besides, Harry never divulges information over the phone. Phones can be tapped. We need to go see him."

I jumped up. "So what are we waiting for? Let's go."

Tom chuckled and pulled me back into my seat by my sleeve.

"Hold your horses. You had a shower, but I didn't yet. If you don't mind, I'd like to freshen up as well. Besides, Harry mentioned it wasn't urgent."

"Oh, okay." I lowered my eyes and dropped into the seat again. If Harry had mentioned it wasn't urgent, it meant he didn't know where Charlie was. I lost interest in seeing him already.

Tom and I had breakfast together after which he took ten minutes to use the bathroom. I used the time to call Marlon and to talk to Sonny. Sue was still in bed. According to Marlon she was still upset but calmer now, and that Sonny helped lift her spirits. I told him I would come over as soon as I could. I refrained from telling him about Dirty Harry's message. I wasn't sure what it would lead to yet.

After calling Marlon and chatting with Sonny, I called Harry. I told him Tom's contact had a lead.

"Kate, I told you. Don't get involved with him, please," Harry pleaded.

"Why not? It's a lead, Harry. I've got to follow it. Grayson hasn't contacted me with any news yet. If this Dirty Harry's lead is a dead end... well, at least I can say I tried."

There was a long silence.

"Okay, but you take care, you hear. Don't do anything stupid. Tom has certain views and ideas, besides having a certain reputation. Don't do anything you don't want to. Keep thinking straight. Keep thinking of Charlie."

"Of course. Don't worry, you know me."

I hung up before Harry could comment on that.

What views or ideas of Tom is Harry referring to? What reckless things has his brother been up to? Why didn't Harry just say what he had to say?

Tom came downstairs and soon we were out the door. He insisted using his car as Dirty Harry may not show if he didn't recognize the car. We took off in the direction of Portland.

"So where do we find Harry?"

"We don't find Harry, Harry finds us," Tom said. "Well, sort of. We use a system where we rotate a few meeting locations. Depending on the time of day, the day of the week, and time of year, he knows where to find us. He'll only show up after we get there. He'll never be there before us. If we don't show, he won't show."

"How do you know he won't show if you're not there?"

"Ha, I found that out the hard way," Tom said. "I once sent someone else in my place when I couldn't make it to the meeting myself due to certain circumstances. Harry didn't show. Had some bad consequences. He told me later he would never work with someone else showing up instead. It's his rules. 'A matter of confidentiality,' he said."

"Wow. He sounds like he has some trust issues."

"I like it," Tom said. "It means I can trust him, too. So far, I've always been able to rely on him. His information has been profitable in about ninety-five percent of the time. The remaining five percent was out of his control."

Ninety-five percent. This meant that there was a very good chance that we would find out something useful. I settled myself a bit deeper into the car seat. It was made of leather and had been cold when I first sat down. Now, the seat heater had kicked in, and it was a welcoming place on this cold day.

We drove into Portland at about 10 a.m. Tom took us to a shady part of town and parked the car around the corner from some nightclub. He then led me into a dark alley. There were a few dumpsters against the wall and the smell coming from them was far from fresh.

"This is where we wait," Tom said.

I rubbed my hands together, and when they were warmed up a bit, I tucked them in the pockets of my jacket. This morning was the coldest of the season so far. Probably because of the clear sky.

My nose picked up a new scent which made it crinkle. The dumpsters smelled, but this was far worse. I looked around but couldn't figure out where it was coming from.

"What's that god-awful stench?"

"Oh yeah, I almost forgot. Whatever you do, don't mention the smell," Tom whispered.

I frowned at him, wondering what he was talking about. Tom smiled, not at me but at someone behind me.

"Who's the broad?" a voice said. It startled me.

I turned around, the stink now hitting me full-frontal. A shadow walked up to us from out of the darkness of the alley. As it neared us, the stench became more and more concentrated. The shadow appeared to be a short, stocky man. Around him clung the smell of sewerage. I consciously kept my hands in my pockets to stop them from pinching my nose. I smiled as well as I could at the man.

"Kate, this is Harry. Harry, this is Kate Clarke, the woman I told you about. She's the one looking for Sasha Morozov." The man looked me up and down. "Don't worry, she's kosher," Tom said as he reached into his pocket and took out a packet of cigarettes.

I didn't realize Tom smoked. I certainly hadn't noticed an ashtray smell on him or seen him smoke outside. To my surprise, he gave the packet to Harry, who immediately took out a cigarette and lit it. He drew heavily on it and blew the smoke into my face. Normally I hated cigarette smoke, but at the moment, I welcomed the smell coming out of Harry's mouth over the one coming from the rest of him.

"I know Kate Clarke, seen the interviews. I know what she's done," Harry said.

Is that a good thing or a bad thing?

Harry hadn't taken his eyes off me. My eyes sought Tom's, anything to take my mind off this strange man and the stench he was emitting.

"You said you had news?" Tom reminded Harry.

Harry took another drag from the cigarette. This time, the smoke escaped his mouth as he talked.

"There's a place six miles out of town, between Turnpike and Forest Lake. Was bought by one S. Morozov about half a year ago." Harry took another drag and blew it in my face.

"Why do you think there's no urgency?" I asked.

"Because the place is for sale again," he answered.

Shit.

"Thank you."

For the information and the smoke.

"Thanks, Harry," Tom said. "You'll find my appreciation in your bank account as usual."

Harry gave Tom a single nod, looked at me one more time, and disappeared in the direction he had come from. Unfortunately, his smell lingered a bit longer.

Tom and I walked back to the car, enjoying the crisp, fresh air as soon as we stepped out of the alley.

"How much are you paying him for the information?" I asked as we reached the car.

"That's something between Harry and myself," Tom said.

"But I requested the information, so I want to pay for it."

"After all you've done? No way. Forget about it." Tom got into the car and gave me the impression that the matter was closed.

What does he mean with 'what I've done?'

A Sign

The place Harry had mentioned wasn't far from Portland, and we arrived there within half an hour. There was hardly any traffic on the roads on a Sunday morning. We didn't know exactly where the house was located, but there only existed one road between the toll road and Forest Lake. We drove along it until we found a for sale sign.

"You think this could be it?"

"It could," Tom said.

"Why don't we drive a bit further to see if there are other properties for sale?"

Tom took his hands off the steering wheel and rested them on his thighs.

"What are you afraid of?" he said. "That they want to sell you the property if it's the wrong one? Do you expect the next sign to say 'Sasha was here'?"

I blinked and turned to Tom. He returned my stare with a gentle smile.

He's got a point.

"Okay, let's check it out."

Tom put the car into drive. The vegetation in this area gave the properties plenty of privacy from the road. Once we neared the cabin, the area cleared, but the perimeter of the place was still screened from the neighbors by bushes and pine trees. It was the perfect place to do clandestine things. Yet, there were no vehicles parked in front of the house, and my heart sank. I would not find Charlie here.

The possibility of finding my love chopped up into pieces entered my mind. My stomach cramped, and my hand tried to clutch it to still the pain.

"Are you okay?" Tom asked.

"I'll be okay in a minute."

He gave me a single nod and got out. He walked around the property and came back to the car. By this time, I had taken several deep breaths and had stepped out, ready to face my fears.

"There doesn't seem to be anybody around. Let's see if we can get into the cabin," Tom said.

Together we walked toward the front porch. The cabin looked like a nice vacation home. It was on the edge of a lake but close to the city. I bet it had cost Sasha a fair bit to purchase the place, even though it could do with a lick of paint. Where would she have gotten the money from, though? She had been in prison for over ten years. Either she saved money while working as a model, or she had contacts, Russian mob contacts.

Tom knocked on the door. Nothing happened. I peered through one of the windows. It was dark inside as most curtains were drawn, but through a slit, I distinguished some furniture. It was hard to tell if somebody had been here recently. There weren't any coffee cups or plates on the table, no personal items lying around.

A sound of scratching made me look aside, and I found Tom fiddling with the lock. Before I had a chance to tell him off, he had the door open. Harry had mentioning years ago how his brother had a set of unapproved friends teaching him unapproved skills. They might have been unapproved, but they certainly were handy skills to have. Tom looked at me and tipped his head toward the open door. I followed him into the cabin.

The first thing I noted was the absence of a rotting-flesh smell, and I instantly breathed better. I took in my surroundings. It was a simple place with a seventies look. Kitchenette, dining table with four chairs, two couches, a small, old-fashioned TV on a little table. On the wall behind the TV hung a myriad of road work signs. Stolen government property. Why would anybody want to collect those? I poked my head into the adjoining rooms. The bathroom was empty and so were the two small bedrooms, their mattresses stripped. It seemed we hit a dead end. Dirty Harry's tip appeared to belong to the five percent statistic. Back in the living room, I found Tom standing with his hands on his hips, looking around with a disappointed look on his face.

"Fuck," I said as I pulled a chair out and dropped on it. "I thought we were going to find some evidence here.

Something to tell me that Charlie's still alive, or at least that he had been here these last few days." A heavy pounding made itself present behind my eyes. I only had had one coffee this morning, and my body wasn't agreeing with the limited supply of caffeine. Pressing my fingers to my temples, I tried to massage the pain away. Tom walked over to the kitchenette and opened and closed the kitchen cupboards. The sounds of the doors closing were too loud, but I held my tongue. It hit me that not finding Charlie here didn't only mean we weren't any closer to finding him. It also meant that the chance of re-attaching his finger was getting slimmer. We only had two more days. Bile rose up in my throat, the nasty surge equaling the rise of my hate for Sasha.

"There's nothing here," Tom said.

"I know. I can see that." I had thought him to be better than stating the obvious.

"I mean, there's nothing here in the cupboards, not even dust. Not a cobweb in sight," he said. "If this place was bought six months ago and not used, there should've been enough dust to write your name in, but there's nothing. Don't you find that strange?"

I looked up. Could he be on to something?

"It could also mean she's really trying to sell the place." I sighed.

Tom wasn't so easily defeated. He walked over to the TV and wiped his finger on it.

"No dust at all. I'm sure this place has been used."

He went into the bathroom, and I heard him lift the toilet seat.

You could at least close the door.

"See," Tom said as he came out a few seconds later. "Even the toilet has been used. The water level hasn't lowered due to evaporation. Same with the wash basin drain. Someone has used this cabin not too long ago and has made sure there are no traces."

I stood up, deprived of any enthusiasm.

"No point in staying here any longer then."

Tom followed me back to the car. My body sagged into the seat which had lost its warmth and made me shiver. Tom got into the driver's seat. I felt his eyes on me. Whatever. I didn't want to communicate right now. I wasn't getting any closer to finding Charlie, and it ate me. Every minute counted. Time was ticking by, and I was getting nowhere. Why would Sasha have bought this place? Why would she want to lead us here? There must have been another reason than teaching us the extent of road work signs.

My eyes opened wider. I nearly broke the door handle trying to get out of the car. I ran back into the cabin. Tom came running after me. He found me in the middle of the room, staring at the road signs.

"What is it?" he asked.

"Look at them. Don't you see something odd?"

Tom took a moment to inspect them.

"No, not really. Apart from being an odd thing to

collect and put up on your living room wall."

"What about that one?" I pointed at a circular sign, one of those 'forbidden to...' ones. It showed a pink pig with a red, diagonal stripe through it.

"Yeah..." Tom said as he scratched his chin. "That's not a real road work sign."

It hung high up on the wall, so I dragged a chair over. I lifted the sign off its hook and laid it on the dining table.

"No pigs. Well, that message is clear," Tom said.

My eyes scanned the surface of the sign. The light beam coming in between the curtains reflected from the fluorescent surface. There were no scratches on it, no rusty marks. It appeared to be brand new, and that Sasha had this sign made especially for me. I picked it up again and turned it around. An envelope was stuck to the back of the sign. My heart now pounded in my chest. I quickly laid the sign down, but before I could take off the envelope, Tom put his hand on my arm, restraining my movement.

"Don't touch it," he said.

Sparring

I threw an annoyed glance at Tom, asking for an explanation for stopping me opening the envelope.

"If I understand this woman a bit better," he said, "I think you shouldn't touch it."

"Why? It may have info on Charlie's whereabouts. The sooner we open it, the better." I tried to continue the movement of my arm, but Tom's strong grip kept me from reaching the envelope.

"Look at how it's bulging. There's something in there. It also smells funny."

I pulled my arm back. "Do you think there's another finger of Charlie in there?"

"No, it doesn't smell like that, but I'm certain we should have the police take a look at it first."

He was right. The envelope seemed to contain something more than a letter. I smelled nothing strange, but I trusted him when he said there wasn't another part of Charlie in there. I wanted to trust him on that.

"But she said no pigs. You said so yourself."

"Exactly. She wants to frustrate you. I'm certain you'll ruin whatever is in there if you touch it. It may even ruin you. She wants you to suffer."

"Well, that's for sure. And she's succeeding."

I sighed as I looked at the fat envelope. It possibly hid a clue, telling me how to get to Charlie, and I couldn't touch it. Suffering was an understatement.

"Call Grayson. Tell him what we found," Tom said.

As I took out my cell phone, I realized I still hadn't put Grayson's number into my contacts. My hand went into the pocket of my jacket, to find the business card Grayson had given me but found it empty. I face-palmed myself as I realized I had put on a different jacket this morning due to the cold.

"I'll have to call the police station. I haven't got Grayson's number on me."

A young man answered the phone, this time very much sounding like George.

"Bullsbrook Police Station. How can I help you?" he said.

"George, is that you? It's Kate Clarke here. I'm looking for Detective Grayson. Is he in?"

"I'm afraid he's not available for the day. Nobody's here at the moment. Can I leave him a message?" George said.

I made a noise of frustration.

"When will he be back?"

"Tomorrow morning, I expect," George replied.

"Okay, we'll see him then." I hung up. "I don't expect the forensic team to work on a Sunday anyway."

Tom had heard the whole conversation as I had put

it on speaker phone, and he didn't ask for a recap. I carefully picked up the sign, and we left the cabin.

***

When Tom pulled the car up in front of my house, I dreaded finding another parcel on my doorstep. My home, the place that had been my safe haven since we bought it, a place of happiness, was now a place of terror. Every time I returned to it, I was afraid of what I might find.

Relieved to find the porch empty, I got out and took the sign with me. Before going in, I turned back to Tom. He had wound the car window down.

"Are you sure you don't want to come inside and have lunch?"

"No, Kate, but thanks for the offer. I've got a few things to take care off. If you want, I can come over again tonight, though."

It was a sweet gesture, but I couldn't keep asking this man to sleep on my couch. I had no idea how long this situation was going to take, and I needed to get used to being on my own in the house.

"I'm fine, Tom. I trust the alarm system. I'll call you as soon as I know more. Thanks for your help."

"My pleasure. You can call me anytime, Kate."

He didn't drive off, and I assumed he waited for me to go inside and possibly set the alarm off. I hesitated momentarily but entered the house. It was exactly as it had been before. Dark, cold, and empty. I disabled the alarm and checked the kitchen, but there was no trace of a break in, no parcel on the kitchen table. Before I took my jacket off, I went back outside and waved to Tom. He said goodbye and drove off.

***

I hoped the baked beans on toast I made myself for lunch would warm me up, but I kept feeling cold. I turned up the thermostat. It made no difference. My hands kept feeling like clumps of ice. I tried to absorb some warmth from the sun rays coming in through the kitchen window, but it was as if the sun had lost its desire to share its warmth. I had to go out of this place, or I would lose my mind.

Before starting my car, I texted Marlon I would be at the farm in a quarter of an hour and hoped we could do a training session.

***

As soon as I killed my car's engine on Sue and Marlon's driveway, Sonny came running outside. He waited about five meters away from the car. I grabbed my sports bag from the back seat, also grabbed Sonny's teddy bear which I had brought, and stepped out of the car. Sonny took three large steps and jumped the remaining distance into my arms. I swirled him around, the both of us laughing. His laugh was so contagious. I missed him but was glad he stayed with Sue and Marlon. It was better for Sue.

"Hey, Little Man. Guess who I brought with me."

"Teddy!" Sonny screamed with delight. He grabbed the bear from me and strangled it in a hug. I let him slide to the ground. My boy was getting heavier every day.

"Come on, Little Man, let's get you inside. It's way too cold for you to be outside without a jacket."

Sonny almost pulled me off my feet as he tried to drag me inside.

"You can help us with the puzzle, Mommy."

"Oh? What puzzle is that?"

"It's a picture of a koala bear, lots of gray hairs. You'll love it."

I didn't contradict him but thought otherwise, especially now I was getting some grey hairs myself.

Sue sat at the dining table in her PJs, the jigsaw puzzle pieces taking up most of the table's surface. She smiled at me, but I noted the sad look in her eyes. I went over and gave her a kiss on the cheek and a hug. Sonny climbed on the chair next to his sister.

"Heard anything about Dad?" Sue asked.

"Well, Tom and I followed a lead this morning, and it seems promising. We'll have to wait until tomorrow before the police can check it out." I caressed her pretty face. "We'll find him, Little Smudge."

Sue grabbed my hand, pressed it against her cheek, and cried.

"Hush now, darling. I told you we have a lead. We'll find him. Keep thinking positive thoughts. Your father wouldn't want you to think negative things now, would he?" I tipped her chin up to make her face me. "Think positive, Little Smudge. We'll get him back."

Sonny stood up on his chair and leaned over to wipe Sue's tears away.

"Mommy will find Charlie. You'll see." He put his arms around Sue's neck. Sue returned Sonny's hug.

"Yes, she will," she said.

The two of them smiled at each other and it made my heart melt. A parent couldn't wish for lovelier children.

"Now, how hard is this puzzle?" I leaned over to examine it.

At that moment, Marlon came out of the bedroom, dressed in his training outfit.

"I thought you wanted to do some sparring, Kate?" he said.

"Mommy?" Sonny's eyes pleaded.

"Mommy's got to stay in shape to fight the bad guys, Little Man. I promise you, I'll only be gone an hour. Then I'll be back and do this puzzle with you if you haven't finished it already by then."

"Don't worry, we have another one," he said, "one with lots of leaves."

"Okay, can't wait to do that one. This one is a bit too difficult for me."

It made Sonny beam with pride as they had already finished half of the puzzle. I kissed Sue on her forehead and Sonny on his nose.

"We'll be back shortly."

***

I drove Marlon to the gym on the farm ground. The girls had always trained their kids in the feeding aisle between the cows, but as the farm was making a good profit these last few years, funds had been freed to build a proper gym.

"She looks better today." Sue's smile had made me happy.

"Yes, Sonny's a great influence on her, keeping her mind off her Dad," Marlon said. "Sometimes she breaks down and cries for no apparent reason, but Sonny helps her get over it. He's a good little man."

"I wished I could do something for her, but I can't. It frustrates me so much." My knuckles went white on the steering wheel.

"It's okay. Sue knows it's out of your control. Getting Charlie back would be the best thing you could do for her at the moment."

"That's what I'm trying, Lon, with all my might."

"So, what's this new lead I heard you talk about?" he said.

We arrived at the gym and got out of the car. I brought Marlon up to speed on the pig sign as we walked into the gym.

"Wow. She really goes out of her way to hurt you, doesn't she?"

"We still don't know what's in the envelope, but I believe Tom. I wouldn't be surprised if there's a bomb in there or something."

Marlon stopped walking, clearly shocked.

"Don't worry. We're on to her." I gave him a playful pat on the back.

Once inside, I used the locker room to change into my karategi and went out onto the mat. I jumped up and down a few times and shook off some tension. I was ready for a good workout. Marlon would have a hard time with me today, for sure. We began with a ten-minute stretching session. I pushed myself to my limits, just beyond the hurting point. I wanted to feel pain. I wanted it to fuel my fire to fight Sasha. One of these days, I would face her, and when that day came, I planned to beat the crap out of that woman.

"What did you have in mind for today? Aikido, jiu-jitsu?" Marlon asked.

"Let's do some aikido first, then some karate, a bit of taekwondo perhaps."

"You sure you don't want to train MMA?" Marlon laughed.

"At my age? Forget about it. You should've asked me ten years ago."

"Ten years ago... Hmm, I was a two-year-old then," Marlon said. "I don't think I knew about MMA when I was two years old."

I shook my head. Talking about time was always tricky with suckers. Officially, Marlon was only twelve, but physically, he was a healthy adult athlete. There was always the nagging question in the back of my mind if their fast growth-rate also meant they would get old twice as fast. I repressed the thought and focused on our katas.

After the katas, we put on our sparring gear. I was pumped up and ready for some action. When Marlon was ready, we bowed to each other and took our fighting stances. With no time to lose, I came down on Marlon, raining punches and kicks. Marlon took it all in, blocking my every move, biding his time, and when I pulled in my leg after kicking his torso, he ducked down and with a stretched-out leg, swooped my weight-bearing leg from under me. Exhausted and surprised, I lay on my back.

"Don't make yourself vulnerable," he said. "You should have been faster and able to block that one with your lifted leg. Always be prepared to block a counter strike." He held his hand out to help me up. "Once you're down, it's very hard to get up again."

Tell me about it.

Having been put on my back too often in the past had made me take up martial arts in the first place. I hated not being in control of my body. Marlon's remark hit the nail on the head. I needed to be more in control during my fighting, not let my attempt to conquer make me open to assault. It was good to blow off steam by lashing out, but winning a fight wasn't done by force alone. You had to keep thinking, being ahead of your opponent, like when playing chess. You needed to have several options in place and make the best move at the right time. We took our stances again and renewed our fight.

Fifteen minutes later, I was exhausted and drenched in sweat. It blurred my vision. We called it a day and did some cooling down stretches.

After we drove back, we took turns in the bathroom to freshen up and get changed. Sue and Sonny had finished the koala puzzle and were now working on laying down the edges of the tree puzzle. I stayed the evening, ordering pizzas for all, and finished the puzzle with them. When it was bedtime for Sonny, he said he wanted to come home with me, but I told him he had to stay with Sue and Marlon until Charlie was back. As I tucked him in bed, I explained why.

"I need you to take care of your big sister for me. It's hard for me to be there for her at the moment as I am working very hard on getting Dad back. I'm depending on you to take care of her for now, together with Marlon of course. Can you do that for me? I know it's a big ask, but I really need your help, Little Man."

"Sue does need my help. She cries a lot. I make her stop. I'll stay and help her."

"That's my boy. I knew I could count on you." I nuzzled his nose and gave him a big hug. "Sleep tight Little Man."

Not long after, I said my goodbyes to Sue and Marlon and drove off.

Before I left the farm, I visited Julie. I would see Grayson the next morning, and I thought I'd better let her know, just in case she wanted to come along. She was, as expected, in her office. Sometimes I wondered if she ever stayed in her apartment at all.

"Hey, sis, what are you up to?"

Julie looked up from her computer screen.

"Covering your ass," she said.

A Mental Case

Cocking my head, wondering what my sister was on about.

"You had an interview scheduled with The New York Times this Tuesday, remember? I also had to postpone a lot of interview requests since your appearance on the Emma show. And I've got to get May Ling to cover all your council meetings."

"Ah, shit. Sorry, I completely forgot." I dropped myself into a chair in front of her desk.

"Apology accepted. You've got more important things on your mind at the moment. The Times didn't mind, but they definitely want to reschedule." Julie leaned forward. "They're very eager to get the whole story on Charlie. An exclusive."

I saw the dollar signs in her eyes.

Scroogina Duck.

"Jules, I don't even know if we're going to get him back in time before Sasha chops him to bits."

My own coolness surprised me. It had been only a few days ago that I nearly had a nervous breakdown about Charlie's predicament. My mind was adjusting from being a nervous wreck into someone who was ready to kick butt. The sparring session got me into gear to make Sasha pay for what she was doing to my Charlie.

"They don't care," Julie said.

My eyes flashed lightning bolts at her.

"Well, I do. Fuck it, Jules, tell them to piss off."

"I know, sis," Julie said as she leaned back again. "Don't worry. I'll deal with them. My way. Now, did you come here to enjoy my entertaining company, now you're on your own on a Sunday evening, or do you have any progress on Charlie's whereabouts?"

This time I leaned closer to her.

"We've got a lead—"

"Who's 'we'?" she said.

"Tom and I. He received information from an informant this morning—"

"This morning? What time? Did he stay the night?"

My god, Julie, you are the worst gossip whore I've ever met.

"Yes, he stayed the night, and no, he slept on the couch. Thank you for your concern for my wellbeing. Now, do you want to hear the news or not?"

"Yes, of course, don't let me stop you," she said.

Right.

I told her about Dirty Harry, the cabin, the pig sign, and the letter.

"Oh my god, Tom's right. There could be a bomb in there. She'd definitely want to blow your head off," Julie said.

"I don't know. Somehow I doubt that. I think there won't be any gratification in it for her. I think she'd want to see me suffer."

Julie leaned back and stared at me for a minute.

"Yeah, you've got a point. But still, better safe than sorry. Thank heaven Tom was a quick thinker. I like him. Especially the way he danced."

I groaned, sinking back into the chair. Julie appeared not to have left the party when Sue and Marlon had, and she had seen me made a fool of myself with Tom.

"Please, don't remind me of that again."

"Why not? You two were quite a sight to see, so in sync. It's good Charlie wasn't there, or you would've had a major fight about it afterward."

"You really believe I would've danced like that with Tom if Charlie had been there? He'd never let me get drunk like that in the first place. And thank you for bowing out by the way. It would've been nice if you'd stopped me from making such a fool of myself."

"Come now, sis. You know as well as I do that you needed it. You were a mess, and you needed to take your mind off the situation. One mental case in the family is enough."

Trouble

My body stiffened upon hearing Julie's words.

"Sorry, I didn't mean it that way," Julie said. "What I meant was that Sue needs you and you must be strong for her."

I stood up.

"I'm tired so I'm gonna go. I'll be seeing Grayson tomorrow morning to show him the pig sign and the letter. Do you want to come along?"

Julie had risen with me.

"I sure do. I'll take any opportunity of seeing that man again. Thanks. Shall I pick you up?"

"Come and get me at nine. The sooner he can open that letter, the better. See you tomorrow."

I turned around and left my sister standing behind her desk without giving her my usual hug. I should have given her one, but she had hurt me with her words, and I wanted her to know it.

When I sat in my car, before I turned on the engine, I realized what I'd just done. Sasha and I weren't so different after all.

***

As soon as I was home and sure nobody had left any parcels for me, I set the alarm and made ready for bed. Once in bed, I thought about the day. It had been a roller-coaster of ups and downs. Too bad it had ended on a down. I loved my sister, but sometimes her uncurbed mouth was a bit too much for me. Maybe getting together with Grayson would tame her a little. I had no idea what she saw in him. He seemed like a boring man to me, but love worked in mysterious ways. I knew that very well. I hoped my sister would finally find the partner of her dreams. With that positive thought, I turned off the light.

In the dark, my thoughts went out to Charlie. Where could he be right now? Would the wound of his finger be throbbing? Had Sasha bandaged it in a sterile way? How was she keeping Charlie confined? Was he locked up or chained to something? Were the chains made of metal or were they those plastic ties. If they were the plastic ties, could he possibly get himself free?

It was hard to keep thinking positive thoughts, and it took me a long time to fall asleep.

***

Julie rang the doorbell at 9 a.m. sharp. I bet she wanted to get back in my good books.

Let it go, Kate. You know she loves Sue.

I opened the front door and let her in.

"Hi, sis. How are you this fine morning?" I knew her face beamed because of the anticipation of seeing Grayson, not me.

"I've been better." It was the truth. I hadn't said it to make her feel bad. The whole situation was just taking its toll on me. I couldn't sleep without hearing Charlie soothing snoring, and I had woken up tired and cranky. To make sure Julie didn't take it the wrong way, I gave her a peck on the cheek and a quick hug. "But I'll live. Let's see how fast Grayson can show us the inside of that letter."

I grabbed the bag I put the pig sign in, set the house alarm, and locked the door behind us. Within a few minutes, we arrived at the police station. Julie had been silent all the way which was unusual for her. After she locked her car, she checked her image in the side mirror.

"How do I look? Is my hair okay?" she asked.

"You look fine." Julie made me laugh. She was in her thirties but acted like a teenager. "Come on, I'm not waiting for you."

George let us into the interrogation room, and not long after Grayson entered. When he noticed Julie in the room, he smiled and said hi to her. Julie returned the welcome. Grayson completely forgot to say hi to me. He wore the same type of clothing as before, but there was something different about him. I couldn't put my finger on it. He had wheeled in a trolley with a TV and CD-player on it and was now plugging the cords into the wall.

"Before you show us whatever you're going to show us," I said, "I want you to see something else first." I took the pig sign out of the bag and put it on the table.

Grayson turned around, looked at the sign, and then at me.

"What is it?" he said.

"Well, I thought it was pretty obvious. It's a 'no pigs' sign."

"Oh, come on, Kate," Julie said. "Grayson can see that. He wants to know why you're showing it to him."

I glanced sideways at her and saw her bashing her eyelids at the detective. Grayson, in return, gave her all of his attention.

Somebody pass me a bucket.

I shrugged, and Grayson reluctantly focused on me.

"Tom received a tip yesterday morning, leading us to this cabin near Forest Lake."

Grayson's smile disappeared as soon as I mentioned Tom's name. He began tapping the remote for the CD-player in the palm of his hand.

"We had a look around and found this sign." I indicated the sign before turning it over. "We found this on the back, but Tom said not to open it. He advised me that the police should have a look at it first."

"I thought I warned you not to get involved with that guy," Grayson said as he looked down his nose at me.

Don't ever tell me what to do.

Tom's words were getting more and more popular with me.

"Well, at least we got somewhere and found something, which is more than I can say for your actions."

"Come on. The police are working very hard to find Charlie. Aren't you?" Julie hadn't taken her eyes off Grayson.

Whose side are you one, sis?

"I sure am," Grayson said and smiled a sickly sweet smile at my sister. "We've received new information. That's why I wasn't available yesterday. I'll show it to you in a minute, but I'll have a look at this first if you want. I suppose you didn't find it lying outside the cabin?"

"Um, no... Not exactly, no." My index finger followed an invisible trail on the laminate table top.

"I thought as much. Stay away from him, Kate. He's trouble. I can't say it often enough. Now, tell me exactly where you found this."

I told Grayson all that had happened. Well, almost all of it. I left out the bit about visiting Dirty Harry and the bit where Tom had picked the lock of the cabin. Grayson didn't ask how we got inside. I guessed he already knew and didn't find it important.

"Why did Tom stop you from opening the envelope?" he asked after I finished my story.

"I don't know. He said the envelope was bulging. Maybe there's a bomb in it?"

I wasn't going to mention to Grayson that Tom had said it smelled funny as I wasn't sure what he had meant with that. One thing was for certain, if I had been alone, I would've opened it. It had taken all of my self-restraint not to open the envelope after Tom had dropped me off at home and I was alone with the envelope. But I knew he could be right. There could be a bomb in it for all I knew. I didn't know what letter bombs looked like. I guess they weren't hand-grenades, but envelopes containing letters usually didn't bulge either.

"Does it matter why he stopped me? All I want is for you guys to open and examine the content. I want to know if there's a clue in it that will lead me to Charlie, without me getting my head blown off."

Grayson studied me for a moment. I stared back at him and refused to look away first. Julie shuffled her foot.

"Okay," Grayson finally said. "I'll have our guys check it out. Although I still don't see any evidence that this has anything to do with Sasha Morozov."

"Come on. The tip we got was that one S. Morozov bought this cabin six months ago. How many S. Morozovs can there be? And six months ago, don't you think it's too much of a coincidence? It's got to be her."

"You should have let the police deal with it. We may

have been able to find more evidence. I thought you learned your lesson when you messed up the previous crime scene. Sometimes I wonder if you really want to find Charlie."

Grayson's words hurt me like a dagger stabbed into my heart. I would give my life to get Charlie out of Sasha's hands. And I was sure that Tom was right about Sasha not leaving any evidence in the cabin, so Grayson's words were empty. He just tried to make me let go of Tom.

Focus on the here and now, Kate.

"What did you have to show us?"

Grayson turned on the TV.

A Family Affair

Grayson pressed the TV's fast-forward button while he talked.

"We found nothing on who could have delivered the package, but we got our hands on CCTV footage of the street where we found the lunchbox. It's from the shop on the corner off High Street."

In the video, you mainly saw the shop window, but it also gave a view of further up that side of the street. Grayson continued to fast-forward to the time of day when Charlie walked home. He went back to normal time when a white van stopped in the middle of the street. Two men stepped out. They wore thick clothing, including gloves, their faces covered with balaclavas, their eyes hidden behind dark glasses. The men were obviously suckers. Only when they grabbed Charlie was it clear he had been walking on the side of the road, alongside the parked cars.

Charlie struggled when the two men grabbed him, dropping his lunchbox. Even though the men moved slowly, they had the element of surprise. They were strong and had no trouble getting Charlie into the van. One of them got into the back with Charlie. The other closed the door and took the driver's seat. Before they drove away, the one behind the wheel threw Charlie's cell phone out of the window. The van drove off within a minute after it had stopped. The kidnap was over before anybody had noticed.

Grayson stopped the video.

"If that isn't proof we're dealing with a kidnap, I don't know what is," Julie said to no one in particular.

"Do you recognize any of these men?" Grayson asked us.

"No, I have no idea who they are," I said.

Julie shook her head.

"The van was stolen a day before. We're looking for it as we speak," Grayson said.

"Two guys," I said. "You mentioned earlier Sasha has two sons, twins. Could they be her boys?"

"That's what I was trying to find out yesterday. It appears that as soon as Sasha was released from prison, the first thing she did was getting in contact with her sons. They had been taken away from her at birth and put in a local sucker internment camp. From there, many were transported to the New York facility when they were five years old, including the twins. Due to SAMM's work, they were released two-and-a-half years ago. The SAMM program helped them to be introduced into society and they were doing okay. Sasha must have gotten a hold of their records as they disappeared a week after she did. I still don't have any proof, but yes, I do think the two men who took

Charlie are her sons."

My heart sank and bled for Charlie. Sasha having two accomplices didn't make things easier for him. They could keep an eye on him day and night. Would the boys hold a grudge against Charlie? Would Sasha have brainwashed them in the past six months to hate him as much as she hated him? We needed to find Charlie, and fast.

I bit my nails almost into non-existence as my thoughts raced. Sasha had left a clue when she bought the cabin in her own name. She had done this on purpose, but now she had sold the cabin, she had to live somewhere.

"What are the boys' names?" I asked Grayson.

Grayson picked up a file from the trolley and had a quick look inside.

"Arkady and Konstantin, a.k.a. Kady and Kostya Duncan."

"Duncan?" Julie and I both said in sync. We looked at each other.

"I always assumed Duncan was his first name."

"So did I," Julie said.

It had been clear Duncan used to be a soldier when he ran his suckers pack during Black October. Only now did it make sense people had been calling him by his surname.

"Does it matter?" Grayson asked.

"No," I said and focused on Grayson again. "My

reasoning was this; Tom and I found the property because Sasha had bought it under her name. It's for sale again, and they're definitely not there, so they must have another place to stay. What if she bought another property, but this time under one of her sons' names?" I looked at Grayson and saw his face light up.

"Good thinking. I'll get on it right away. Grab a coffee in the meantime if you like." He disappeared before I could ask him where the coffee machine was.

My disappointed glance fell on the TV. I grabbed the remote of the CD-player Grayson had left on the table and rewound the video footage. I played the kidnap scene again. This time, I did notice Charlie walking on the side of the road before the van came into view. Longing filled my heart. He looked up innocently when the van stopped beside him. The abduction happened so fast. After watching the footage about three or four times, I was sure Charlie realized the men were up to no good by the time they had reached him. It was a shame the boys were wearing balaclavas and that I couldn't see their faces. Would Charlie have recognized them?

I was about to rewind the tape again when Julie put her hand on my arm.

"Come on, let's grab a coffee," she said.

I hung my head. Reluctantly, I let go of the remote.

George pointed us to the coffee pot in the little kitchen. They had a snack machine in there as well, and

I was tempted to grab myself a chocolate bar. Thinking of Charlie, chained or locked up and possibly starved, I restrained myself from doing so.

Julie and I got ourselves a cup of coffee, returned to the interrogation room, and waited. I took little sips. The coffee tasted horrible, but my caffeine addiction made me sip it again and again.

"He's looking even better today than when he came to the farm," Julie said after a while. She was staring happily at the wall opposite us. I agreed with her.

"He shaved," I said, glad I finally figured out why he looked different.

"You noticed it too?" she said. "Do you think he did it so I'd want to kiss him? I'd kiss him with or without a stubble."

Grayson entered the room as Julie finished the last sentence. Her cheeks turned crimson, and Grayson's eyes desperately avoided hers. He cleared his throat and tried to focus on my face. It was no use, his eyes kept drifting toward Julie's.

"We've had a hit. There's a storage box rented by a Kostya Duncan on Kennebec Street, Portland."

"When are we going?" I said as I got up.

"Hold your horses," Grayson said. "I need to get a warrant and a team together first. This will take time. I'll let you know how it went."

"What do you mean 'how it went'? Aren't we coming?" I couldn't believe he wasn't going to let us in on this.

"Too dangerous, Kate. Just sit this one out."

Grayson opened the door and held it to let us out.

"Thank you," Julie said.

"My pleasure," Grayson replied.

The pheromones flying through the air were making me feel sick, so I went outside as fast as I could. It took Julie a bit longer before she appeared through the doors. She sported a huge smile. No doubt she had been able to chat with Grayson on a topic that had nothing to do with finding Charlie. I zipped up my jacket.

"Finally. Let's go."

When we sat in her car, she didn't start the engine. Instead, she turned to me, but didn't say anything. The twinkle in her eyes said enough.

"Are you thinking what I'm thinking?" I said to Julie.

"If you're thinking storage facility on Kennebec Street, I sure as hell am."

I smiled, and she started the car.

***

We found the place in no time. It was the only storage facility in the street. Julie and I entered the reception area and found a pock-scarred, thirty-something redhead manning the desk.

"Good morning, ladies. What can I do for you?" he

asked with a friendly smile.

"We'd like to know if you're renting out a storage unit to a guy named Kostya Duncan," I said.

"I'm sorry, but I'm not allowed to give you information on any of our customers," the man said politely. He had made quotation marks in the air with both hands when he said the word 'customers.'

My heart sank, and I turned away.

"Look, mister," Julie said, not giving up as easily as I had. "My sister's partner was kidnapped, and his finger has been chopped off. We already know Kostya Duncan has hired a storage unit here. What we want to know is, has anybody complained about the unit? You know, like, have there been any sounds coming out of it, funny smells, that sort of thing. We're talking CSI Miami kind of scenes."

Julie did a great job trying to make this guy talk. I would've talked. It seemed to work as the man was following her every word.

"Wow," the man said when Julie finished her plea. "I can't wait to tell this one to my friends. But, unless you have a warrant, I can't give you any information." The smile hadn't left his face. "Well, do you?"

"No, we don't. But it's coming, don't you worry about that." I sat down on one of the plastic seats available, and Julie joined me. Her face set into a dark mood.

"Of course, ladies. Of course." The man went back

to whatever he was doing before we came in and ignored us for the time being.

After a few hours of being bored to death, Grayson and five cops busted into the small reception room, all dressed in full protection armor including cuffs to protect their necks. I was convinced this team knew how to fight suckers, should the boys be here.

Grayson stormed at us as soon as he saw Julie and me sitting in the corner.

"What are you two doing here? I told you to go home."

"Yeah, I heard you," I said. "But I wanted in on the action. If Charlie's here, I want to be there for him."

There was nothing Grayson could do about it. This was a public place. He threw an angry glance at Julie, who smiled a very unconvincing smile at him, and with her hands gestured it was my idea.

Thanks for the backup, sis.

Grayson then stepped away from us and waved the warrant in front of the guy behind the reception desk.

"Where do we find the box rented by Kostya Duncan?" Grayson said.

The poor guy didn't know what had happened when his reception room had filled with policemen dressed like ninja turtles and armed to the teeth. He typed away on his keyboard and stuttered as he answered.

"It's... it's... box number thirteen at... at... the end of

the corridor. Box thirteen... at the end of the corridor. Left-hand side."

"You've got to be kidding me," I whispered to Julie.

"Why?" she said, also under her breath.

"Did you see the street name at the end of the building? The one we drove on to get here?"

"No. What about it?"

"It's Elm Street."

Mail

Julie looked at me, her eyes as wide as saucers. A bad feeling settled into the pit of my stomach.

"You two wait here," Grayson said. "I'll let you know when the coast is clear."

Said the man standing a few miles from the second largest oil port on the east coast of the country.

The police team, including Grayson, exited the reception area and filed into the corridor. One of the squad members carried a large bolt cutter, and I supposed it wouldn't take long for them to get into the unit. I hated not being able to see what was happening, but I could understand why Grayson didn't let us in on the action. I didn't want one of the twins going for my throat either.

"Has the unit been used lately?" I asked the guy behind the reception desk.

He checked his computer data without an objection this time.

"No, not at all," he said. "The guy rented it about two months ago, but he's never been back since. I thought it was weird as he waited specifically for one to become available at the end of the corridor."

Julie's eyes met mine, and we both knew Charlie

wouldn't be here. The anxious feeling in my stomach settled. I hoped they'd find a clue though.

Within minutes, Grayson was back.

"It's empty," he said.

"Completely empty?"

"As empty as a serial killer's conscience," Grayson answered. "But I'll let forensics have a go at it. Maybe they'll find something seeing as you haven't ruined any possible traces this time."

Yeah, yeah, rub it in.

I didn't feel like telling Grayson what we had learned from the employee but told him anyway. I didn't want them to waste their resources on something I knew wasn't going to help.

"Thanks for letting me know, but I don't want to miss any opportunities this time," he replied.

"Okay, your choice. If they find anything, when will we know?"

"It depends on what they'll find and if they need to process that evidence in some way or another. I can't tell you anything more specific. What I can tell you is that I did some digging to find out a bit more about that relief teacher, John Smith. Didn't find anything of interest, I'm afraid. He owns some houses, rents them out, and works as a janitor at Bullsbrook High, but you knew that already."

John owning and renting out houses was new to me. I guessed it was his way of earning a bit on the side since janitor wages weren't much. How he got the money to buy multiple houses was anybody's guess.

***

On our way back to Bullsbrook, I kept my eyes peeled to the road in front of us. I had to keep looking to the future. It was the only thing I could do if I didn't want to go insane.

When we arrived in Bullsbrook, Julie drove me home.

"I'm sorry we didn't find Charlie today," she said as I unbuckled myself.

"Yeah, but at least we didn't find him cut into pieces either." I gave her a hug.

"That's the attitude, sis. Keep thinking positive."

I gave her a quick smile back.

When her car was no longer visible, I turned toward my house. I had already noted there were no parcels on the porch. That was good. I fished my keys out of my pocket and opened the front door. As I threw my keys in the dish on the sideboard, the alarm went off. The sound was deafening. Returning to the control panel next to the front door, I turned it off. An angelic silence followed. I suddenly remembered I hadn't looked for mail for a few days. Charlie normally took it in when he came home from school. I walked to the mailbox next to our drive and opened it. There were a lot of supermarket pamphlets and a few letters, one looked like the electricity bill. I grabbed them all and went back inside.

In the kitchen, I threw the mail on the table, hung my jacket over a chair, and put on the kettle. I scooped a spoonful of instant coffee into a mug and sat down with a kitchen knife to open the letters. One of them bulged a little. It reminded me of the envelope stuck to the pig sign. I turned it over. It looked the same. Not bulging as much, but there was definitely something inside it. It had my name and address written on it this time, but there was no stamp, no sender's details. 'Fuck it,' I thought and opened the envelope with a knife.

A Date

Inside the letter I found a folded piece of paper. My stomach contracted around ye olde brick as I unwrapped the content. With trembling hands, I held up the paper. It read, 'You didn't listen. Maybe this will help.' I unwrapped the tissue paper I found inside the letter and stared at Charlie's ear.

I didn't faint or vomit. Instead, only anger and worry rushed through me. I sat looking at the ear for a moment before I hurriedly wrapped it back into the tissue paper and put it on a shelf in the fridge. I took my cell phone out to call Grayson after I had retrieved his card from my other jacket. As I waited for him to pick up, I opened the freezer to look for ice. It was difficult to pull the drawer out with only one hand available. Once it finally budged, I pulled it out with too much force, spilling its content onto the floor. I cursed as I jammed the drawer back again and put the spilled items back. I continued to curse as Grayson took his time answering.

"Kate, I'm busy. Can't this wait?" he finally said.

"They sent me Charlie's ear in the mail."

I short silence followed.

"I'm still in Portland. I'll send George to pick it up."

George arrived within a few minutes, plastic bag in hand. In the meantime, I had put Charlie's ear on a frozen bag of peas. Fortunately, George didn't tell me off for opening the envelope. He wrapped the ear in the bag of frozen peas, put it all in one of those forensic bags, put the letter in another, and left.

Grayson and I hadn't talked about the 'no pigs' warning, but it was all I could think about. The fact that the box had not been used since it was rented only told me one thing; its only purpose had been to hurt Charlie, to hurt me. Sasha wanted us to suffer and took every opportunity she could get. Now Charlie was missing an ear. First a finger, now an ear. What would she be chopping off next?

When I called Grayson, I had noticed there was a message from Harry. I called him and told him about the investigation's progress. Harry was shocked. He told me the flyer was still up at the medical center, but nobody had come forward. He told me he felt frustrated there was nothing else he could do. There was nothing I could say to make him feel any better, so I said I'd keep him up to date and hung up.

After I had pressed the 'end call' button, it reverted back to the contact list, and I saw Tom's name. Without thinking, I pressed his icon and the call button.

"Hey there, Sunshine, do you have Charlie back yet?" he said cheerfully.

"Well..."

I told him what had happened since this morning.

"And when I got home, I found a letter in my mailbox, very much like the one we found on the back of the pig sign. It contained Charlie's ear. So, yeah, I've got a little bit of him back," I said and recalled my earlier reaction after my conversation with Dr. Strang.

"Let me guess, a 'no pigs' warning."

"On the dot. The police have their hands full on the storage place and now Charlie's ear, apart from the letter and the finger. I don't think they'll be doing anything else in the near future as far as I know. It's already been three days since I received Charlie's finger. So... I was thinking, maybe we could team up again. Look for another clue?" I tried to bite a nail that was too short already.

"Sure. Great idea. As Sasha and her boys seem to focus on the Portland area, why don't you and I go check out the nightlife there? I'll come and pick you up at twelve. We'll call it a date."

"Um, okay, till then." I ended the call and checked the time. It was only 4 pm, eight hours to go still. I hoped I could stay awake until midnight. I grabbed my bag and jumped in my car. Sonny would surely keep me awake.

***

While driving to the farm, I rehashed the conversation with Tom. Why did he call it a date? I was in a relationship with Charlie. I really needed to make it clear to him I wasn't available.

Sonny was over the moon to see me again. Sue was happy as well, but I could tell by her tiny pupils she was drugged up to her eyeballs. Marlon confirmed my suspicions. They had gone to see Dr. Strang that morning, and Sue was prescribed new drugs. I hated her taking medication but realized it was the better option at the moment.

I decided not to tell Marlon about Charlie's ear. It wouldn't make a difference to the situation, and I didn't want to burden him with knowledge he couldn't discuss with the people around him.

Sonny, Sue, and I went for a walk to give Marlon a break. When we got back, we had a cup of soup with toast for dinner and puzzled some more. After I tucked my Little Man into bed, I said goodbye to Sue and Marlon and popped into Julie's office to let her know about the afternoon's event.

"Still working?" I said when I found her behind her desk again.

"A farmer has no days off," she said as she continued typing.

"I wonder how you do it. Anyway, I wanted to let you know Sasha sent Charlie's ear in the mail today."

To say it out loud made me uncomfortable. The

horrible news sounded like I was talking about something I bought on the internet. I wanted to cry, but I was too angry. Angry at Sasha and her sons for hurting Charlie. They should be hurting me, not him.

"Oh my god, that's awful," Julie said.

I had her full attention now.

"It came in the mail. I found the envelope with the ear in it in my mailbox just after you left. I called Grayson and George came to pick it up. There was a letter with it. It said, 'You didn't listen.' Sasha doesn't want me to get the police involved."

"Kate, this is not a TV series. You must let the police deal with this."

"I'm seeing Tom tonight. He got the tip about the property where we found the pig sign. Maybe he can help me find another."

"Grayson told you not to get involved with him, sis. Stay away from Tom."

I looked at my sister. What was her issue with Tom? She hardly knew the man. Tom had been nothing but helpful and kind to me. Why did everybody have a problem with him? I liked him, and he actually gave me the feeling we were getting somewhere.

"Whatever. I'll keep you up to date." I got up from the chair. "I'm expecting the police to soon have some results from all the stuff we've given them. I'll give you a buzz when I'm going to the police station, so you can meet Mr. Right again."

"Um, I'm seeing him tomorrow actually, for lunch," Julie said. She took in my reaction.

"Good for you." I walked around her desk and gave her a hug. "It's about time you had a date. See you soon."

"Chin up, sis. I'm sure they'll get that bitch one of these days."

Yeah, but I wanted it to be yesterday.

"Do you want me to close the door?"

"It's fine. Just leave it. The cold will keep me awake," she said and was back to typing on her keyboard before I turned around.

Bat Beats

When I arrived home, I had a power nap. If I intended to stay awake all night, I needed to sleep at some point, so it was better if I did it sooner rather than later.

Afterward, I took a shower and passed the time trying to figure out what to wear. It had been ages since I'd been out clubbing. What was the fashion nowadays? It was even harder than deciding what to wear for Harry's party.

When the doorbell rang, I opened the front door wearing a black dress. It had long sleeves and no décolletage at all. I found the dress a bit plain on the front side and had chosen to spice it up with a long necklace. It had a blue butterfly pendant resting at stomach height. Tom stood on the porch dressed in black chinos, a white, silk shirt, and a black jacket.

"Wow! Who are you and what have you done with Kate," he said when he saw me.

"Says who? You look pretty good scrubbed up yourself." I stepped aside to let him enter.

He chuckled. "Hey, I always look good."

I closed the door behind him and Tom whistled when he saw the back of me. The front of the dress was simple. Its focus was the plunging back.

"Do you think I should wear something else?" I asked as I turned. I suddenly realized I wasn't twenty anymore.

"Absolutely. I wouldn't be able to have a normal conversation with you due to all the other men trying to get your attention."

My hand went up to check the platting I had managed to put in my hair. Redressing would very likely ruin the hairdo.

"Are you sure?"

"As much as I would like to give you a negative answer to that, I'm afraid this won't do. Where we're going, this outfit will be classified as severely overdressed. Something slightly less classy would be better."

I sighed and slumped my shoulders.

"Okay, give me a few minutes." I disappeared upstairs. As I took the dress off, Tom's cheeky smile visualized in my mind's eye. The image of an English detective sprung to mind. I tried to remember the detective's name or the name of the old TV series— Inspector Lynley, that was it. I liked that guy too. He was classy.

"Do you mind if I turn on the TV?" Tom called after a minute or so.

He probably expected me not to emerge within the next hour.

"No, of course not," I called back to him.

I checked my wardrobe for something else to wear. After a few minutes of looking through the outfits I had gone through earlier, I chose something resembling Tom's outfit. Dark blue pants, a white blouse, and a silky, dark blue vest fancifully embroidered with dark blue beads. It was a favorite of mine, but I'd only worn it once to a Christmas party at school.

I pulled my hair out of the plat, brushed it, and let it hang loose. Checking my look in the mirror, I decided it would have to do.

When I came into the living room, Tom immediately turned off the TV, got up from the couch, and smiled.

"That's much better. You still look great."

"Thanks. Let's go."

I was eager to get more information. We were nearing the deadline Charlie's finger could be reattached, but we also had an ear to worry about now.

Tom insisted driving his car again. I didn't bring a jacket, but I knew the seat warmer in Tom's car would warm me soon enough. Staring out into the darkness ahead, I asked Tom where we were going.

"First," he said, "I thought we could visit 'Bat Beats,' a club on the outskirts of Portland. If we don't find anything there, we could go to 'Lust Lair.' There are plenty of other joints we could go to, but they're not as busy as those two. If Sasha's boys like to party, that's where they would probably go."

The name 'Lust Lair' didn't entice me to visit the place of my own free will. I could imagine the name of the club sparking interest with young males and wasn't surprised Tom knew about it. Whether or not he had done it on purpose, I was glad he had suggested going to 'Bat Beats' first. I kept my fingers crossed we didn't have to look any further after visiting it.

"Do you think they'd go out?" I said, thinking out loud. "I don't think Sasha would let her sons go out to party, to be honest." Sasha seemed very organized to me, anticipating every step of the investigation, and making sure everything was down to a tee. Boozing boys would not fit her plans.

"Well, there's only one way to find out," Tom said. His smile was enough to convince me.

We arrived at 'Bat Beats' within the hour. It was as if a big cube had dropped from the sky into the flat landscape. All around it was one, big parking lot, and it was completely filled. Even though the cube was huge, I imagined people packed like sardines in there.

We got out of the car and Tom took my hand, putting it on his arm. Arm in arm, he walked me past the line of people waiting to get in, straight to the bouncers.

"Mr. Wayne, how nice to see you again," one of the burly men said and removed the thick cord blocking our entrance.

"Thank you, Hank. It's good to be back." Tom put

some dollar bills into the man's breast pocket.

As Tom guided me through the crowd inside and toward the stairs, his hand in the small of my back, I stared at him. He acted as if this was all normal behavior. At the stairs, we met with more large-bodied staff. Tom exchanged more pleasantries, parted with more money, and they allowed us to go up to a less crowded level. We found us a spot where we could sit along a balustrade, looking down onto the packed crowd on the dance floor below.

"Suzie, the usual, please, and a sweet martini for the lady," he said to a waitress. "I do hope you like martinis," he said to me after she'd left, worried.

"I don't know. I've never had one."

"Why now, you've got to try everything at least once." His smiled his cheeky smile.

"Why did the bouncer call you Mr. Wayne? Isn't your surname Moore, like Harry's?"

Tom laughed. He leaned forward, his lips close to my ear, his ocean-breeze scent filling my nostrils.

"Of course it is, but they don't have to know that."

Why does he want to keep his name a secret?

"Wayne, as in the superhero character?" I raised my eyebrows.

The waitress brought the two drinks, a red one for Tom and a clear one for me. Tom pulled his wallet out to pay the girl. Either he knew the prices by heart and they were bloody expensive, or he included a large tip.

"So nice to see you again, Mr. Wayne," she said and winked at him before she walked away.

Tom lifted his glass, and so did I.

"Nothing wrong with having a childhood fantasy," he said and clinked his glass to mine before we both took a sip. "Do you like it?"

The name or the drink?

Tom looked worried again as my lips puckered up and my eyebrows squeezed together. When I swallowed, the alcohol burned my esophagus, and I quickly took a breath to ease it. My eyes flung wide open, dispersing the tears induced by the burning sensation in my lungs.

"I like it so much, I'll be sipping it the entire night." My voice was a pitch higher than I had intended.

"So sorry, girl. Do you want me to order you something else?"

I waved my hand toward him. "No, no. Give me a sip of yours to wash it down and I'll be fine."

"Um, I'm pretty sure you won't be impressed with this one either."

"Okay, I'll just take it very slow with this martini then."

"Well, on the bright side, at least I won't have to put you to bed drunk again."

"Aargh. Please don't remind me of that night." I tried to hide my face behind my hand. "I made such a fool of myself." I wished I could shrivel up and blow away that very moment.

Fortunately, Tom's attention was taken away by the appearance of a tall, slim woman in a long, red dress, covered by a long, white fur, a sleeveless cardigan kind of thing. Golden hair cascaded down her back. The woman draped herself over Tom's body, kissing him three times; twice on the cheeks, the third one on the mouth. He didn't seem to mind.

"Fomka, kak dela? How are you?" she said in a heavy Russian accent.

"Normalno," he answered.

"It's been what, three months? Where have you been?" She brushed a strand of hair from her face. Before Tom could reply, she spotted me. "No, say it's no true." She looked from me to Tom and back at me again. "You are Kate Clarke, no?"

"Yes, I—"

My words were cut off as she had jumped off Tom's lap, and she hugged me like I was her long lost, favorite teddy bear. She was hopping on the spot, despite her six-inch heels, and gave me three kisses, the third one also on the mouth.

Hello to you too.

When she finally pulled away from me, she sported a huge smile, and I noted her fangs.

"Kate," Tom said, "may I introduce Olesia to you. She's a good friend of mine. Olesia, this is indeed the famous Kate."

I frowned at Tom's words, but he ignored it.

"I'm so honored to meet you," Olesia said, grabbing my hand and doing something of a curtsy. "You changed my life and that of many others." Her voice was low and full of awe. I felt my cheeks warm. Frantically, I thought of something to say.

"How... how do you know Tom?"

I hoped to divert her attention away from me. Maybe she could help me get more info on my mysterious companion. Olesia turned to Tom, her excited facial expression softening to a warm glow.

"Tom is my savior. My... what is word... guiding light. I would not be now without this special man." She kept looking at him with adoring eyes. Tom rubbed his lips and looked away.

"That's enough now, Olesia," he said.

"I'm so sorry. You came here with Ms. Clarke. I will not interrupt." She turned to me and said, "priyatno poznakomit'sya, Katya." Then she left.

"What did she say?"

"It means 'nice to have met you.' She is very thankful for what you have done for the sucker community."

"Yes, I gathered that. Are there many suckers here?" I scanned the people around me and began noticing more and more fangs. Suddenly, the name 'Bat Beats' made sense to me.

"What did you expect?" Tom said. "A nightclub is like a mall for suckers, a place to meet and greet."

I was amazed. This was a part of sucker-life I hadn't been introduced to yet. The sucker children of Julie's farm girls all were daywalkers. What SAMM was mostly concerned about was to make the life of nightwalking suckers as normal as possible, and for the unturned communities to accept that suckers existed, to integrate them into their everyday lives. We had made sure there was blood available for them in the supermarkets, so they wouldn't have to live in dark alleys, killing innocent passers-by. We had made sure they could get a proper education. We tried to make sure they weren't discriminated against when applying for jobs, so they could earn a living and not depend on government handouts. What we hadn't thought about was what they did in their spare time. An idea popped up in my head, and I made a mental note to discuss it with Julie later.

"Wow," I said. It was all I could think of.

After an hour of sitting and sipping, I began to wonder what we were doing here. I turned to Tom.

"Isn't there something we should do?"

"We are," he said.

"What are we doing?"

"We're waiting."

"Waiting for what?"

"Waiting for them to contact us."

A Warning

I tried to figure out who Tom meant by 'them.' Surely he didn't think Arkady or Konstantin were going to walk up to us and say hello. The music was too loud to carry on the conversation, so I let it go. I figured that if he wanted me to know who 'they' were, he would have told me. I finished my sweet martini sooner than I anticipated and ordered a new one. The taste of it was growing on me.

A man came to stand next to Tom. His face had a scar on it and it made him even uglier than he already was. Although it had nothing to do with his looks, I instinctively didn't like this man.

"Tom, kak dela?" he said. It sounded as if the words came out of a grater.

"Vanya," Tom replied. They hugged and did the kissing thing. I gathered this joint was a Russian gathering spot and the kissing fetish a Russian tradition. "Normalno. May I introduce Kate Clarke to you? Kate, this is Ivan Golubev."

Make up your mind. Is his name Vanya or Ivan?

The man stepped toward me and greeted me the American way, only giving me one kiss on the cheek.

Apparently, the feeling is mutual.

He turned away from me, dismissing me, directing his attention back to Tom. I busied myself looking at the people below on the dance floor yet straining my ears to follow Tom and Ivan's conversation over the loud music.

"Long time no see."-Ivan.

"It's been a while."-Tom. "I need a favor. I'm looking for two boys, twins. Arkady and Konstantin Duncan. Have you heard of them?"

"I have. That's why the Boss wants to talk to you."

I stopped leaning on the railing and turned to the two men. Adrenaline rushed through me. My eyes caught Tom's, but he shot me a warning look back.

But the man knows something!

"I'll come immediately," Tom said. Without a word, he put his glass down on the little table between us, got up, and moved in the direction Ivan had come from. I moved to follow, but Ivan turned to me, blocking my path.

"Only Tom," he said.

His ice-cold stare frightened me. It was not the fear you got when you wanted to tell your father you didn't like his chicken soup. This fear was more the 'if I tell him something he doesn't like, I'm not going to live much longer' kind of fear.

Ivan turned around and caught up with Tom.

I wanted to come along so badly, to find out what 'the Boss' had to say about the twins, but I couldn't.

Why hadn't I been invited? It was my quest after all. Why didn't Tom ask me to come along? Who was this boss person anyway? Was he a Russian mafia Don? If so, would he know everything that went on in the Russian community? That would be good news. A wide grin crept onto my face. I had to be patient. News would come. Excited I would soon find out more on Charlie's whereabouts, I leaned on the railing and passed the time studying the people on the dance floor. They were bobbing to the music, drinks in hand. The music was loud and the bass strumming, putting the people in a trance.

I caught the eye of Olesia in the crowd below, and she lifted her drink to me. I picked up my drink and lifted it to her. Then the sucker standing next to her lifted her drink. I acknowledged her too. A third sucker did the same, and another one. One by one, all the suckers on the dance floor turned to me. They began chanting to the beat of the music, something in Russian, while lifting their glasses to me. I turned to look behind me, thinking that maybe the Boss was behind me, and they were paying tribute to him. But the suckers I found there were also lifting their glasses to me. Desperate to find somebody whom I could find refuge with, someone acting normal, I frantically looked around. I found no one.

The sudden pressure made it impossible to think straight, and I had nobody to give me advice on what to do, so I lifted my glass a bit higher to the crowd below, and then downed the remaining martini in one gulp. The sudden wave of alcohol burned its way down, making me gasp for air again. I lifted the empty glass, tears streaming down my face, and threw it over my shoulder.

The glass smashing on the floor behind me wasn't heard over the roaring crowd below. The applause thundered in my ears while the DJ pumped up the volume of his music. The people below began jumping wildly to the beat. The whole experience gave me a high I had never felt before. I wiped my face and turned around to go downstairs and join the heaving mass of bodies.

I bumped into Tom, who stood right behind me. His oceanic scent surrounded me. I patted his shirt back into place. Not that it needed it, but I thought it was the least I could do for bumping into him so rudely.

Bumpety-bumpety-bump. What a lovely six-pack.

"Hey, you, let's go dancing," I yelled at him over the music. I moved to get past him, but he grabbed me by my upper arm.

"No, we're leaving," he said. His face was set awfully grave.

"What? No, I'm having a good time." Tom didn't change his expression. "Wait. What? Do you've news? Whatis it?" If Tom had heard bad news from this Russian Boss, he'd better tell me right now. The high I had just experienced disappeared within a second.

"Come on, let's get out of here first. Then I'll tell you." He took me downstairs, pushed me through the crowd of suckers who tried to congratulate and kiss me. I tried to hug each and every sucker back, but Tom was unrelenting, pulling me by my arm toward the door. It was like a déjà vu.

Once outside, he guided me to his car, away from the bouncers and the people in the line.

"Tell me. Wh-what did ya hear? Who's this Boss dude?" I hung off Tom's arm, my legs hardly able to keep my tipsy body upright in the ridiculously high and fragile heels.

Why hadn't I changed these shoes when I changed my outfit? I shouldn't have drunk that second glass. Man, it's cold out here.

"That was the head of the local Russian mob I just talked to. The Russian people in this area owe him a lot and do his bidding. He also knows a lot of people, especially Russians. He knows about the boys, and he knows about Sasha."

Tom stopped talking, grabbing me with both hands by my upper arms. Did he do this to keep me upright or to get my attention? I couldn't help my eyes closing as often as they did. Tom shook me a little.

"He told me to stop looking for them, to butt out of the whole situation."

Old News

Did I hear him correctly? I couldn't believe my ears. They were still buzzing since leaving the club. I frantically tried to read Tom's face.

"Whatcha mean? Why can't we look for 'em? What hazzee gotta do withit?"

"He didn't tell you off, Kate. Only me."

I understood his words now loud and clear. I tore myself loose from his grip as he hadn't given me any notion of disagreeing with the message either.

"Wellee can go ffuckimself! An you too!"

I tried to kick the tire of his car in frustration. My foot missed, and I lost my balance. Tom caught me before I hit the ground. As he tried to pull me upright, I began lashing out at him, my fists pummeling his body.

"Fuckyou, Tom. Fuck the Russian mob. Fuck y'all! I want my Charlie back, an I'm not gonna stop. With or withoutcha." My fists did nothing to his chiseled chest. "I hate 'em. I hate 'em!"

My adrenaline was spent sooner than I wanted, and any energy to keep myself upright vanished. As my legs gave way, Tom swooped me up. I put my arms around his neck and, for a moment, held him tight without saying a word. Then I began to sob. Tom let me. I felt safe being held in his arms, but it didn't take away the fact I had never felt so lonely before in my entire life. I didn't know if I had the strength to keep going.

"Shhh," Tom whispered as he put his forehead against mine. "I didn't say I was going to listen to them."

It took me a moment before his words sank in. I lifted my head, fully aware I did a pretty good panda bear imitation, but I didn't care.

"Whadidya say?" I wiped the snot from my upper lip.

Tom let go of my legs and my feet touched the ground. He held me close against his body with one hand in the small of my back, just in case, and brushed a strand of hair from my face with the other. With his thumb, he caressed my cheek.

"I said, I'm not going to take their advice. I'm still going to help you find Charlie."

How I loved that smile. I threw my arms around him and hugged him as tight as I could.

"Thankya. Thankya sso much."

***

The next morning, I had another hangover. Not as bad as Saturday, but still bad. Trying to recall exactly what had happened the night before, I vaguely remembered

Tom saying on the way home he didn't want to give the Russian brotherhood, or the Bratva as he called it, the notion he wasn't going to comply with their 'request.' The current pounding in my head made it hard to focus, yet I forced myself to remember more. I had been in no state at all to go anywhere else after those two martinis, but my drunk self had tried to convince Tom to go to 'Lust Lair.' As I had been adamant we go there, he had made me look at myself in the side mirror of his car, after which I had conceded to go home.

My arm stretched out to Charlie's side of the bed, but it reached nothing but empty space. The longing in my chest for him grew and became painful. It actually hurt. I always thought when they said 'love hurts,' they were talking metaphorically, but now I knew it was a physical pain. It made me curl up into a ball, and I cried, the pounding in my head rhythmically increasing with my sobs.

When my cell phone rang, I had been on the brink of falling asleep. I pulled the duvet over my head. The cell kept on ringing, not doing much for easing my headache, so I finally answered the call. Maybe it was Sonny or Sue. I couldn't let them down. Maybe, just maybe, it was Charlie, telling me he was coming home.

"Kate, I'd like you to come to the police station."

I considered hanging up for a moment.

"Why?" I pinched the bridge of my nose, trying to squeeze away the headache.

"I have Ms. Anderson here," Grayson said. "She's a friend of mine and a profiler with the Portland police. She might tell us a bit more about Sasha."

"Give me half an hour."

I fell back onto my pillow and immediately regretted the fast movement. I slowly turned my head toward the bedside table and smiled. Tom had again put a bottle of water ready for me. The box of aspirin tablets was still there from Friday night.

I showered but skipped breakfast, my stomach couldn't handle me even thinking about food today, and I was at the station within the expected thirty minutes.

"Hi, George," I said as I walked in.

George looked up from what he was doing and smiled as he buzzed me through.

"They're in the interrogation room," he said.

"Thanks."

When I entered the room, Grayson stood up. The woman next to him, with her hair into a tight bun, did the same. She stuck her hand out to me.

"Kate, this is Joanne Anderson," Grayson said. "She's a profiler with the force. Joanne, this is Kate Clarke."

I shook the woman's hand. Her long, cold fingers reminded me of alien tentacles. They wrapped themselves around my hand in an iron grip as if trying to drain my soul.

"Nice to meet you, Joanne."

"Likewise," she said, curt and businesslike. There was no pleasant smile accompanying her greeting. Her demeanor certainly didn't appear to be as fluffy as her auburn, mohair sweater.

"Please, sit down," she said.

Did you think I was going to stand for the next half hour or so?

I sat down opposite the two. Grayson kept quiet.

"I've dug up as much as I could about Alexandra Morozov-"

"Sasha," I said.

Joanne's stare tried to pierce through me.

"Her name is Sasha. That's what she calls herself."

"I know that," Joanne said. "Please don't interrupt me again."

It appeared I wasn't the only one who should have stayed in bed today.

"Sasha was born Alexandra Katharina Maria Morozov. Her father is unknown. Her mother, Anna Katharina Josephina Morozov, was the youngest of four. All of Anna's siblings were born in Nekrasovka from working-class parents. None of them had great lives. The two older brothers became thieves, went in and out of jail. Anna and her sister Maria became prostitutes and addicts. Maria died when she was twenty-four, accidentally gunned down in a street war, making Anna even more drug dependent. She became pregnant with Sasha half a year later. At the age of eight, Anna made her daughter available to clients. When Sasha was sixteen, one of those clients happened to be Giovanni Caballo, an Italian fashion designer. He took Sasha out of the country, paying Anna a substantial amount for her loss of income, who died shortly after from an overdose. Caballo cleaned Sasha up, put her through rehab, and used her in his shows. Not long after, others saw her potential, and she was hired for more and more shows. She traveled the world with the greatest fashion designers until she came to Portland for a show in 2004. I am assuming you know what happened thereafter."

I nodded. I wasn't going to let her tell me off again. So far, the story didn't give me any more information than Grayson had already told me, and I wasn't impressed. Perhaps the real information was about to be told, so I kept quiet.

"Coming from such a poor background, her eyes opened up for the possibilities when Caballo took her to Italy. It made Sasha want for power and wealth. She did everything to get it, including sleeping around. It was the way she was brought up; you could trade sex for anything you craved. Not having a father around make her seek a father figure, a sugar daddy, and she clamped herself to any man who offered her a better life. Having seen her family go down the wrong path, she was very picky about who she clung to, always striving to become better off. She only picked the men who would help her climb up the ladder. It gave her the name of 'diva calcolato' or 'the calculated diva' in the fashion world circles. She continued her reputation when she befriended James Duncan during Black October. With his background as an army commander, he took control of a sucker pack, and she took her chance to become the alpha female. So far, all understandable actions on her part. She fell out of character when she left Duncan to start a pack with Caleb Murphy. Murphy—

Caleb.

"—was not a typical leader. The second son of a captain, he grew up following his father's footsteps, and became, like his older brother, a ship's mate. His career would be a dragged-out one, eventually leading to the title of captain. This, however, was long-term planning, not something Sasha would have had in mind. Murphy did become a pack leader when he left Duncan's pack, and this may have been reason enough for her to become his partner. Yet his pack was smaller than Duncan's, so she dropped down in status. Unless she had been thinking of overthrowing Caleb and running her own pack, which is also a possibility.

What about love? She may have done it out of love. Does that word appear in your dictionary?

"During her internment, Sasha appeared to have been following you in the news. She didn't have newspaper articles hanging on every wall of her cell, but inmates claimed she was obsessed with you. However, she behaved immaculately otherwise. The evidence given during her trial had been vague and limited. Next to this, she always claimed she had acted the way she did due to the virus. The prison board had no objection against releasing her when the general view on suckers changed and the law to keep them locked up was overhauled.

So, you're now rubbing it in that SAMM caused Sasha to be released so she could seek revenge upon me?

The painkillers didn't work against the thumping in my head and Ms. Fluffy's words only made it worse. I had enough of this waste of time.

New News

Before Ms. Fluffy could continue, I spoke my mind.

"And nobody found it necessary to mention this to me when she was released?" I leaned forward. "Nobody ever thought that the person who was obsessed with me, the person who killed her lover, who maimed her, who put her in jail for twelve years, nobody thought she may be out to get me? You guys are a fucking joke."

"Kate, please," Grayson said. "We only found this out after we did some digging after you received Charlie's finger." His eyes flitted toward Joanne, who had made herself tall in her seat, her stare colder than it was before.

"So what? Do I have to feel all sorry for Sasha now? Because she didn't have a hula hoop as a child? Did those people on the prison board forget that she tortured and killed people during Black October? Sucking people dry when they didn't comply with her wishes? Did they forget how she and Duncan kept people prisoner in their pack, gave orders to shoot them when trying to escape? I guess they did, didn't they? Because poor, little Sasha was so well-behaved in prison, rehabilitating into a model citizen. But they weren't there during Black October. They didn't see the murdering bloodlust in her eyes. Well, I did. The woman is a calculated killing freak. But how could I know?" I now directed my speech toward the woolly woman. "I didn't study for years to become a profiler, did I? No, I'm just plain Jane. I know nothing."

I got up and walked over to the window. There was nothing to be seen through the matted glass. It didn't matter as I wouldn't have seen anything through the blood red of my rage anyway. My chest pumped air through my lungs like I was running a marathon, and I clamped my jaws shut to prevent me from hurling more verbal abuse at the two persons sitting behind me at the table. Who was this woman to come and tell me what Sasha was like? She knew nothing, hadn't been there, seen her. She had no idea. Sasha had only one thing on her mind; revenge. And I knew she planned it to be as cruel as possible.

Chairs scuffled over the floor, and then the door opened and slammed shut. When I thought I was alone, I hugged myself, dug my fingers into my arms as I screamed in my frustration of not being able to rescue Charlie. The image of Charlie, alone, chained up, and hurt, popped up in my mind, and I fought to hold back the tears. I couldn't.

Suddenly, I felt a hand on my shoulder. It was Grayson's. I twisted from underneath it.

"Please, Kate. She's only trying to help," he said.

"I know it's not Joanne's fault Sasha's out or that she

is a raving lunatic. I hope she doesn't take it personally. But still... she didn't tell me anything I don't already know. Nothing that matters, anyway. She doesn't know Sasha. She wasn't there. She has no idea what the bitch can do."

"I think she does. She's better at her job than you think. We discussed her research before you arrived, and she wanted to tell you how dangerous Sasha is. According to Joanne, she's really out to get you. She will stop at nothing to hurt you."

I wiped my tears away.

"As if I don't know that already."

"Yes. Yes, I guess you do. But I want you to be careful. I don't want you to get hurt. Please don't underestimate Sasha. She's maimed Charlie already, and we don't think she'll stop at that."

I grabbed a tissue from the box on the table and blew my nose.

As I didn't react to his words, honestly, what was there to say, Grayson excused himself to go talk to Joanne. I made use of the time to wipe away as much as possible of the mascara streaks on my cheeks.

When the door opened again, Grayson entered alone. He held two cups of coffee in his hands, and a folder under his arm.

"Joanne has left. She wishes you all the best," he said as he handed me one of the coffees.

I took the cup but remained quiet. Grayson put the

folder on the table, it had Charlie's name on it, and we both sat down. Why did he have a folder on Charlie? He took out a paper. It looked like a report of some sort, but I had never been good at reading upside down.

"First things first," Grayson said. "Forensics studied the envelope you found at the cabin."

"And?" For the first time that morning I felt a little optimistic.

"There was an acid bomb inside."

"Holy shit, you're kidding me?"

"No. If you had opened the letter, a trigger would have exploded a small vial of sulphuric acid. It appears this woman really wants to hurt you."

I rubbed my face with both hands, counting my luck that Tom had stopped me from opening the envelope. *How did he know?*

"Well, to be honest," I said, "I can understand why. I set her head on fire. Touché. Did they find anything else? Was there a letter in there? A clue of some sort?"

"Nothing. No fingerprints or any other clue. It seems that she knows what she's doing and that this lead existed purely to maim you. You were very lucky."

"No shit."

Grayson put the paper back into the folder and took out another one.

"I have more news," he said, eyeing me with his fatherly look.

"What is it?"

"Now, I want you to remain calm. Remember that we're doing everything we possibly can to find Charlie." He put his hand on my wrist, but I pulled it away.

"Just say it, Grayson."

"We received the lab result back from Charlie's finger and ear. They tested the blood on them and proved both to be his. He was alive when they were cut off."

"Old news, Grayson."

I bit the nail of my thumb. This visit was such a waste of time. Why wasn't he looking for Charlie, instead of in his file?

"They also tested it for the *Succedaneum* virus, standard procedure nowadays. His finger was negative, but his ear tested positive."

Pressure

I jumped up, not sure for what purpose, but my brain called for action.

"What?!"

"A sucker, one of the boys most likely, we're not sure yet," Grayson said, "must have bitten Charlie. He now has the virus in his body, turning him into a sucker."

Grayson's words hardly registered. The words 'tested positive' were still ringing in my ears. My heart beat like a drummer on acid and a thousand thoughts flew through my mind. Someone bit Charlie. It could be Sasha, but she had been vaccinated. She may have let herself be bitten and turned or she made one of her sons bite Charlie. They weren't daywalkers. Forget re-attaching his finger and ear. If we didn't find Charlie soon, he'd be a sucker forever, having to live in darkness for the rest of his life. Sasha was doing this on purpose. She was trying to create a wedge between the two of us. If she couldn't have Caleb, I couldn't have Charlie.

I looked up at Grayson. He was still sitting at the table.

"What are you waiting for? My permission to go and find him? Do something!" I yelled.

"Kate, calm down. Like I said, we're doing everything within our power to get Charlie back. It's just... right now, we don't have a lead. We don't know where to look." He sighed and sat back as he held my stare.

I had thought my contempt for Grayson couldn't get any worse. I was wrong. Here he sat, washed and fed, with a cup of coffee in his hand. While out there, somewhere not too far away, Charlie was being held captive, mutilated, bitten. The image of the multitude of pamphlets of missing persons up on the notice board flashed by again. Sasha wasn't the only one too clever for the police. Maybe it was just that they didn't have the resources to do their job properly. If I wanted Charlie back, I needed to do it myself. I needed Tom's help again. Maybe Dirty Harry could find something on the whereabouts of the twins. He didn't seem to be under the yoke of the Russian mob, or the bureaucracy of the police.

I left Grayson to drink his horrible cup of coffee on his own.

Once in my car, I decided to drive to the farm. Before I contacted Tom and did whatever we could do, I wanted to see my children. I missed them. I missed Sue's funny remarks and Sonny's sunny smile. Not having them and Charlie around me was like not having any sunshine in my life. I needed them as a tonic, to stay positive.

As I drove through the countryside, despair grew inside me. It was as if my insides were burning, consuming me. Would Charlie still be alive? 'He was alive when they were cut off,' Grayson had said. I had automatically assumed Charlie had been alive, but Grayson was right. I wouldn't put it past Sasha to kill Charlie. If only to hurt me. An eye for an eye.

My chest constricted, and it became hard to breathe. Deep breaths, I had to take deep breaths. The words Charlie had once said to me made my anxiety attack exponentially worse. I had to pull over and let the wave of angst pass. When I regained my composure, I checked my look in the rear-view mirror and wiped my face dry. My mascara was as good as gone now.

Buy waterproof mascara next time, girl.

I focused on seeing my children during the rest of the drive, to keep me from sliding further into the rabbit hole.

***

Sonny jumped into my arms when I arrived at the farm. Instantly, I felt better. We went for a walk again, taking Sue with us. After walking the perimeter of the farm grounds, we decided to go to the barn and say hello to Marlon. He was shoveling a mixture of corn and grass silage into the feeding troughs. While Sonny and Sue were feeding one of the calves a bottle of milk, Marlon took me aside and asked me if there was any progress in finding Charlie. I hesitated to tell him the news about Charlie's ear and about him being turned, but as I figured he would find out sooner or later, I told him everything. He was visibly taken aback.

"It's okay, Marlon. I'm going to get him back in time."

"Are you sure? How?"

"The million-dollar question. I have no idea, but I'll come up with something. One way or another." I hitched up my shoulders as my skin showed goosebumps all over.

We both turned to watch Sonny and Sue. They were so happy feeding the calf.

Marlon and I refrained from saying any more on the matter. I walked Sonny and Sue back, said goodbye to them, and stopped by at Julie's office. I knew Julie was going to meet with Grayson for lunch, and I wanted to be the one to tell her about Charlie.

"Hi, sis. How're you holding up?" she asked as I entered her office.

"I'm okay," I said as I took off my jacket, threw it over a chair, and sat down. "But Charlie isn't."

Julie's eyes opened wide. "You've heard from Charlie?"

"No, but Grayson told me the lab results from his finger and ear. He's infected, Jules. The bitch or one of her sick sons has bitten Charlie. He's turning into a sucker as we speak. And there's nothing I can do about it."

Jules drew a in breath in shock. My leg shook as I tried very hard not to bite my nails. I got up and paced the room.

"I don't know what to do, Jules. We need to find him. Fast. He only has three weeks before the infection is permanent. We need to get him back before then to give him the vaccination."

"If she hasn't chopped him up completely before then," Jules said.

I shot her a look of fire.

Well, aren't you a little ray of pitch black.

"Sorry to be so pragmatic, sis, but at the rate she's going, there won't be much left of him after three weeks."

I sat down again.

"You're right. We need him back as soon as possible. But Grayson said they've hit a dead end. They have no lead. What can we do?"

"Yeah, if only there existed a lead generator."

A thought formed in my mind.

"That's it! Jules, I love you."

An Epiphany

I jumped up, moved to the window, and stared into the green distance. My hands were on my hips, and a smile was on my face. The sun shone through the clouds for a moment, like a sign from the gods, lifting my spirits even higher.

Julie had swiveled her chair around to follow me.

"Come on, sis. Tell me. What are you on about?" she said. "What did I say?"

I turned and leaned my hands on both her armrests, my face close to hers.

"A lead generator." She pulled her head back as far as the chair would let her and frowned.

"Sorry." I withdrew as soon as I could and continued. "We need people to come forward with leads."

"But we've put up flyers, and nobody's come forward with anything," she replied.

"No, but that was local. I don't think Sasha's anywhere local. We need to go further out. We need to go on Maine television." I couldn't contain my excitement. "Aren't you having lunch with Grayson today?" I picked up my jacket.

"Yes, but what's that got to do with anything?"

"I'm coming with you."

Julie winced.

"Fuck, Jules. Don't be such a cow. This is to get Charlie back. You can hook up with Grayson anytime. After, that is. I need to ask him if it's possible to do a public appeal on TV. If we can, people from the whole area will be looking for Sasha and her sons. They won't be able to go anywhere without being noticed. Somebody will see something at some point, won't they?"

Julie's phone rang. She looked at who the caller was before looking at me as if to ask for permission to pick it up.

And the farmer, he plowed on.

"Pick me up at twelve-thirty," I said in the doorway.

Julie nodded in agreement and picked up the call.

***

As miserable as I was driving toward the farm, I was elated on my way back home. I couldn't wait to tell Tom about the decision. I hoped Grayson would agree with a TV appeal. Damn, why hadn't Grayson thought of it? And sooner. Surely, he must have dealt with missing person appeals more often. He should've known better. Then again, most missing persons weren't turned, and if they were, it most likely wouldn't be known in advance, and there wouldn't be such time pressure. The missing persons I had seen pinned on the board were standard. The husband who'd had enough of family life. The teenager rebelling against parental rules. The wife who'd had enough of her abusive husband.

But Charlie was different. First of all, he was kidnapped, not a runaway. Secondly, he wasn't a standard person. He was the rock in my life, the only one who could make me see sense in this world. I was lost without him.

My hand went to the pendant hanging between my breasts. I had put it on this morning as it made me feel closer to Charlie. He had given it to me for my birthday a couple of years ago. It was an intricate design of silver wires. I had asked him what it was supposed to be, and he had said it portrayed my hair on a Sunday morning. It looked like a knotted bunch of wires to me, to most people actually, and I supposed that was exactly what my hair was on a Sunday morning. Yet it was very special to me. Not because it was supposed to be my hair. Not because it was made of silver. It was special to me because Charlie had made it for me. I smiled as I imagined him secretly studying my hair on Sunday mornings.

Charlie often stared at me. Once, I had asked him what he was thinking, expecting him to say he was wondering why he loved me. It was the question I was always wondering about him. Deep down, I didn't think I was worthy of him. He was always so caring and reliable, loving me unconditionally. In return, I had rejected him multiple times before realizing I loved him, and three years ago, I had been unfaithful to him. More recently, I had hurt him deeply with my comment before I flew to California for the interview. Why in heaven's name did he love me?

Charlie had answered that he was admiring me. It had taken me by surprise. I hadn't known what to say, so I had kissed him, and we had made love. Charlie had the most kissable lips. They were so soft and responsive. I loved kissing them. I loved making love to him. Charlie had the most agile hands. His fingers were strong and gentle at the same time. The things he could do with those fingers.

My hand slowly moved down. My fingers disappeared between my legs and applied pressure. Butterflies fluttered in my belly and muscles contracted as I thought of my most recent intimacy with Charlie. I wanted him, needed him. I missed him so much. However I was going to do it, I was going to get him back.

Entering Bullsbrook traffic requested my full attention. I had to put my hand back onto the steering wheel, and I brought my mind back to the here and now.

Once at home, I called Tom.

"Hey, Sunshine. What are you up to today?" he said.

I twirled a strand of hair around my finger.

"I'm going on television."

"I must get your autograph, girl. You're becoming quite the celebrity," he said.

I'm sure I blushed although I didn't know why.

"No, no interview this time, silly. I'm going to do an appeal on local TV to ask if anybody has seen Charlie or Sasha and her sons. I've got to discuss it with Grayson first, but I hope he agrees. We haven't got any leads at the moment and hopefully, somebody will come forward with some information."

"That's a great idea. I'm sure the phones won't stop ringing, and you'll be able to get Charlie back."

It didn't escape me he said 'you' instead of 'we.'

"Can you come over this afternoon?" I bit my lip, not sure what his answer would be.

"It seems you have everything under control. Why would you need me?"

I stopped moving around, my body suddenly rigid.

"Well, I... Um, I'd hoped you could help me with my speech."

Tom remained silent.

Did I push him too far? Had I sounded too eager? Did the prospect of getting Charlie back make me less interesting all of a sudden? Did it matter? Why was I upset about his words?

"Sure, I'll come over and help you with your speech," he finally said.

"Thanks, Tom. You're the best. I'm seeing Grayson for lunch. I'll let you know what he says when I'm back home."

"I'll be looking forward to your call," he said, his voice as smooth as velvet again.

What was I to think of Tom, of the conversation? Yesterday, he had told me he wasn't going to listen to this Russian Boss. If so, then why was he reluctant to come and help me now? Did he change his mind? He could've just told me if he had. I was at a loss of following this man's thoughts.

I decided to wash the windows of the living room and the kitchen to keep my mind occupied with other things. I was just putting the bucket away in the kitchen when Julie honked her horn. I grabbed my jacket and jumped into her car.

It appeared she had set up the meeting at the 'Dilly Dally' lunchroom. It was new and looked clean and fresh with its light-green-and-white checkered half curtains and white interior. I felt bad for spoiling Julie's possible romantic get together with Grayson, but getting Charlie back was more important. Besides, Grayson already sat at one of the window tables. It showed his eagerness to make the most of their time together, and that he wasn't trying to hide their relationship either. If anything went wrong between the two today, Julie could always blame me.

Grayson's smile dropped as soon as he saw me.

Third Wheel

I slid into the space opposite him, and Julie sat down next to me. Grayson hadn't bothered to get up. I bet Julie was pee-ed off she didn't get a nice-to-see-you-again kiss. I'd be if I were her.

"Sorry, Grayson, but I have an urgent matter to discuss with you." I put the menu flat on the table, so I didn't have to look around it.

"Okay. For a moment I thought I got a two-for-one deal," he said dryly.

Julie smiled briefly but didn't hold his stare.

"No, we're not that cheap. Sorry to burst your bubble," I said. "Now listen, how about I go on Maine TV to do an appeal to the public to look for Charlie?"

"Let's order our food first," Grayson said. "Then we'll talk business."

My leg twitched while we were looking at the menu, and my gaze kept darting at Grayson across the table. Was he making up his mind about it in the meantime? Was he thinking of ways to tell me it wasn't going to happen? If only I could read his mind.

While we studied the menu, Grayson only had eyes and ears for Julie, and I realized my mistake. I should have waited until after lunch to meet him at the police station. He would probably have been in a better mood, and I wouldn't have suffered the nausea I experienced every time the two were flirting. The flick of her hair, the over-the-top comments on her looks, and the feigned interest in every word they said made me want to puke. These were grown-ups for Pete's sake, yet they were acting like teenagers. It irritated me they had time for this crap while Charlie was being mutilated and turned into a sucker.

After we ordered our meals, a farmers' quiche for Julie and myself and a steak sandwich for Grayson, he finally leaned back and noticed me again.

"Now, tell me. What exactly did you have in mind?" he said.

I slid the pepper and salt shaker around each other over the smooth, laminated table surface as I explained.

"I want to go on the Maine TV evening news. To tell people Charlie's missing and that Sasha and her sons have him. I want to show photos of the four of them, asking people to call the police if they've seen any of them since Thursday." As I waited for Grayson's answer, I stopped fiddling with the shakers.

"Sounds like a plan," Grayson said after about a minute of contemplation. "It has one flaw, though."

"What's that?"

"There's still no evidence that Sasha or her boys are involved. The CCTV footage shows two men abducting Charlie, but we can only speculate they're her sons."

"But... but what about Charlie's ear? They sent it to me after we opened the storage box rented by one of her sons." Feelings of helplessness and frustration tried to settle in my stomach. I fought them off with all my might.

"Circumstantial," Grayson said.

Julie kept quiet. I assumed she knew as well as I did that he was right.

"But..." Grayson said as he sat up a bit straighter. "As there's no lead to follow at the moment and time is of the essence, it's a good idea. Showing the boys' photo is of no use though, they cover themselves in daylight. Next to the fact we have no evidence they have anything to do with this, they have no criminal record. We can show Sasha's photo as she skipped parole and there's an APB out for her anyway. She's the main person we want to find. We'll also show a photo of Charlie. We can say we think Sasha has Charlie and that she may be in the company of two men, to inform people they're not looking for a woman on her own."

"Excellent thinking," Julie said.

Grayson smiled at her.

His words put a slight damper on my enthusiasm. I wanted everyone to look for the boys as well. The more individuals people were looking for, the greater the chance somebody would see one of them, particularly because the sucker community may not be inclined to help the police find them. However, I had no choice but to take what I could get.

"Okay, deal. Do you organize it or do I?"

"Our communications officer will organize Maine TV to come to the station, and I'll take it from there. I'll call you when I've got a time set up."

"Great."

I kept quiet during the rest of lunch, letting the lovebirds have their moment. I was already going over a speech in my head and couldn't wait to discuss it with Tom.

Before we left the lunchroom, Julie asked Grayson if he wanted to meet again. Of course he wanted to. They made me promise I wasn't going to attend. They really needn't worry about it as I had no intention of witnessing another courting ritual.

While they made their arrangements, I texted Tom that I would be home within fifteen minutes. He texted back he'd be there in thirty.

When Julie stopped her car on the street in front of my home, I asked her to wait for a moment before taking off.

"Why?" she said.

"Just let me check my mailbox."

"Oh, okay," she replied. "I'll wait." As annoyed as she'd been with my presence during lunch, her caring smile let me know she still loved me.

With trepidation, I check the mailbox after I got

out. It was empty.

"Clear," I said to Julie.

She waved and left.

I loved my sister. She could be quite a character sometimes, but she was there for me when I needed her.

As I made myself comfortable on the couch, I received a call from Grayson. He told me they organized Rosanne Bennett from Maine TV to come and do the live broadcast. I had done some interviews with her for SAMM, and I remembered her. Grayson told me they had agreed to the time of 4 p.m. for a meeting at the Bullsbrook police station. This meant it could be shown in the six o'clock news. I thanked him and hung up.

I immediately texted everyone about the arrangement but didn't text Sue. Instead, I asked Marlon if he could make sure Sue and Sonny didn't watch the news that evening. I felt like I was cheating on my own daughter, but I had to do what was best for her. Right now, that was having her know as little as possible about what was going on.

It wasn't long before I heard Tom's car turning onto the driveway.

Moral Support

I opened the front door and saw Tom fetching something from the passenger seat. For a moment, I thought he was Harry. They were so much alike; they could have been twins. If it weren't for his slightly darker hair, lighter eyes, leaner body, and dress sense of course. He certainly dressed better than Harry. Not to mention that oceanic smell.

Tom walked up to me wearing jeans, a black-and-blue checked flannel shirt, and a denim jacket. It was such a surprise that I laughed.

"What?" he said when he walked up the porch steps, a six-pack of beer in one hand, a bag of potato chips in the other.

"How much wood could a wood chopper chop if a wood chopper could chop wood?"

He gave me a peck on the cheek before he inspected his outfit.

"You don't like it?"

"No, no, I do. I just didn't expect you to wear checked shirts. I thought that wasn't you."

"Never assume you know me. I'm full of surprises," he said as he walked straight to the kitchen. He took two cans out of the rings and put the rest in the fridge.

"What?" he said as he saw me standing with my hands in my back pockets, biting my lip.

"Honestly? Beer? At two in the afternoon? Have you forgotten I've got to go on TV later today?"

Tom threw me the packet of potato chips and grabbed the two cans. He swaggered over and put one arm around me, directing me back into the living room.

"Ever heard of alcohol-free beer, my dear?"

I took the can from his hand and inspected the label. It was indeed alcohol-free beer.

"I wanted you to feel good about your speech, but I know from experience you'll be talking gibberish if I make you drink any alcohol." He smiled his cheeky smile at me.

Did I smile back at him for being a practical thinker or because he knew me better than most people?

"Thanks for another reminder of my poor intoxication record." I sat down on the couch, and he chose the nearest chair this time. "Are you aware, by the way, that since I have been acquainted with you, your presence and two of my drunkennesses have coincided? One could swear you're a bad influence on me." I opened the can and took a swig. It tasted like any other beer.

"When I hear you say that, I could swear you're drunk already." He opened his can and drank. I think he downed half the can in one go.

"Well, I'm not. I only had a diet coke at lunch."

Tom wiped his mouth and sat back.

"How's my dear friend Grayson? Is it any fun to have a non-work-related conversation with him?"

"Ugh. Don't start me on him. He keeps drooling over my sister." I stuck my finger in my mouth and pretended to gag to express my feelings more clearly. Tom laughed.

"Well, as much as I don't like him," he said, "I can't blame him. It must be her family genes that have that effect." He cleared his throat and looked away for a moment. "So, what did you have in mind to say during the broadcast?" He took another long swig from his beer.

Was that a flirt? Did he honestly have a crush on me? I couldn't deny there was some sort of an attraction between us, but he knew I was involved with Charlie. I loved Charlie with all my heart, and I would never betray him again. Would Tom actually know about my one-night-stand with Caleb three years ago? Harry wouldn't have told Tom voluntarily. I didn't put it past Rhona though. Perhaps he had figured it out himself. Sonny wasn't what you called the spitting image of Charlie. Tom hadn't met Sonny, but there were family portraits all over the house. And he did watch the Emma show.

"Earth to Kate," Tom said as he snapped his fingers in my direction.

"What? Oh, sorry. Too much on my mind at the

moment." I smiled at him but curled my toes in my shoes.

"I'm here to help you ease your load," Tom said. "Now, how about we start with you telling me what message you want to convey during the appeal."

For the next ninety minutes, we talked about my speech only. Tom helped me choose words that would draw a sympathetic response from the public, words like shocking, urgent, and freedom. Together we made it as concise, yet as tear-jerking as possible. We wanted as many people as possible to jog their memory and to look for Charlie, Sasha, and her sons in order to try and help us find Charlie.

At about three-thirty, we were as good as done.

"If you don't mind, I'm going upstairs to make myself presentable. Why don't you have the last beer in the meantime?"

Tom got up.

"Um, I think I better go," he said. He collected the empty beer cans and scrunched up the empty chips bag.

"Going? Why?" I tugged at my earlobe.

Tom let his stare wander around the room while he spoke.

"You don't need me. You know your speech by heart. There's nothing I can do for you."

I opened my mouth and closed it again, racking my brain for words to convince him.

"But... I need you... for... moral support."

Tom walked toward the kitchen.

"You don't need me, Kate."

I followed him on his heels. He was right. I didn't really need him, but I liked having him around. I frantically tried to think up a reason for him to be there.

"Yes. Yes, I do. I do need you. I need you to be there for me." Why didn't he want to help me? Why didn't he say what the problem was? He promised me he'd help me.

Tom put the cans and bag in the trash. He didn't turn around for a moment. When he did, I didn't like the look on his face. Something told me that I wasn't the problem. There was another reason he couldn't come with me, and he didn't really want to let me down.

"I'm sorry, Kate, but I really can't."

TV Appearance

Apprehensive, I closed the distance between us.

"Why, Tom? Why can't you be there? Is it a girlfriend? If so, you can tell her not to w—"

"It's not that." He struggled to find his words, looking this way and that. Then he sighed. "Oh, all right. I'll come with you. But I'm not going to stand next to you if that's what you had in mind."

I rolled my eyes and felt slightly giddy. Was there really no alcohol in that beer?

"Don't worry, you won't need to hold my hand. I only want you to be there for emotional support. Before and after."

He took a deep breath and let it out slowly.

"I can do that."

I'm sure my smile reached both my ears.

"Thanks, Tom. I don't know what I'd do without you." I gave him a quick peck on the cheek before I ran upstairs.

***

Tom and I left for the station at a quarter to four. I didn't want to be late. When we arrived, the Maine

News van was already in the parking lot, and the cameraman was taking his gear out. A burley woman was talking to the guy. She stopped talking when she spotted me and hurried over.

"Hi, Kate. How're you holding up? What terrible news about Charlie."

"Hi, Rosanne. Thank you so much for doing this. I know it was rather short notice." I gave her a hug, and my face disappeared into her curls.

"It's okay, dear. You know I'm always looking for a story. I'm so sorry to hear it's a terrible story about your partner this time. Let's hope this will help get him back." She squeezed my arm in sympathy.

"Rose, you want to do close-ups and medium shots or just medium shots?" The cameraman demanded Rosanne's attention.

"Just a sec, Jake," Rosanne said over her shoulder. "I'll see you inside," she said to me and squeezed my arm again. She then turned to instruct Jake.

Tom and I went inside where George buzzed us through. If his grin was any wider, the top of his head would fall off. I reckoned this was his first brush with TV.

"They're in the interrogation room," he beamed.

"Thanks, George.

I guided Tom to the room. He was awfully quiet. We entered the room and found Julie talking to Grayson. Rhona was there as well. Harry had to work of course, so I hadn't expected him to be there. I hadn't expected Rhona there either, for that matter. I gave her a hug.

"Hi Rhona, thanks for showing up. I really appreciate you being here."

"No problems, honey, but why's that asshole here?" Rhona said as soon as we parted. She glowered at Tom.

"Love you too, sister-in-law. Oh no, wait. I don't."

Tom's remark made me bite the inside of my lip as I didn't want to upset Rhona.

"Tom helped me write my speech. He's been awesome."

"Are you sure that's all he did?" She squinted her eyes as she looked at him, leaving no doubt about what she really wanted to know.

"Yes, Rhona, that's all he did. Now stop being so unkind. I can't deal with that right now." I took a deep breath and looked in Grayson's direction.

"Sorry, hon. You go do your stuff. Good luck." Rhona moved into a corner of the room. Tom moved into another. Whatever it was between those two, I wasn't going to deal with it right now.

I moved closer to my sister, trying to get into Grayson's field of view.

"Ah, you're here," he said when he finally noticed me. "As you can see, we've got the stand here for you to put your speech on. The TV crew can attach their microphone to the front. And I've arranged for

Charlie's and Sasha's photo to be enlarged. I thought having them in the background would be a good idea. What do you think?"

"It looks great, but I don't have a paper with my speech. I've learned it by heart."

Grayson scratched his eyebrow.

"O-kay, I really wished you had it written down. A lot of people forget what they want to say once the camera starts rolling, you know."

"You forget I've been on camera before."

I turned to Julie before I could get more annoyed with Grayson.

"Jules, how do I look? Is my hair okay?"

"You look fine, sis. You always do."

Was that a compliment or was she fobbing me off for being annoyed with Grayson? I couldn't tell.

George let Rosanne and Jake into the room. It took Jake a moment to set up his camera and the microphone.

"Are you ready?" Rosanne asked me.

I wiped my sweaty hand on my jeans.

"Yeah, I am."

"Okay. Now, I'll explain the situation to the audience first, then Jake will focus on Grayson, who'll give the details of who they want people to look for. Next is your turn, honey, to make it personal, but keep it short. Then I'll close off. How does that sound?"

"Fine with me."

Rosanne turned toward Grayson.

"I want you behind the stand when we start. Give way to Kate when you've done your speech. Do you have a police uniform to wear?"

"I'm a detective."

"Ah, sorry." Rosanne blushed. "I thought it would give a more authoritative look."

"We can ask George to be in the picture?" I offered and looked at Grayson.

Rosanne frowned questioningly at me.

"The guy who let you in. He's in uniform."

"That's a great idea." Rosanne's face lit up.

"George!" Grayson yelled from the doorway. "Get in here!"

George was there before Grayson finished his sentence.

"What is it?" he said, still sporting that huge smile.

"My dear boy," Rosanne said, "today is your big day. You're going on television. I want you to stand in the background. You don't have to say anything, just represent the police force. Do you think you can do that?"

"I sure can," George said.

I thought his head was going to explode from excitement. The crimson of his cheeks certainly wasn't normal.

"Jake, are you ready?" Rosanne asked.

"Yep, I can roll whenever you say the word," he said

without looking up from fiddling with his camera.

Rosanne put George and me in front of the headshots of Sasha and Charlie and asked Grayson to take his center spot.

"Remember, guys. Keep it short and snappy. No long, outdrawn sagas. Okay?"

Grayson and I nodded.

"No saga, not to worry," Grayson said.

Rosanne went to stand at a ninety-degree angle in front of the stand.

"And roll," she said to Jake.

Jake indicated with one hand that the camera was rolling. Rosanne introduced herself before announcing where she was, why she was there, and what had happened to Charlie. As she spoke, I felt butterflies in my stomach. I had been annoyed with Grayson that he didn't trust me to remember my lines, but going on TV always made me nervous. Even though it wasn't a live broadcast, the idea that every move you made was going to be judged by thousands of watchers was unnerving. I slowly breathed in and out through my nose to settle myself.

After Rosanne introduced Grayson, Jake pointed the camera at him. He talked about Sasha, telling people she may be involved in the disappearance of Charlie. He also mentioned her sons briefly. Halfway through Grayson's speech, Jake focused on the photos in the background while he talked.

When it was my turn, I swapped places with Grayson. I put emphasis on the emotional side of the situation. How Charlie was taken against his will, depriving him from his freedom, taken away from his children and myself. I asked for the person holding Charlie prisoner to please release him. I also told Charlie we loved him, that we would find him soon, and not to give up hope.

Jake then turned the camera a further ninety degrees. Rosanne had moved around the back of him and was ready to pick up from where I had left off. Tom had not expected the move and ducked out of view. Rosanne didn't see it and finished the broadcast with the request for people to call the police if they had any news regarding the whereabouts of Charlie, Sasha, or her sons.

Jake lowered the camera when he was done.

"How did that go?" Rosanne asked him.

"Perfect," he said and began packing away the camera and microphone.

"Can we do it again?" Tom asked.

"Why? Jake just said it was perfect," Rosanne said as she collected her microphone wire.

"I think I'm in it," Tom said. He put both hands on the top of his head, his eyes darting from Rosanne to Jake and back. I hadn't seen him this anxious before.

"We hardly see you. People will not be watching the background anyway." Jake had a matter-of-fact attitude.

"But I don't want to be on TV," Tom said.

"We'll block your face in post-production, how about that?" Rosanne had one hand on her hip as she awaited Tom's answer.

Tom nodded.

"Okay. I suppose I can live with that." He didn't look overly happy about it though.

"Are you worried your ex-girlfriends are going to find you and take revenge?" Rhona said out of the blue. I had forgotten she was there.

"Why don't you go take a super-hot shower to practice burning in hell?" Tom stormed out of the room before I could intervene.

Rhona raised her eyebrows.

"I think I hit a nerve there. You better watch yourself, missy," she said to me.

"I'm not sure if it's what you think, Rhona, but something's definitely not right."

I thanked Rosanne, Jake, Grayson, and George, said goodbye to Julie and Rhona, and hurried to the car park.

Tom sat in his car, his radio blasting. I got in but didn't say anything. Without a word, he started the car and drove me home.

"You want to come in for another beer?" I asked.

"No. Thanks, but no thanks."

He didn't look at me. Whatever the problem, he was

worried about it. I had no idea what it was that was upsetting him so much, but it was obvious he didn't want to talk about it.

"See you soon?" I asked after I got out.

"We'll see."

"Fine."

I slammed the car door shut and stomped up to the house. Without looking back, I went inside. His tires squealed on the tarmac as he pulled out into the street and sped off.

Murder

Once inside, I threw my jacket over a chair in the kitchen and made myself a cup of coffee. I really needed some caffeine right now. Why had Tom acted so strangely? I didn't think it was nerves. He actively tried to duck out of view. Who wasn't allowed to see him on TV and why? Was Rhona right? Did he have a couple of ex-girlfriends who wanted revenge? What did I really know about Tom?

I took my coffee into the living room and let my mind wander. Tom had been awfully curt toward me on the drive home. The fact that he didn't want to come inside and talk about it with me told me he was really pissed off. But what had I done? He was a grown man, wasn't he? I hadn't forced him to be there. He could have said no.

He did say no.

And stick to it.

I sat upright, pulled out my cell, and hovered my thumb over his call button. I pressed the home button instead. He was probably still on the road and couldn't answer. Besides, it was better to let him calm down a bit about the whole situation. I would give him a call the next morning.

***

At 6 p.m., I turned the TV on and changed the channel to Maine TV. First, they showed the international news. Rosanne's interview was up next. I hated hearing my own voice and thought my hair was sticking out on all sides. Julie could've said something about it. When the camera moved to Rosanne after I had spoken, I saw Tom clearly ducking out of view in the background. They hadn't blocked out his face.

I didn't know why I felt anxious, but I knew this was bad. Was it Tom's reaction that made me so worried? There was nothing I could change about it now, though. Whatever the damage, it was done. Tom had a good claim to ask for compensation as he had clearly stated that he didn't want to be in the shot, and they had promised him he wouldn't be. I'd vouch for him as a witness. It was the least I could do. Yet somehow, I didn't think Tom was the claiming type of person, but like he had said himself, he was full of surprises.

I turned the TV off and tried to call him. He didn't answer. As there was nothing I could do about it, I made myself a microwave dinner. Cooking had never been a hobby of mine and at the moment it was at the very bottom of my 'to do' list. Whilst spooning the hot-yet-bland meal into my mouth, I texted Sue. I told her I wasn't stopping by as I planned to have an early night.

The last few days had exhausted me mentally, and I decided to go straight to bed. Hopefully, my internal clock didn't object it being so early in the evening.

Once in bed, my mind kept milling over one thought. Four days ago, I had received Charlie's finger. Now, according to Grayson, it couldn't be re-attached anymore. That worry was over and done. I didn't care much about the ear as it wouldn't be missed underneath Charlie's half-long hair. What consumed me most of the night was the thought that Charlie might become a night-dwelling sucker forever. I couldn't stop thinking about it. Round and round it went through my head. My body tossed and turned all night in the big, empty bed.

***

The next morning, I woke up before my alarm went off. I checked the time; twenty-five past six. I rubbed my eyes. Did I sleep enough already? It was still so early. I wanted to get up, but a bone-felt tiredness still occupied my body.

Then I heard the noises coming from outside. There were voices and sounds of car doors slamming and the likes. It must have been what had awoken me. I got out of bed and pulled the curtain aside. Cameras flashed like strobe lights, blinding me. What the hell? I quickly let go of the curtain.

To make sure I wasn't dreaming, I took another peek. Once again, the cameras blinded me. Reporters and film crews were all over my lawn. Vans from various news stations lined the street. I moved away from the window, uncertain of what to do. After a few minutes of biting my nails, I left my bedroom to have a shower. Stripping naked while there were more than a dozen people standing on my front lawn, waiting to get a glimpse of me, wasn't easy, though. My shower was the shortest I'd ever taken.

By the time I was dressed and had breakfast, the noise had grown to a steady hum. What was I going to do all day? Not confronting the paparazzi, that was for sure, but if I wanted to get out, I had a problem. They blocked my drive with their vehicles, making it impossible for me to leave. I was about to call Julie when she rang me.

"Jules, you never guess what's going on here." I took another peek through the living room curtain to make sure I wasn't making it up.

"Kate, I need to talk to you. Will you be home?"

"I don't think I have another choice."

"Good, I'm on my way."

She didn't ask me why I had said I didn't have another option. Her mind apparently was preoccupied with something that was more important. As I hung up, the hairs on my arms stood on end. Julie's voice had sounded off, like she was afraid. What was it about this

TV broadcast that had people so freaked out?

I awaited Julie's arrival with trepidation. Slowly moving the edge of the curtain a slither, I assessed the situation outside. How the hell was she going to get through all the paparazzi? Where was she going to park? Would they even let her get inside without harassing her?

My heart skipped a beat when, about fifteen minutes later, I heard a knock on the kitchen door. It was Julie.

"How did you get here?"

"I jumped your neighbor's fence," she said.

"Your car?"

"Back on High Street. As soon as I got here and saw the frenzy, I drove on and went back to High Street. I wasn't going through all that to get to you." Julie's voice still sounded off. It had an edge to it, making me feel uncomfortable.

"Why did you want to talk to me this early? Shouldn't you be milking or something? Is it about the TV broadcast?"

We sat down at the kitchen table.

"Kate, you've got to stop working with the police." Julie held my gaze. Only now did I notice her red-rimmed eyes.

"Why? What's going on? Have you been crying? Jules, what's wrong?"

Tears welled up in my sister's eyes. I couldn't

remember the last time I'd seen her cry. She had been the one in control, the one who could handle everything, no matter what life threw at her. These last few years, she had been my role model.

"They murdered her, Kate. They killed her, cut her head right off."

Miscommunication

Dread filled my thoughts as I wondered who Julie meant when she said 'she' had been murdered. Tears poured down her face, and I quickly put my arms around her. Her body shook, but I wasn't sure if it was from grief or anger. Was it Sue? Was it one of the farm girls?

"Who, Jules? Who did they kill?" I held my breath with fear.

"My prize cow, sis. They killed my prize cow." Julie was a blubbering mess.

A wave of relief washed over me.

"But... how? I mean, why? What has your cow got to do with me? With Charlie?"

I let Julie take the time she needed to gain control of herself.

"It's the no pigs sign, remember," she said. "Sasha warned you not to get the police involved. She even sent you Charlie's ear to warn you, and you ignored her. Now she's trying to intimidate you by hurting me, your family. I don't even want to think about what she could do next."

I sat staring at her, scary thoughts flying through my mind. The loudest one being what Sasha could do to my kids if she so easily could get to the farm.

"I'm so sorry, sis, I really am, but I had to do something to get Charlie back."

"I know. But I've worked so hard for the past thirteen years to put the farm on the farmer's map. She killed all that when she killed my baby. I know she's not a human…" Her face scrunched up into a crying fit again. I rubbed her arm in a feeble attempt to soothe her.

"Don't say that. I know what she meant to you. She was like a family member." The photograph hanging in her office of a proud Julie standing next to her prize-winning cow sprung to mind, and the absence of any of ours.

"Still, she's only an animal," Julie said, wiping her nose. "I'm not that stupid. I'm just worried, Kate. What will Sasha do if you involve the police again? It's clear she can get to us whenever she pleases as none of us have heard her sneak in, not even the dogs. You've got to stop doing what you're doing. What if she got to Sue or Sonny? Is that worth it?"

Those last sentences didn't have the right ring to it. They stuck out like a couple of ugly witches at a Miss Universe competition. My eyes shot at Julie's.

"What do you mean?" I said.

"What do you mean by 'what do you mean'? I thought I was pretty clear."

There's obviously some miscommunication going

on here.

"Stop doing what you're doing? What did you mean by that?" Involuntarily, my body inched minutely away from her.

"Well," Julie said and cleared her throat. "Is it worth trying to get Charlie back if Sue or Sonny could get injured or killed in the process?"

I couldn't believe my ears. Slowly, I stood up.

"Get out."

Julie didn't move. "Come on, Kate. Think about it. Of course I want you to get Charlie back, but do you really want to risk our lives for him? My life, your children's lives? Do you really want to risk losing Sue or Sonny? Do you think Charlie would want that?" She looked at me with pleading eyes, as if any of her words contained any form of logic.

"Get out, Jules, and don't come back."

I left the kitchen and went into the hallway as I couldn't stand having her in my sight right then. There was a short moment of silence before I heard the backdoor open and close. Julie had left.

Not wanting the paparazzi to get a glimpse of me through any curtains, I locked myself in the toilet. Sitting on the closed lid, I ran my hands through my hair. My throat had closed up and an empty feeling took over my whole body, making me double up in agony. How could she do this to me? Why? She knew what Charlie meant to me. She wanted me to abandon the search for Charlie, the father of my child, my partner, the love of my life. How could I ever abandon him? He wasn't a stupid cow.

Obviously, I didn't want to risk the lives of my children either, but I had to get Charlie back. If Sasha hurt my children, I... I didn't know what I would do to her. What I had to do was get Charlie back and get Sasha locked up before any of that could happen. Simple.

I calmed myself by taking deep breaths, letting the clean air in and breathing all the bad stuff out. I had to keep thinking straight. And practical. Who could I rely on?

I called Tom's number. The phone kept ringing, and I bit my nails. I hoped he had been able to sort the issue of the broadcast by now. Finally, the call was answered, and my mood lifted instantaneously. It dropped straight away when he didn't speak.

"Tom, are you there?"

"Yes."

"Great, I need your help."

I explained what had happened on the farm and about my conversation with Julie.

"Oh fuck," Tom said.

"Yeah, she's one screwed up bitch."

"No, I mean you two have got it all wrong."

"Wrong? How?"

What did he mean?

"The cow wasn't killed by Sasha, Kate. Did you ever watch that movie The Godfather?" Tom asked.

"Um, I may have, a long time ago."

"Well, remember that part where this guy finds his horse's head in his bed?"

I remembered the scene. At the time it had shocked me immensely that anybody could do that to an animal. Instantly, I realized what Tom was getting at.

"You mean to say that was the reason you were so upset about being in the footage yesterday?" The angst in the pit of my stomach was confused for a moment, not knowing if it should stay or not.

"Exactly. I was afraid something like this was going to happen. The Boss told me to stay out of the situation between you and Sasha, and I clearly didn't. I know for a fact he loves old movies, and this is his way of saying he meant what he said."

"Holy shit, he does mean business, doesn't he?" I leaned back and let my shoulders drop.

"Yeah, he does mean business."

"Now what?"

"Now I must lie low for a while. By the time he's calmed down, I'll apologize. And I probably will owe him a favor," Tom said as a matter of fact.

"Oh dear. Is that bad?"

"Nothing I can't handle. Don't you worry about me. Why don't you go to the farm and explain it to your sister. I don't want you two arguing about something that didn't happen."

My jaws clenched shut, and I wrapped my free arm around my body.

"It's too late for that. She spoke her mind, and I heard it, loud and clear. This is one thing that can't be undone. Besides, I couldn't get away if I wanted to."

"What do you mean?" Tom asked.

"There are paparazzi all over my front lawn. They're filming and photographing every move I make. My car's blocked in by their vehicles, and I can't get out, even if I wanted to.

"Hmmm..." Tom said. "You won't be able to get Charlie back if they follow you everywhere. My guess is Sasha will be even less impressed with paparazzi than she already is with the police. How about I come and pick you up, and you stay at my place for a while? We can stay low together for a few days. If they follow us, I'll lose them on the way over. I'm pretty good at that."

His complete turnaround had me confused.

"Are you sure? They just killed Jules's cow because of your involvement and now you offer to accommodate me? Is that a clever move?"

Tom laughed. "If I owe them anyway, I better owe them good," he said. "Don't you worry. Will you be okay for a little longer?"

"Yes, but when you come, you better pick me up from High Street. You won't be able to get anywhere near the house without the paparazzi spotting you. I'll escape via the back door and jump my neighbor's fence. Just send me a text when you're there."

"Okay, Sunshine. See you soon."

Tom hung up, and I was alone with my stalkers again.

I went back to the kitchen to make myself a coffee when I heard a loud noise. It wasn't clear what it was. I hurried into the living room to find out what had happened. Inside, all was normal. When I pulled back the curtain, I jumped when an egg hit the window. Its smashed remains dripped down the glass.

When I was over the shock, I looked beyond the window. A man stood in the middle of my lawn. I didn't know him. He had a carton of eggs in one hand, an egg ready to throw in the other. His eyes met mine. If looks could kill, I would have been incinerated on the spot. The intensity made me take a step back.

"You stupid bitch!" he yelled. "It's all your fault!"

Escape

The man threw the egg at my window and picked another one from the carton.

The paparazzi loved it, shooting the drama from a safe distance. One reporter tried to interview the man, who continued to scream obscenities at me. Apparently, he wasn't too keen on me helping suckers, something to do with his wife dying. Maybe the broadcast hadn't been such a good idea. Even though I had been on TV before, I had never said where I lived. As Rosanne had mentioned Bullsbrook during the broadcast, it hadn't taken sucker-haters long to find me.

Especially not with all the news vans in front of my door.

I let the curtains fall and called Harry. He always knew what to do. I explained to him what was happening. Before I could tell him to go the route Julie had taken, he said he'd be there soon and hung up. He must have been in a hurry as he needed to go to work.

Five minutes later, the noise outside rose to another level. With a coffee in my hand, I peeked through the curtain. Harry and Rhona were trying to make their way to the front door, but the man who had been throwing the eggs harassed them, along with some new anti-sucker friends. They were calling them all sorts of vulgarities which Rhona replied with fervor. To my surprise, the haters yelled words like 'sucker lovers.' As if that was something foul.

I opened the door to let Rhona and Harry in. There was a bit of a scuffle when they were pushed and shoved by the protesters trying to prevent them from entering my home. Harry had to rudely push the protestors off as otherwise they would've gotten inside as well.

"Phew, we made it alive," Rhona said. "How can you put up with those dickheads?"

We hugged.

"Thank you so much for coming, guys. I appreciate it. You want a coffee?"

"Sure," Harry said. "In the meantime, we'll think about what we can do about this situation. You can't stay here, not with that crowd out there." He peeked through the curtains at the commotion outside.

I went to the kitchen and put the kettle on. I took the mugs out of the cupboard and scooped instant coffee into them, one spoonful of sugar for Rhona. Looking out of my kitchen window, I wondered if I would ever live a normal life again. Was it really too much to ask to want to live with Charlie in peace and quiet?

Thoughts of Charlie made my stomach tie itself into a knot. I did my breathing exercises and focused on the task at hand. I returned to the living room and handed out the coffees.

Now Rhona stood at the window, peeking through the curtains.

"What a mess out there. Was the broadcast worth it? Did you get any clues?" Rhona asked.

"I don't know yet. I haven't heard anything from Grayson since it went out. To be honest, I had expected to hear something from him by now."

There was a knock on the door. I peeked through the spy hole before opening. It was Grayson.

Summoned by the devil.

I let him in and quickly shut the door, muting the noise from the protestors.

"Did you get a lead?" I asked. I hoped that this was the reason he showed up at this hour.

Grayson indicated with his thumb outside.

"One of the news guys called me when they started throwing eggs at your window. I heard some people also attacked you?" He looked at Harry and Rhona for confirmation.

"It was nothing," Harry said. He wiped the issue under the carpet as he usually was more worried about the bigger picture.

"She can't stay here," Rhona said to Grayson. "It's too dangerous. God knows what those motherfuckers are going to throw at her window next. What if the morons start throwing bricks? She's got a little kid, you know. It's not fucking safe."

Grayson's jaws clenched before he turned to me.

Is he offended by Rhona's flowery language or by the fact she insinuated he thought otherwise?

"Do you have anywhere else to stay?" he asked me.

"I can stay with Tom."

"Kate..." Harry said. He couldn't finish what he was about to say as Rhona went into a tirade.

"Oh, for fuck's sake, Kate. How often have we told you not to get involved with that motherfucker? He's bad news. You can stay with us, or you can stay with Julie, anywhere but with that fucking psychopath."

"And have them throw eggs or bricks at your place? Putting you and your daughters in danger? I don't think so." I knew she meant well but staying with them was not an option.

Rhona put her hands on her hips and her mouth opened to say something. Nothing came out.

"What about Julie's place. The farm is safe," Harry said.

"The farm's not safe." I folded my arms, but my fingers kept plucking my sweater.

"Why not?" Grayson looked at me in alarm.

Surely, Julie would've told Grayson about her cow first thing. Did she really not call him? Is she that afraid?

"Julie's prize cow has been killed. A warning from the Bratva."

"Bratva? What's a fucking Bratva?" Rhona said.

"It's the Russian mob," Harry said as he slowly sat down.

"Is Julie okay?" Grayson asked.

"Yeah, she's fine. Upset, but fine. She'll live." I wanted to tell him what Julie had said at my kitchen table, get it off my chest. But Grayson wasn't one of the family, yet, so I kept my mouth shut.

"The mob?" Rhona's eyes grew large as she looked at Harry. Then she abruptly turned to me. "What did I tell you? He's a walking fucking disaster. That son-of-a-bitch should be locked up."

"Rhona..." Harry tried.

"I don't give a shit about him being your brother. He's putting other people's lives in danger." She turned to Grayson. "Can't you lock him up or something?"

"For what?" he answered.

"I don't know. For being a ball-ache pain in the ass, for all I care." Rhona plumped herself next to Harry on the couch.

"Would you like a coffee?" I asked Grayson.

"I'd love one."

Going back into the kitchen, I felt my cell buzz in my back pocket. There was a message from Tom. 'I'm at High Street,' it read. While preparing Grayson's coffee, I contemplated my options. I couldn't stay with Harry and Rhona, not wanting to endanger them. Julie's place wasn't an option right now, even if it had been safe at the farm. And over my dead body was I going to endanger Sue, Marlon, and Sonny by staying at their place. Should Grayson mention a safe house of some sort, I would have my every move monitored by the police. Basically, I had no choice but to go with Tom.

Rhona and Harry were arguing in the living room. Grayson tried to give his opinion now and again, only to get his head bitten off by Rhona. As quietly as I could, I grabbed my jacket from the kitchen chair and put it on. I carefully pushed the handle of the back door down. It didn't squeak for a change. Inhaling deeply, I threw the door open and spurted toward the back fence. I half-jumped, half-climbed over it, ran through my neighbor's garden, and was out in the open on High Street. Tom's car sped up to me, and I jumped in. My escaped took less than a minute.

The Penthouse

As if racing for our lives, Tom drove us out of Bullsbrook. I had to hang on for dear life not to be thrown about in the car, even with my seatbelt on. I didn't think anyone was following us, but Tom kept racing until we were out of town. Once we were on the freeway, I got my cell phone out.

"Who're you calling?" Tom asked, throwing a quick glance at my cell's screen.

"Harry."

"Why?"

I couldn't answer him as Harry answered the call immediately.

"Hi, Harry... No, I'm okay. I'm with Tom..." Rhona screeched in the background. Harry apparently had put the call on speaker. "Just listen to me, Harry, please. I only wanted to let you know that I've made up my mind. I didn't want to put any of you in danger. Tom knows what he's getting himself into. It's my decision. I'll keep you up to date. Tell Grayson he can contact me on my cell anytime." I hung up before they could lecture me.

Tom's eyes briefly met mine.

"You just left?"

I didn't imagine the thrilled look on his face. I sighed and sank deeper into the car seat.

"They wanted me to stay elsewhere, with people throwing eggs at my home and all, but they didn't want me to stay with you. They would've never let me go if I'd told them beforehand."

"People were throwing eggs?"

"Yeah, and I had just washed my bloody windows. Would it surprise you that not everyone agrees with my work? Some people can't forget Black October. They even tried to prevent Harry and Rhona getting into my home."

Tom remained silent. I guessed there was little for him to say. Apart from some acid remark about how he agreed with not letting Rhona inside, perhaps. Leaning against the door, I took Tom in as he drove. I wondered what experience he'd had with sucker-haters. He clearly was a pro-suckers guy and must have had a brush with the people opposing the change, like all of us had. Would he have had far worse experiences? Would that be why he kept quiet?

I had to stop thinking about the past, keeping focused on the future.

"Where are we going? Your place?"

"Yes, my place. One of my places," Tom said.

"You have multiple places?" I always wondered how people could afford more than one place, especially people like John Smith.

"A couple. They're not big, but they give me some options."

Do you also have enough money for someone to clean them all, or is cleaning your hobby?

"So, are we staying in the penthouse or in the one with the lake view?" I said.

Tom chuckled. "Like I said, they're not fancy. But you'll be free from the paparazzi for the time being."

We soon entered Portland and Tom drove the car into a multistory parking garage. He parked the car, and we got out.

"Do you live nearby?"

"Just follow me."

He took me to another level where he produced another set of keys and opened a red sedan. We got into the car and out of the parking garage. Not only did he own multiple apartments, he also owned more than one car. My curiosity for Tom's profession grew by the minute.

We drove around for another fifteen minutes before he parked the car in an indoor private parking in an alleyway. Through an internal door that lead to a flight of stairs, he took me to the top floor where he opened a door.

"Madam, may I present to you 'the penthouse.'" Tom held the door open and bowed.

"Liar," I said with a grin on my face as I entered.

"I never said I didn't have a penthouse." He followed

me inside and locked the door behind us.

The studio wasn't small, but it was still only one room with most of its space upward. It contained all the comforts of modern living, and like Tom had said, it wasn't fancy. He hadn't done much to do up the old factory building accommodation. He had tried to decorate the place with some paintings, statues, and lamps, as well as adding an old mahogany wardrobe and a large, wooden, four-poster bed. I guessed there was a bathroom behind the only other door in the room. It amazed me that the place was clean. Even my house had more dust lying around.

Maybe cleaning truly is his hobby.

"Um, there's only one bed." I had walked up to it and admired the intricately turned style at one of the corners, too embarrassed to face Tom.

"Don't worry. I'll sleep on the couch. I do hope you don't snore. Otherwise, I'll have to move you to the bath."

When I imagined Tom carrying my snoring, sleeping body from the bed to the bath, I realized I didn't bring anything for a sleepover, including PJs. I'd have to borrow a shirt and a toothbrush from him when the time came.

I hope he doesn't sleep naked.

"Do you mind if I use your bathroom?"

"Mi casa es su casa, Sunshine," Tom said and busied himself making coffee in the kitchen.

I went through the door with the large, mottled glass window. When you lived alone, you obviously didn't worry too much about privacy. I looked back at Tom and the big bed before shutting the door behind me. Harry and Rhona were wrong about him. Tom might have been a romantic, but he didn't seem to be a seducer. Wouldn't he have suggested sharing the bed otherwise?

I found myself in a dark room that was about half the size of the living room. Unlike the other room which had large windows in the ceiling, there were no windows here. In the dappled light through the door window, I could make out a toilet to the left, a sink to the right, and in the middle stood an old cast iron bath on four legs. There was a shower at the far end of it, but no shower curtain. I bent over and thought I could see a drain in the center of the concrete floor underneath the bath, a relic of the place's olden days. I wondered what the factory had manufactured. Like the living room, Tom had made no effort to do the place up at all, and it had a cold feel to it, the darkness and cold temperature not doing much for the atmosphere at all.

As I didn't fancy sitting in the dark, I searched for the light switch. It was an old, black Bakelite box on the door post. I flipped the switch, and instantly the whole room lit up with a warm glow. How could I have missed the thousands of Christmas lights hanging from the plumbing that crisscrossed the high ceiling? It made the room look like something from a fairytale with the lights reflecting off all the enamel and ceramic surfaces. The lights were also mirrored in the polished concrete floor, making the room even brighter. My jaw dropped, and I almost drooled.

I used the toilet and washbasin, all the while being dazzled by the multitude of little lights. I regretted having to leave the room.

"Wow, that bathroom is amazing," I said to Tom as I reluctantly turned off the lights and closed the door.

Tom handed me a coffee, and his fingers brushed mine. His touch lingered only momentarily, but I could sense it was done purposefully. Had I been wrong about him? Trying to ignore him, I inhaled the smell of hazelnuts drifting up from the coffee and busied myself warming my hands on the mug. The temperature of the water coming from the tap in the bathroom had been as cold as the temperature outside.

"Thanks, I did it up myself," he said smugly.

"I can see you're quite the decorator." My eyes fell on the plaster of the wall behind the TV. The plaster that was more absent than present.

"It still needs some work, but not much," Tom said as he sat back in the black leather couch, admiring his place.

I sat down next to him as there weren't any other comfy seats.

"No, not much." I smiled and sipped the coffee. It

was the best coffee I'd ever had.

We sat in silence for a moment, enjoying our warm drinks, before Tom turned on the TV. He flipped from one news station to another. Now and again, the topic of Charlie was touched, but it always ended in the presenter stating there still was no further information. Every fifteen minutes or so, I checked my cell, but there was never a message from Grayson.

Around 1 p.m., my stomach grumbled. I pulled a couch cushion against it and hoped Tom hadn't heard.

"I'm sorry. You must be hungry," he said, obviously not suffering from a hearing impediment. "I'll have a look at what I've got in the refrigerator."

Before he could get up fully, I pulled him back into the seat. I used his weight as leverage and was on my way to the kitchen before he could stop me.

"You stay put," I said. "I'll have a look and make you something. It's the least I can do."

I opened the refrigerator, and right next to the bread, milk, and vegetables, lay bags of blood. Stacks of them. I took one out and stared at it. 'O-negative,' the label read. Tom now stood beside me, running his hands through his hair, making that scent of his whirl around me.

"There's blood in your refrigerator," I said.

"Yeah, there is..."

We both stared at the bag in my hand. Tom couldn't be a sucker. He had had a normal dinner with me, with vegetables, and we had had potato crisps and beer together. But then why would he have blood in his fridge?

"Do you often have sucker friends over?" I asked.

Tom's eyes met mine, and he smiled.

"Yeah. Sometimes." He took the bag out of my hand and put it back on the shelf. "But I think you'd be more interested in a ham and cheese sandwich."

"Can you grill it?" I loved the idea of a warm lunch. This place was freezing.

"I sure can," he said and flicked on the grill in the oven before getting ingredients out of the fridge. "You sit down, Kate. This is my home. Let me do my magic."

"If you insist."

"I do."

I took a seat on one of the bar stools on the other side of the cooking island, nearly falling off as the seat turned.

"Careful there, or it's no booze for you," Tom joked.

It was fun to watch Tom do his thing. He appeared to enjoy cooking, something that I had often tried but always failed to do.

"Tom..." I said after watching him in silence for a while, chin on my hand, my elbow resting on the countertop.

"That's my name, don't use it in vain," he gave me a quick smile before returning his attention to the frying of diced onions. His culinary creation was going to be far more than the simple ham and cheese sandwich I had in mind.

"What do you do for a living?"

He now washed some veggies underneath the tap.

"I told you. I'm in the information business," he finally said as he began cutting up some mixed bell peppers.

"Yeah, but you didn't tell me what sort of information."

Tom stopped cutting the peppers and looked at me.

"Sometimes, it's better not to know certain things. This is one of those times and one of those things. Pepper?" He held out a little piece of yellow bell pepper.

I took it from him and chewed on it. It tasted sweet.

"Okay, no more questions about your work." I pushed off the countertop and spun my seat around, taking in the place, until I faced him again. "How did you get this apartment?"

"I thought you just said you weren't going to ask me questions about my work," Tom replied.

"Oh, sorry. I didn't know this was a fringe benefit. Your boss must really like you. Is that Bratva Boss your boss?" I realized I wasn't keeping my word, but I was curious as hell to find out.

Tom put both his hands on the countertop and sighed.

"No, he is not. Now cut out the questions about me. Let's talk about you for a change." The corners of his mouth did that sexy thing again.

"What do you want to know?"

"Oh, I have so many questions, for example—"

A knock on the door interrupted Tom's question. We both looked at each other in alarm.

Unexpected Help

There was another knock on the door. This time more urgent.

"Are you expecting anyone?" I asked Tom.

"Not that I know of." He wiped his hands and went to the door. Briefly, he peeked through the spyhole.

"It's Olesia," he said, then opened the door. Olesia walked into the room. "Olesia, what're you doing here?" Tom checked the landing and stairs, but there appeared no one else coming on this unannounced visit. He closed the door.

"What kind of welcome is that, Fomka?" Olesia said as she kissed him left, right, and center. She then walked over to me and gave me the same welcome.

"How are you sailing?" she asked me.

"Sailing?" I said. "Oh, you mean faring. I'm doing okay."

Olesia waved her hand in the air. "Excuse my English, please. I don't speak it so good. Tom, you help me, yes?"

"Of course." He had walked over and turned the stove to a lower setting. Tom didn't say anything, but it was clear from his expression he expected an explanation from Olesia for being in his studio.

I wondered if Olesia was his ex-girlfriend and whether she had more problems letting him go than Tom had letting her go.

"I'm here to help Kate," Olesia said. She turned to me and smiled the sweetest smile. I returned it even though I had no idea how she could possibly help me. "I saw the television news. I know where this Sasha woman is."

I jumped off my seat.

"What? You do? Where? Are you sure?" I was dying to know the answers. Tom was also very interested in what Olesia had to say now.

"I know about the preduprezhdenive."

I frowned and looked at Tom.

"Warning," he said.

OMG. As well as cooking and cleaning, he speaks Russian.

"But when I saw Fomka on the television news," Olesia continued, "I knew he no listen anyway. I thought I help you too."

Tom and I looked at each other and both of us smiled.

"So much for worrying about nothing," I said to Tom before directing my attention back to Olesia. "What can you tell us?"

"I know where she is. It's a place close to here." She told us the address, but I had no idea where it was. I pulled out my cell phone and looked it up. It was indeed not far from where we were now.

"How do you know?" I said. "No one has come forward since the TV broadcast."

Grayson would certainly have called me if he had received a lead.

"This man rents out places to Boss," Olesia said. "I heard Boss talk to him about Sasha and where to put her. And the reason you have no heard from anybody is because the... warning... is not only for Fomka. Everyone has been warning."

"Warned," Tom said absentmindedly. He frowned and seemed in deep thought. "This means that this Sasha woman is important. Why else warn everybody off?" he said to no one in particular.

"She is," Olesia said. "She was lover of Boss before Chornyy Oktyabr', before Black October."

I didn't care why Sasha was important. I only had one thing on my mind.

"When are we going?" I asked Tom. I was full of energy all of a sudden.

"Hang on, we need to think about this first," he said. "Besides, I've got this lovely food nearly ready. Olesia, would you like to join us for lunch?"

"Yes, thank you," she said and threw her long coat over one of the other bar stools.

My hands drummed the countertop the entire time Tom was cooking. Waiting while knowing where Sasha was, where Charlie possibly was, was torture. But I couldn't leave, aware it wasn't a good idea to go in alone, guns blazing. Even if I'd had guns.

Tom finished his cooking and put a lovely, gourmet-style, cheese-and-ham sandwich in front of me. For Olesia, he pulled out one of the blood bags from the refrigerator and poured it into a wine glass. He himself also ate a gourmet sandwich. If I had previously thought Tom might possibly be a sucker, my mind was now one hundred percent at rest.

I finished my sandwich in no time. It was delicious, but I wanted to get lunch over and done with. Once the other two had finished their lunch, which was like watching grass grow, Olesia said goodbye and wished me all the best. Tom told Olesia to keep a low profile for the time being. He obviously was worried for her safety now she had defied the Bratva Boss as well.

Before Tom had shut the door when Olesia left, I had stuffed all the dishes in the dishwasher.

"Ready when you are," I said with a huge smile on my face.

"Sit down, Kate," Tom said. "Let's talk this over first. We need to do some surveillance before doing anything else."

I plunked myself down on the leather couch, my mood following me to a lower level. Tom sat down beside me.

"We need to know if she's alone in this place," he said.

"She's not. Charlie is with her. Her sons probably too."

"See, that's three to two. Too much for us to handle. If she hasn't got help from anybody else, which we still don't know. We also don't know the layout of the place. Is there another entrance or exit? Do they have access to a getaway car? Those sorts of things. We need to make sure Charlie is there before we go in. And, maybe most importantly, do you want to tell Grayson?"

I looked away. He was right, we had to find out more before going in, but I didn't want to tell Grayson. Even though it was the Bratva that had killed Julie's cow, according to Tom, Joanne, and my own gut feeling, I wouldn't put it past Sasha to retaliate with something more horrible if I involved the police again.

"Okay, you're right. I don't want to tell Grayson, but I agree with doing some surveillance first. Then we can figure out what to do."

"Okay. We'll stick to the plan then," Tom said.

"I do think we should go now, though. Because Sasha's sons are suckers, they won't be out and about during daytime and we have a better chance of not being seen snooping around."

"In that case, let's go."

I jumped up, adrenaline spiking again.

I would finally do something to get Charlie back, and I could hardly contain my excitement. Why had everybody been so opposed to me getting involved with

Tom? He was the best thing around.
I grabbed my jacket, and Tom led the way.

An Unexpected Visit

Tom drove us to a block away from the address Olesia had given us. It wasn't the best area of Portland to live in, but I guessed plenty of people in the world would give their right arm to live in a free-standing house. Maple trees lined the streets, and the leaves had turned a beautiful fall color. From an esthetic point of view, it wasn't that bad here at all.

We got out of the car and walked to the corner of the street where Sasha was supposed to live. We counted the houses, and it appeared the house we were looking for was the fourth house on the right, across the road. It was an old house, nothing special about it.

The sun's rays came out from behind some clouds, but the wind was still freezing. I put my arm through Tom's and huddled close to him. Maybe because it was cold or maybe because, despite aesthetics, this place was giving me the creeps.

"Let's walk," I said.

Tom grinned back at me. "It sure is a nice time for a stroll."

I rolled my eyes.

We ambled along the street, pretending to look around and admiring the scenery. I didn't see anybody around to see us and think we may possibly have other intentions, but you never knew who was lurking around a corner.

We had walked about three-quarters of the distance toward the house when I heard a door open. The sound came from the house in question. Tom and I looked at each other. We didn't expect Sasha or her sons to be outdoors for another hour, when it would be darker. We were only one house away and extremely visible. Without a word spoken, we ducked behind the steps of the house we were passing. A car door slammed, and a motor started. Before we knew it, a black van came out of the drive and took off. They must have dumped the white van and stolen another one. The windows of the van were tinted, but I was sure I saw a young, hooded man sitting in the driver's seat.

When the van was out of view, Tom and I stood up and continued our walk, pretending nothing had happened. From the corner of my eye, I studied the house across the road. It had a red front door and plenty of windows, all of them with block-out window treatments. Trees planted closely around the house had enough foliage to prevent as much light entering as well. An empty drive alongside had a dilapidated garage at the back of it.

As we walked on, my eyes fell on the front door again. Was it ajar? I nudged Tom in the ribs and indicated with my head toward the door.

"The door is open," I whispered.

"Keep on walking," he said casually, looking the other way.

I didn't agree with Tom. This may well be our only chance. If one of the sons had left, this meant one opponent less. Tom was a healthy and fit man, and I knew my martial arts. Together we had the element of surprise.

I let go of Tom's arm and spurted across the road. I ran as quietly as I could up the steps. My heart pounded in my throat as I flattened myself against the wall next to the front door. Tom had followed me and flattened himself against the wall next to me. He mouthed, 'What the hell are you doing?' I smiled and slid through the opening of the door.

Inside, the hallway was dark. I had expected this, but it still took me a little while to get adjusted to it. We inched along, and I stopped before we got to the first door on our left. Tom moved past me and pushed me back. When he put his foot down to get past the door, the floorboard screamed like a hungry baby in the middle of the night.

There goes our stealth mode.

I held my breath. I heard a movement from inside the room, and the door opened before we could react. Sasha stared at Tom. Then her glance fell on me.

"YOU!" she shrieked.

She flew at me, but Tom threw his arms around her.

Sasha's claws only just missed my retreating body as he held her back. He gave her another tug and together they fell into the room. I didn't waste any time and flew up the stairs. I assumed they kept Charlie in one of the bedrooms. As soon as I got to the landing, I opened every door I came across. Behind the third door, I found him.

Charlie lay on a bare mattress on the floor in the far corner of the room. His right hand was tied with metal handcuffs to a central heating pipe. His head was bandaged and so was his left hand. Dark stains marked the spots where Sasha had mutilated him. A horrible smell filled the room. I couldn't place it immediately.

"Smudge, it's me," I said and rushed to him. "Smudge, I'm here to get you out."

Charlie didn't react at first. I shook him by the shoulders and called his name several times. A pang of fear shot through my chest. Charlie finally opened his eyes and tears of joy and sadness streaked my face. I hugged him as he, too, began to cry. This close to him, the stench of a week's sweat filled my nostrils. That, and the smell of excrement. I looked over Charlie's shoulder and spotted a bucket.

Animals!

I let go of Charlie and yanked at the cuffs, but they didn't break. I noticed the wounds on Charlie's wrist, evidence he had already tried to break free many times. So that option wasn't going to work. A pain in my chest made it hard to breathe, and tears in my eyes blurred my vision. I heard Tom and Sasha fighting downstairs. I put my foot against the wall and yanked the cuffs again, putting my full weight to it, while trying to think of another way to free Charlie.

"Kate..." Charlie whispered. "Kate, don't."

"What...?"

"Kate, go. Get out... Leave me... Let me die..."

My breathing stopped, and my heart shrank almost to non-existence as I looked at Charlie.

"No, no, no, don't say that. You can't say that." Taking his face in my hands, I caressed him, kissed him. "I love you. I won't leave you. You're coming home, Smudge. I'm getting you out."

Charlie tried to escape my caresses and kisses. Tears streamed down his face, but now I worried they weren't of happiness.

Would he be too embarrassed about the state he's in? Did he really want to die? He was a mess for sure. His hair was matted, his shirt stained, his pants torn. There were also little holes in his shirt and pants. I had no idea what horrible things besides cutting off his finger and ear they had done to him, but I swore they were going to pay for it.

"No, Kate. Get out. Leave me. Go."

We sat staring at each other. I couldn't believe he was giving up. I finally found him, and he was giving up. Well, I certainly wasn't going to give up on him, even if he had. I took his face in my hands and kissed him hard on the mouth.

"You're coming home with me, Smudge."

"Think again," said a voice behind me.

A Shot in the Dark

It was the voice of one of Sasha's sons, and he was behind me before I could defend myself. With one hand he grabbed my left wrist and put his other arm around my throat. He pulled me upright which was in my favor. I walked up the wall and threw my weight over his head. Gravity pulled him onto his back and the shock of the fall loosened his grip on me. I turned around before he had a chance to get up and sat with my knees on his upper arms, my full weight preventing him to use them. Unfortunately, he wasn't so easily defeated. He threw his legs up and hooked one of them around my neck, pulling me backward and off his arms. As I now lay on my back, he moved to get on top of me. My legs were still between us. I put my feet on his chest and pushed him away with all my might. He hit his head against the wall and was momentarily dazed.

I grabbed the chance to jump up and pull his arm into a wrestling hold. I knew he was far stronger than me, but Marlon once told me no one could escape this grip unless they didn't mind getting their shoulder dislocated. Marlon had been right, and my opponent couldn't move anymore. I had the upper hand. The only problem was that I couldn't let go to get to

Charlie. I had to wait for Tom to come and take over. A sense of accomplishment washed over me, despite the situation I currently was in. Until I heard a shot downstairs. Fear took over. The boy tried to get loose, but I wouldn't let him, keeping him in my grip while my thoughts run riot.

Tom didn't bring a gun. I didn't see him pack a gun, did I? Would he have had one hidden in his boot, like in the movies? Would he actually pull the trigger? Had he shot anybody before? Someone was coming up the stairs. Was it Tom or Sasha?

My thoughts were brought to an abrupt hold as my enemy walked into the room. She was even uglier than she had been in the photo of her file. The scars on her face were an angry red, twisting and turning, forming pits and bumps, making her once perfect skin look like a moon landscape. She limped and moved as if she was hurt. Did Tom shoot her? Then I noticed the gun in her hand. I realized Tom's fate and a primordial scream roared from my throat. The boy screamed with me as I tightened my grip on him in my anguish.

Sasha took one second to assess the situation. I feared she was going to shoot me even though I had moved her son in between us. Instead, she walked up to Charlie, yanked his head up by his hair, and put the gun to his head. The boy in my grip tried to move again, thinking I'd let him go, but I held firm. He screamed in pain and stopped moving.

"Let Kostya go or I'll kill him." Sasha's voice sounded surprisingly casual. "I don't really want to do it, yet. I had planned to toy with him a bit more, but here you are, spoiling my plans again." She waved the gun about while keeping her grip on Charlie's hair. I didn't miss her having fangs again. She adjusted the black wig that sat crooked on her head since she entered the room.

"Never," I hissed.

"I'll do it!" She pulled Charlie to his feet.

I held my breath. I didn't want Charlie dead, but I wasn't sure that wasn't going to happen if I surrendered. What was I supposed to do? My heart pounded in my chest and blood drained from my head. I struggled between fainting and throwing up.

"Wait, wait…" I tried to buy more time to think. My eyes met Charlie's, and he slowly shook his head.

"Don't do it, Kate," he said. I could hardly hear him. His voice was so weak.

Next, he grappled for the gun. Sasha probably thought he was trying to shoot her. I feared Charlie had other ideas, so I had to act fast. Tom appeared in the doorway, his face badly beaten and bleeding. He held what looked like a ripped-off table leg, ready to strike. I let go of Kostya and threw him in Tom's direction. I saw Tom wield the piece of wood as I threw myself at Sasha and Charlie. The three of us struggled for the gun. Until it went off.

We backed away, and the gun fell to the floor. I kicked it out of reach. I wasn't sure who had fired it, and if anybody got hit. I certainly didn't feel any pain. Sasha's eyes went wide, and I followed her stare. A red spot in the middle of Charlie's chest grew larger by the second.

"Nooo!" I yelled.

Charlie saw it too. He stumbled and fell sideways against the wall, hanging from the cuffs. He slid down, leaving behind a red stain. Sasha looked back at her son who was now unconscious in a chokehold by Tom. She didn't think twice and threw herself through the window. I tried to grab her, but she already had too much momentum for me to hold on. She was gone.

I hastily turned to Charlie.

"Charlie, stay with me, you hear. Don't you die on me!"

I was frantic, knowing that if his heart or major arteries were hit, there wasn't a miracle on earth that could save him. The blood-smear on the wall gave me hope, though. He had fallen with his side to the wall which meant that the bullet had passed through him at an angle. It might not be a fatal shot. I lifted his shirt and moved him, so I could inspect his back as well as his front. What I saw confirmed my suspicion. When Charlie breathed in, I could hear the air being sucked into both wounds. I quickly pushed his hand on the wound on the front, pushing my own hand on the one on his right side.

Charlie looked up at me.

"I love you," he whispered. He coughed, and blood spattered out of his mouth. Stopping any more air getting in hadn't stopped the bleeding.

"You be quiet now, Smudge. Forget about your death speech. You're not going to die. The bullet went through your lung, not your heart. You're going to live. Lean toward your right, put pressure on your side." I helped him move, but it was hard with his hand tied to the plumbing.

I made a choice and jumped up. Kostya was still half-unconscious, and I searched his pockets for the keys of the cuffs. I could almost jump for joy when I found them. Quickly, I untied Charlie and helped him get into the position I had learned during a first aid lesson years ago. More blood came out of his mouth and his breathing was shallow. He was as white as a sheet. I guessed his right lung had collapsed, either by the air being sucked in through the wounds or because of the bleeding. He needed medical attention as soon as possible. I pulled out my cell phone and called for an ambulance. When I thought Charlie was as stable as I could get him, and there was nothing more I could do for him, I helped Tom put the cuffs on Kostya. Tom tied him to another heating pipe.

"I've got to go," Tom said.

"Wait, what?" I had kneeled next to Charlie again to

put my hand on the side wound. "Now? But you need medical attention too." My eyes hadn't missed the puddle of blood Tom was standing in slowly getting bigger.

"I'll live. With the ambulance, paparazzi will come. I'd be a fool to be caught on TV again. You understand, don't you?"

I hung my head.

"Yes, I do."

Tom limped over to me and gave me a one-armed hug as he bent down with difficulty. I hugged him back as well as I could while holding on to Charlie.

"Wait," I said as Tom turned around. I put Charlie's other hand on his side wound as good as I could, hurried over to Kostya, whose head was lolling about now, and ripped his T-shirt off. I rolled it up and tied it around Tom's leg above the shot wound. "There. Now I feel better to let you go."

"Thanks," he said.

"No, thank you. Thank you so much." I gave him another hug.

"You can thank me later. I've really got to go."

I let go of Tom, but before he left, he turned to Charlie.

"You take care now, Charlie. This woman has been hell bound to get you back, so you better not die on her."

Charlie managed a quick smile.

When I turned to face Tom, he was gone.

It didn't take long for the ambulance, the police, and the paparazzi to arrive.

Karmasutra

The paramedics worked fast and professionally. Nevertheless, Charlie had lost consciousness by the time they wheeled him into the ambulance. They said it looked like he had lost more blood than was expected with the gunshot. They let me ride with him, but as soon as we arrived at the hospital, Charlie went into surgery, and I had to part with him. A Portland detective took my statement. After this, I was on my own.

I called Sue and let her know her Dad was back. Sonny screamed with joy in the background. I told Sue that her father was on the operating table and made sure I kept the message positive, like Dr. Strang would've wanted. I told her he was going to make it. It was bullshit, of course, as it would be hours before I heard if he would pull through. Anything could still go wrong, blood clots were always a possibility, but I wanted Sue to know that he was in safe hands, to make her feel better. She had immediately wanted to come to the hospital, but I told her he would be sleeping after the surgery. I promised her they could visit him tomorrow.

I also called Julie. She was so relieved to hear that

Charlie was safe again. She tried to talk about what she'd said, but I cut her off, saying I had to go. I didn't have a real reason, but I didn't want to talk about her right now. Initially, I intended to call Harry and Rhona, but after my conversation with Julie, I was drained of energy. So I left a text message on their phones, saying that Charlie was safe but in hospital, and that I would call them when I had more news on his health status.

Grayson showed up at the hospital after about an hour. His large strides and grim face told me he was going to chastise me this time.

"What the fuck did you think you were doing?" he said as he sat down next to me.

"Nice to see you too. Oh, and yeah, I think Charlie's going to make it."

"He could've been killed, Kate."

"He could've been killed if you had tried to get him out."

Grayson didn't know what Charlie had said to me before he was freed. I hadn't told anybody. Neither had Grayson seen the state Charlie had been in, although I guessed the hospital staff had informed him before he came to see me.

"I could arrest you for obstructing justice."

"I could tell you you're an asshole."

Grayson sat back and sighed.

"Look," I said, "I did what I thought best in the circumstances. I didn't want Sasha to retaliate the way the Bratva did, or worse. I had to do it on my own."

Grayson looked at me with narrowed eyes.

"Without the police, I mean," I said. "Charlie and I probably wouldn't be alive if Tom hadn't been there. I still don't know why you have such a grudge against him. Tom's a good guy. At least he gets things done." I folded my arms. Grayson could talk all he wanted, but I wasn't going to change my mind about Tom.

"Tom and I go back a long time. From a teenager on, he's always been running into the law. He may have been a good guy once, but not anymore. Over time, his crimes have been escalating, but somehow I can never nail him. That's my grudge against Thomas Moore."

He used Tom's full name. Obviously, Grayson wasn't aware Tom was using an alias. Or he didn't want me to know he knew it. I shook my head.

"Whatever it is between you and him, you stick to the rules and get slowed down by bureaucracy. Tom doesn't, and like I said, he gets things done. He knows people. I found the house that Sasha owned, through him. We found the road sign together. He got me away from the paparazzi. And now he got me the lead to find Sasha and helped me get Charlie back."

"Don't forget he also got your sister's prize cow killed."

"It's a fuckin' cow, Grayson!" I was shocked by my own vehemence. I loved animals. "Who cares about cows when human lives are at stake. Jules can breed another one in no time. She can do whatever the fuck she wants, for all I care." I got up and walked away a few steps.

"I know what happened between you two," Grayson said.

"Excuse me?"

"Julie had the same reaction about you when I came to the farm this morning. It was obvious you two had a tiff or something and... after some encouragement, she told me. She's sorry, though. She realizes she shouldn't have said it."

"Fuck off, Grayson. It's none of your business."

"Okay, have it your way." He stood up. "I just came here to tell you that we have Kostya in custody at the Portland police station, and we'll be interrogating him soon. If you're up for it, I'd like you to be there. We may need you to get him to talk, you know, confront him, making him spill the beans on Sasha's whereabouts. If you don't want to, I understand."

"I'd like to be there. After the surgery." My eyes pleaded with Grayson. Over my dead body was I going to ask him.

Grayson sighed, again.

"I'll hold it off for as long as I can."

I gave him a nod, and he walked away.

The hospital corridor was empty, apart from the occasional nurse walking past. The ping of elevator doors opening sounded in the distance. In my mind, I went over what had happened at the house. What could I have done differently to prevent Charlie getting injured? I hadn't expected him wanting to die. He had only been away one week. What had Sasha done to him that made him give up all hope? What had they told him about me that made him not want to come back to me? Was it really them that were to blame? Had I misled him all these years? Had I forced him to accept and raise Sonny? Had I not shown him enough I loved him beyond imagining?

The thought that Charlie may not want to come back to me after he recovered went through my head again and again. What would I do if he didn't? I couldn't blame him, really. I was constantly working for SAMM, going out to every council meeting that could possibly have an effect on suckers, and giving interviews to anybody who wanted to listen. I was always in the public eye; on the radio, on TV, and in magazines. It was not the life Charlie wanted. Hell, it wasn't the life I had wanted.

I, too, yearned to live quietly in suburbia, taking care of my little family, being happy. Nothing more. Having two sucker children had made this impossible. I had to make sure they were safe in this world, and that they could look forward to a bright future. Together with Julie, I had achieved quite a lot these last three years. I wouldn't change any of it if I would be given the chance. Yet here I sat, my daughter suffering from

PTSD and refusing to talk to me about her trauma, and my husband on the operating table due to a lunatic wanting revenge for something I did thirteen years ago. The both of them had never done anything wrong. Charlie had always been there for me, through thick and thin, my rock to cling to. And with one little sentence, I had driven him away.

You don't know that, Kate.

Why hadn't Sasha taken me? Why torture others when she could have the real thing? Why did I always cause misery to the people around me?

Sonny sprang to mind, my little ray of sunshine. He was the only one not affected by me. Sometimes I wished Caleb could see what a wonderful, happy, little boy he was. I always imagined Caleb looking down upon us from heaven or wherever when we were having fun. Charlie and Sonny could have such fun. Charlie would tickle him, and Sonny would laugh his contagious giggle, they would work in the garden together, or they would surprise me with breakfast in bed on a weekend. I knew Charlie loved Sonny as his own. I couldn't imagine he would give up on him... unless he hated being with me more.

My cell phone rang. I was glad for the distraction. It was Sue.

"Hey, girl. I don't have any news y—"

I couldn't finish my sentence as she was screaming hysterically.

"Hey, calm down. I can't understand a word you're saying. What's wrong?" I held my free hand clamped to my chest.

"Mom, he's gone. They knocked me out with chloroform or something and took him. They took Sonny!"

Life was really trying to screw me in the most creative ways right now.

Another Perspective

I jumped up and ran toward the exit of the hospital. My motherly instinct pulled out a state of hyperactivity that instantaneously took precedence over my tiredness.

"Where are you? How long ago did it happen?" I skidded into the main foyer, out the doors, and jumped into the first cab I could find.

"I took him to the playground to celebrate Dad's return, and they took him! He's gone!"

I gave the cab driver Sasha's address.

"Go home, Sue. Lock the doors. Don't let anybody in except for Marlon. I'm going to get Sonny back. I love you."

How in heaven's name was I going to deal with Sue's new ordeal while trying to get Sonny back?

I called Marlon and asked him to stay with Sue until all this was over. Afterward, I texted Julie to warn her. I wasn't ready to talk to her yet, but I didn't want her to come to any harm either. She was still my sister. I told her to take care of her girls. I didn't want anybody else taken and hurt by Sasha. I also warned Harry and Rhona. Neither of them answered my calls immediately, so I left them another message. Last but not least, I called Grayson. I informed him what had happened, and that I was on my way to Sasha's house.

"That's of no use," he said.

"Why not?"

"Because the forensic team is still there, so Sasha won't be. You better come to the station as we're about to interrogate Kostya. I can't delay it any longer. He's your best bet to get info on Sasha's whereabouts at the moment."

I told the cab driver to change course and to take me to the Portland police station. He turned the car around without complaining.

***

The police station was larger and more modern than the one in Bullsbrook. As soon as I explained who I was and why I was there, I was asked to follow an officer. He showed me into a dark room. Through a one-way mirror I had a good view of Kostya sitting at a table, being interrogated. I wasn't the only one observing. Several other men and a woman were cramped into the small room. I had no idea who they were as I had never seen them before, but their FBI badges were clearly visible. I assumed they were involved due to Sasha's involvement with the Bratva Boss. They acknowledged my presence but didn't bother introducing themselves to me. They were all too focused on the conversation.

As these people were all taller than I was, I worked my way to a front row position.

Grayson and another man were in the room with Kostya, who was facing the mirror. His hands were cuffed and tied to the table, his legs tied to the floor. There was an armed police officer in full anti-sucker uniform at the door.

It was the first time I had a good look at Sasha's son. Kostya was the spitting image of his father although Duncan had gray hair and more wrinkles. Kostya had the same maniacal look as Duncan in his contemptuous eyes, though. I shook off a shiver as I hoped they would never let Kostya's father out of prison.

Grayson slammed his hands on the table, bringing my attention back to their conversation.

"You're lying," he said. His voice sounded different through the speakers. He got up and walked around the room.

"The fuck I am," Kostya replied. His upper lip was raised as he talked, showing off his fangs, and there was no mistaking of his loathing for Grayson. "You all think she's an angel or something. Well, she ain't. She's an evil, fuckin' bitch."

I don't think he's talking about Sasha, kiddo.

"She stole my mother's lover and killed him. She fuckin' mutilated my mother's face, and that son-of-a-bitch dwarf shot my Mom while she was out cold. I still don't understand why they didn't go to prison. Why did my mother have to suffer? Why did Kate get to raise her children while we were taken away from our mother? You're all a bunch of hypocrites."

Grayson's eyes flicked to the mirror for a moment, and I felt all the eyes on this side of the mirror on me too. I kept my stare straight in front of me, my jaws clenched tight.

"We're talking about you now." The other man in the room said. "You kidnapped Charlie, you tortured and mutilated him, made him a sucker. You attacked Kate. You could go to jail for a long time if you don't cooperate. Tell us where your mother is, and we'll see if we can get some time off your sentence."

"You think you can scare me? You think I'm afraid of going to prison? I've been in a prison my whole fuckin' life. It'll be like going home. And nothing compares to what they did to my mother. Do you know what she had to go through when she was young? Well, let me tell you. She was put into prostitution when she was eight years old. Eight! Do you know how small everything is when you're that age? No? Well, I can show you my dick and tell you it won't fit. They used and abused her as an object, did all the filth you can think of with her, made her do things you can't even imagine in your worst nightmares. I know you all look down on her because she became a crack whore, but you would've done the same, just to have a moment to forget the real world. And she survived. She made a life for herself. Got out and on top of things. She got off the crack and made a name for herself. Life was finally going well for her. Okay, Black October happened, but she still did okay until that fuckin' bitch showed up. She made her lose the man she loved, shot him in front of her eyes. She fuckin' set her face on fire. What person does that? It was the only thing my mother had going for her. She was a model; her face was her income. And your goodie-two-shoes Kate ruined it. Mother was thrown in jail like a criminal, and my brother and I were taken away from her, the only thing she had left. Can you put yourself in her shoes for a moment? Can you?"

A lump welled up in my throat. I couldn't imagine what sort of a life Sasha had had growing up. I almost felt guilty of my actions hearing Kostya's side of the story. I felt sorry for doing the things I did to her. Until Grayson reminded me why Sasha went to prison. He had moved his face right in front of Kostya's.

"Don't think I don't know what your mother did during Black October. She abused, tortured, and killed people. We have witnesses, so don't tell me it isn't true." Grayson said his words with a fire I hadn't heard from him before, as if it was a personal matter.

Kostya lowered his eyes, avoiding Grayson's.

"Yeah, well... she had to do what she had to do to survive. Just like everybody else."

"Everybody else didn't abuse, torture, and kill." Grayson moved away from Kostya, took a deep breath, and sat back down again. "Now let's get back to the point. Tell us where we can find your mother. Where is she keeping Kate's son?"

Kostya met his eyes for a moment. Then he looked away, remaining silent. I didn't believe he was ever going to tell Grayson anything. He may not even know where his mother went after the unscheduled turn of events. Knowing how calculated Sasha was, I was sure she had another hideaway, but this didn't mean Kostya knew of it. This interrogation was going nowhere. I needed to find Sonny, and fast. My stomach knotted thinking about what Sasha could do to him.

I hurried out of the stifling room and took a few deep breaths before calling Tom.

"Hi, how's Charlie doing?" he asked.

"I don't know. I'm at the police station in Portland."

"O...kay, what happened?"

"Sasha's got Sonny. They're interrogating her son, but he's not talking. I need to get to my son, and fast. God only knows what she's going to do to him right now." Bile rose in my throat, burning everything on its way out. I needed to find myself a bottle of water to dilute the vile stuff.

"Well, you better come to my place, because I can help."

The Truth

I could kiss Tom right now if it wasn't for the miles between us.

"How?" I asked, not really caring at all as long as his words were true.

"After we tied the boy to the plumbing, I took his cell phone from him. I didn't want him to call his brother for help."

I pumped my fist.

"Tom, when this is all over, remind me to kiss you."

"Can you say that again, so I can record it as evidence?"

I suppressed a smile.

"I'll get a cab to the Transportation Center. Pick me up from there."

"I'll be waiting for you."

I hurried out of the police station and called a cab. Before long, I was at the Portland Transportation Center. I recognized the red sedan pulling out down the line.

"Show me," I said as I got into Tom's car. After I buckled up, I gasped when I saw Tom's face. It was now showing the full extent of the injuries sustained when fighting with Sasha. His left eye was swollen half shut and purple, his lip cut at multiple places and swollen, and there were bruises on his face. I was sure there were more on the rest of his body. "Holy crap. Are you okay? How's your leg?"

"I'll live," Tom said as he pulled into traffic and hit the gas pedal. "Sasha only nicked me, said she had no beef with another sucker. I guess I was lucky she didn't know I wasn't one. It's not the first time my natural fangs have saved me. And sorry, but I haven't got the cell phone on me. It's at my place."

"Why?" Nearly all of my breath escaped my lungs while I tried to figure out this man's thinking.

"I didn't want Sasha or her other son jumping me and getting it back. I thought my place was the safest."

"And you don't think they can steal it from your place while you're out here, picking me up?"

Tom glanced sideways at me for a moment.

"No."

We did another car swap in the garage, this time into a black 4WD terrain vehicle.

Car number three. How many cars can one man own?

When we got to his place, Tom turned aside a painting on the wall and opened a safe. A wall safe. Behind a painting.

I guess you really don't deal in IT.

From the safe, he took Kostya's cell phone and handed it to me. I tried to activate the cell, but it asked me for a password or fingerprint.

"Damn, it's locked."

Tom stuck his hand out. "Can I...?"

I gave the cell to him. He looked at it, pressed a button, and I heard it ring out. He passed it back to me.

"What did you do?"

"Emergency contact," he said.

I held the cell to my ear and waited for someone to answer the call. My insides squeezed tight. What was I going to say if Sasha answered? What if somebody else answered?

"Kostya?" Her voice was anxious, borderline surprised.

"No bitch, not Kostya. You left him behind, remember. Now we've got him. I know you've got my son, so if you don't want yours to get hurt, you better not hurt Sonny. If you do, yours will feel the consequences a multitude of times. I know you want your son back, and I want mine, so I suggest a swap. I'll call again with further instructions." I then pressed the 'end call' button.

My chest worked hard to replenish my oxygen level. I felt like I had been out of my body during the call and forgot to breathe. Tom stared at me.

"What?" I said.

"My admiration for you grows every day."

His words were the droplet that made the bucket overflow. The stress of the situation with Sonny being kidnapped right after getting Charlie back was all I could handle. I couldn't deal with Tom's shit as well.

"Okay, what is it with you? You've been acting weird toward me since the day I met you. You know I love Charlie, yet you keep making passes at me. Is it my imagination or are you that thick?"

Tom and I stood looking at each other for an uncomfortably long time. I tried to read his facial expression, but it was just dumbstruck. I wished I could take back my words and choke on them. Finally, he spoke.

"I'm... so sorry. I... I didn't mean to give you that impression. At least, not consciously. You have no idea..." He sat down on the couch.

I sat on the armrest, not wanting to be too close to Tom.

"About what? I have no idea about what, Tom?"

I know I'm marvelous, but I still can't mind read.

He turned to me, moved closer, and took my hand in his. I wanted to pull mine back but didn't. I didn't want to hurt his feelings. Yet his gesture hinted that I wasn't going to like what he was about to say.

"Kate, you don't know me—"

"I do. You're Harry's older brother, you do dodgy business deals, and you're rich."

Tom waved a hand in the air.

"No. That's what everybody thinks. Yes, I was a scoundrel when I was younger, but not anymore. And

I'm far from rich. Kate, I work for the FBI."

What the...?

Tom chuckled when he saw my expression.

"It's true. During the end of Black October, I worked with the armed forces to find stray suckers. The military were impressed with my abilities and contacts, and my natural fangs helped me infiltrate any groups in hiding. Word got around, and the FBI recruited me. I've been working undercover ever since."

"You're joking."

"It's true, Kate. How else do you think I can afford multiple apartments and cars?"

"Well, you know... I thought you did dodgy deals that made you rich."

"That's wishful thinking. Crime usually doesn't pay that well. No, the FBI pays for it all."

"Why didn't you tell Harry?" I said.

"Because I didn't want to burden him with that knowledge. It was better for everybody if my family didn't know about me. What you don't know can't hurt you. It's the reason why I didn't have any contact with them for years after Black October. The only reason I made contact again not so long ago was because the world is changing. It's changing because of you, Kate. When I was picking up suckers in hiding, doing my job, I began seeing their situation, the misery they were living in, and I wasn't making it any better for them, knowing a lifelong imprisonment lay ahead of them. I began feeling bad about what I was doing and wanted to change things for them, but I didn't know how. And then you happened."

His eyes were full of admiration. I pulled back my hand and backed away. I didn't like the direction this conversation was going in.

"It's not just me, you know," I said. "Many people have been working to make this world a better place for suckers. Julie, for one. She's worked as hard as I have, if not harder. And then there are the girls at the school. There are many others across the globe that are doing all they can to make this world a better place for suckers. I'm... I'm not the only one." I walked away from Tom. I stuck my hand in my armpits, trying to make myself as small as possible. I didn't want this sort of attention. I had done what I had to do because nobody else did it. That was all.

Tom had gotten up and followed me.

"Yes, but you have been the instigator. You're the one that made people listen. You're the voice that gave hope to all those suckers out there. You are their savior."

I stopped in my tracks, shocked by his words. Tom turned me around.

"Kate, I admire you. I love spending time with you, and I soak up every minute of it, loving you more and more, but I know you love Charlie and would never get in between that. I don't think I ever could."

Yeah, you've got that right.

"I want you to know that I would do anything for you." Tom's icy-blue eyes seemed to be melting.

I blinked and turned away, away from his eyes and his scent which was so strong right now. It made me feel things I didn't want to feel which made me blush.

Stop it, Kate. Don't tease him.

I turned back around, cocked my head to the side, and looked up into those gorgeous eyes.

"If you mean it, help me get Sonny back."

Taking a Turn

Tom grabbed two cans of beer from the fridge and handed one to me. I noted it was alcohol-free.

"To teamwork," he said.

"To teamwork."

He tapped his beer can against mine and we drank.

"Now," Tom said, putting the cold can to his swollen eye. "I'll let you know something, but you can't tell anyone. And I mean anyone."

I sat down on one of the kitchen island bar stools.

"I'm all ears," I said.

Tom leaned closer.

"When I fought Sasha, it was a close call. She's turned."

"Yeah, I know. I noticed her fangs."

"Well, I really don't want to be in that situation again."

"What are you getting at? Are you saying you want out now?" I had been about to take another swig of beer but put the can down. I really couldn't follow this man's thoughts.

"No, please let me finish. I want to do the opposite." I frowned, upon which he smiled. "I'm going to turn, so I match her strength."

My jaw dropped.

He's kidding. Tell me he's kidding.

"You're serious?"

Tom apparently had one blow too many to his head. Who wanted to turn in their right mind? There were suckers out there who would gladly give their right arm to be unturned.

"It's not what you think, Kate."

"You're not an idiot?"

"Remember I said I worked for the FBI?"

"So what?"

Tom moved even closer. His scent filling my nostrils again.

"Well, they haven't been sitting still these past thirteen years," he whispered. "They've developed a strain of the virus that works much faster. With it, the turn happens within a few hours, making you reach maximum strength in that limited amount of time. It's gruesome to go through, but you already know the obvious benefits; super strength, heightened senses, faster healing..."

I stared at Tom, at his swollen eye, his split lip, the bruises, his leg. I remembered his fast moves, his acute hearing, his great sense of smell. Then, I stared at his refrigerator, and the penny dropped.

"You've already used it."

Tom nodded fervently.

"Multiple times. That's why I've got some residual

senses and traits. I'm not healing fast enough without it, though, and most of the time, it's better to turn to go undercover. I've also got the antidote, to turn back again after the job's finished."

Multiple possibilities flashed through my mind for a second. Only one thought lingered. I looked Tom in the eye.

"I want to turn too."

Tom moved away, depriving me of his scent. It was almost cruel, and I wondered if he did it on purpose.

"That's not going to happen." He had a 'not in a million years' look on his face.

My words rolled out like a runaway train.

"You literally just promised me you'd help me get Sonny back. Sasha's out there with her other son, Kady, holding my son hostage. You've seen what she's done to Charlie. We've got to stop her. She's definitely turned, and the boy's a sucker child, most likely trained in martial arts if he was raised in an internment camp. We can't do this with only you being turned. The fact that I beat Kostya was pure luck which I doubt will happen again."

Tom pulled a face as if he was in pain. Was it my words or his leg?

"I don't think it's a good idea." He scratched the back of his head and looked away. It was a sign to me that he was actually contemplating it. I had to make the most of the moment, so I grabbed both his shoulders and made him look at me.

"I need to do this, Tom. They have my son. I need to get him back. I have been training martial arts for three years. I know what I'm doing. I would do anything to get my boy back."

Tom tried to avoid eye contact, but his gaze kept coming back to mine. I could see he was weighing the pros against the cons.

"I can do this, Tom. You know I can."

His stare now tried to pry into the depth of my soul. I didn't look away. Finally, he lowered his eyes.

"Okay, we'll do this together." I jumped for joy. "Don't get too excited. It's like going through hell," he said gravely. "But it's only for a few hours. Just keep focused on that."

I took his face in my hands and kissed him hard on the lips. "Thank you."

Tom got up and went to the refrigerator. Was there a blush on his face? He took out two ampules from a little box in the door and two syringes from a kitchen drawer. He prepared the needles and injected himself first. Just before he stuck in my arm, he hesitated.

"Are you sure?"

"One hundred percent!"

He then injected me.

Next, he pulled out a box from a cupboard and took out four white tablets. He handed me two and a glass of water.

"Let me guess. Painkillers?"

Tom smiled and swallowed his.

"Now what?" I said.

"Now we wait. Come and lay on the bed with me."

I looked at Tom apprehensively. He took my hand and pulled me off the seat.

"Don't worry, I'm not going to try anything. But you're going to thank me later."

I followed him. We kicked off our shoes and lay down on the four-post bed. Lying on our backs, we stared at the canopy. Tom's hand, which was only a few centimeters away from mine, radiated a heat that warmed my skin. I had to resist the urge to hold his hand as I was freezing. This place was so cold. When I looked at Tom, he smiled back at me. I guessed he was happy I was this close to him, lying on his bed, even if we were fully dressed and knowing he could never have me.

I didn't have to wait long. Within fifteen minutes, the virus took a hold of my body, and it was as if I was hit by a train. Every inch of me began aching at the same time. The mattress was soft, easing the pain a little, and I made a mental note to thank Tom later indeed. I twisted and turned, hoping that a new position would stop my muscles cramping and hurting, but when I thought it couldn't get any worse, the agony level was ramped up. My pulse pumped maniacally through my arteries, and my body temperature rose. Even in this fridge of a place, perspiration drenched my clothing and the very touch of them on my skin irritated me.

I turned to see how Tom was doing. To my surprise, he took off his shirt. He noticed me watching him and hitched up his shoulders apologetically. He needn't worry I was offended as I followed his example, clawing my shirt off as well. I didn't stop there. I also removed my pants as they became far too tight with my muscles growing so fast. My stare dared Tom, and he followed suit. We now lay on the bed in our underwear. Cramps contorted our muscles, sweat dripped from our bodies, and strange noises erupted from our throats as we tried to deal with the pain.

When Tom groaned a particularly heartfelt groan, my hand touched his shoulder in sympathy. Feeling his naked skin under my fingertips and smelling his heavenly sweat made my hormones go into overdrive, begging me to take this man, to become one with him. I eased my body toward him, but thoughts of Charlie popped up, lying on the operating table, fighting for his life. I fought too, not for my life but for my sanity as my mind fought my body from letting nature take its course. My heartbeat pounded, and my muscles ached while I struggled to get rid of this urge to have Tom. I couldn't and wouldn't do this to Charlie. Not again. And every skin cell of my body fought me, yearning to feel Tom's skin against mine.

Tom had turned toward me at my touch. He was

breathing heavily, and his eyes were wild. His stare drifted down my body as his nostrils flared. Did my scent do the same to him as his did to me? His gaze lingered slightly longer on my curved parts. When his eyes met mine again, I was shocked to see such raw passion in them. Before I knew it, he had cupped my face with his hands and pressed his lips against mine. They tasted salty, matching his oceanic scent which had fascinated me from the beginning. With one hand he moved my hair out of my face, trailing his fingers down my spine, pulling me close when his hand reached the small of my back. When my belly felt his arousal, I couldn't help myself and wrapped my leg around his, kissing him back. I parted my lips, letting his tongue touch mine. The pain dulled as my mind took flight in ecstasy while our lower bodies moved in sync.

Only after a few seconds did I realize what I was doing. Hastily, I put one hand on his chest and pushed myself away from Tom. I was shocked by my own actions.

"Tom, I can't. I'm sorry, but I can't," I whispered. My eyes focused on his collarbone and the muscle above it that seemed bigger than it had been just a minute ago.

"But I want you, Kate. I need you. I need you now more than ever. I can't take this anymore." His voice was filled with anguish.

My heart bled as I felt his pain. I didn't want Tom

to feel this way, but I didn't want to hurt him either. Yet how was I going to do this without giving in? Somehow, I had to reject him. He knew where I stood. Hell, he had even promised me this wouldn't happen.

Suddenly, I remembered this part of the transition. I cursed my memory for only bringing it up now. The realization of what was happening was like a cold shower. When I had turned so many years ago, I had nearly killed Charlie after he had refused my passionate advances. My emotions had gone haywire then, too. So, I had to be very careful with Tom in this dangerous state.

I tried to untangle myself from him, but Tom wouldn't let go of me. He tried to push his lips back onto mine.

"Tom, listen to me," I said. "I'm going to get off the bed and go to the kitchen. I'm going to get you a bag of blood. You're thirsty."

"Yes, I'm thirsty. I'm thirsty for your lips, Kate. Come here and let me drink the passion from those heavenly pillows of love."

I suppressed a giggle. This was getting funny. While I kept smiling as sweetly at him as I could, I inched myself toward the edge of the bed. Tom followed, shuffling on after me. When I got up, Tom held on to my wrist. He frowned, and his grip became tighter, less romantic. Had I pushed him over the edge?

There was no other way. I loved living too much.

Please excuse me, Charlie, but I have to do this.

I leaned over and kissed Tom. Immediately, his icy eyes softened. He smiled at me and again moved a strand of hair out of my face.

"I've wanted you for so long," he said. "Even before I met you."

That doesn't mean you're going to get me.

"That's very sweet, Tom. Now, come with me."

To my relief, he got up. I wasn't so pleased that he embraced and kissed me again, but it was to be expected. To go with the flow, to keep him happy, I let him but inched toward the kitchen in the meantime. Tom didn't seem to realize what I was doing. We made it to the refrigerator and, still kissing, I managed to take out one of the blood bags. As soon as I held it up to Tom, he snatched it from my hand and drank it. I pulled out another bag for myself. Oh, how I had missed the taste of blood.

Tom finished his bag sooner than I did mine, and he began kissing my throat, his bloody kisses moving lower and lower. He undid my bra and his lips caressed my breasts, his fangs dragging circles around my nipples. He then moved down my belly, around my navel, and onward. Ripples of pleasure radiated from where he touched me. My body urged him to keep on going down, relishing the fact that his touches made the excruciating transition bearable, wishing his touch to get to the place where he could make it all go away. Still, my mind fought hard, and won.

I grabbed another bag from the shelf and held it in front of Tom's eyes. He focused on it and I lifted it up. He let go of me for a moment. That's when I turned and ran, the bag still in my hand. Tom chased me. I jumped over the bed, the couch, and back over the kitchen island. I ran as if for my life. Tom laughed as he dodged all the obstacles I threw in his path. We both laughed each time he nearly got me, and I escaped in the nick of time. It became a game between us, Tom pretending to want the blood while I knew his energy came from wanting me. I had to use everything to stay out of his hands; my martial art skills, my love for Charlie, my desire to save Sonny. Anything to force my mind off wanting Tom as my hormones didn't care who I gave my passion to at the moment. Tom didn't give up easily and was a worthy opponent.

After what felt like hours of playing the cat-and-mouse game, I got so tired of the chase that I decided to let him grab me. I fell onto my back on the couch, and he pinned me down, his sweaty body moving in beat with my breathing.

A New Me

We were panting like sprinters who had just crossed the finish line, and Tom pressed his forehead against mine.

"What d'you say?" I wheezed.

"About what? he panted.

"About calling it quits and going back to lying down." Hopefully, he didn't have any more energy left as I was spent.

Tom regarded the bed and nodded.

"That's an excellent idea." He pulled me up and, we dropped onto the bed. Exhausted and hurting, I fell asleep in his arms.

***

When I woke up, my tongue felt like a flip-flop in a desert.

"Here, drink this," I heard Tom's voice say.

Before I opened my eyes, my hands found I was still wearing my panties underneath the sheets. I turned around and saw Tom sitting on the edge of the bed, completely dressed.

You did it, girl. You made it back from hell.

I sat up, pulling the sheet with me, and grabbed the

blood bag from him.

"Thanks," I said, before emptying the bag in one go.

He passed me another. I finished three bags in total. I wiped my mouth and took Tom in. It was obvious he wanted to say something but struggled to do it.

"What is it?"

"My sincere apologies," he answered. He was looking me in the eye, so it had to be something important.

"For what?"

"For not keeping my word."

"Yeah, about that..." I handed the third bag back, my hand now clutching the sheet closer to my chest. "Didn't they ever tell you emotions are heightened during a transition?"

"They have, now you mention it, but how was I supposed to know those feelings were going to become so uncontrolled? I've never been through a turn with somebody else around. I must say it was... most interesting." He couldn't hide his sexy grin. Something told me it wouldn't be the last time he was going to do it.

Just not with me.

"Holy shit, did we do this?" I scanned the apartment. The place was trashed.

Tom looked around at the damage.

"I'm afraid so. I've checked the news, but as far as I know, no whirlwind passed through town." He chuckled. "I better make sure I don't buy any fancy stuff in the future."

"At least not for this place."

"Good idea. I like your thinking," he said and winked at me.

I abruptly held my breath. He may have taken my remark the wrong way.

Here we go again.

Tom gently put his hand on my knee.

"Don't worry. What happens in this apartment, stays in this apartment."

I smiled a half-hearted smile, not sure if he knew something I didn't.

"Besides, nothing did happen, so there's nothing to be worried about, anyway."

Was he disappointed? It sounded like it. He patted my knee, got up, and disposed of the empty blood bags in the kitchen. I took the opportunity to wrap the sheet around myself and disappear into the bathroom.

***

I finished having a shower in the fairytale setting, only to realize my clothes were still on the floor next to the bed.

"Um, Tom, would you be able to hand me my clothes?" I called to him from behind the door.

"Sure, no problem."

He must have developed an acute visual impairment because it took him forever to find them. In the meantime, I admired my fangs in the mirror above the sink. They were the only thing I had missed from being turned. They looked and felt awesome. I thought I might keep them when all this was over as a souvenir. Tom knocked on the door, and I opened it a little. He passed me some clothing which, I was one hundred percent sure of, wasn't mine.

"What's this?" I said.

"Your clothes reek of sweat and are torn. I found you something else. It's the only thing I think will fit you. I think it also would look nice on you. Let me know if you're not happy with it, and I'll try to get you something else."

"O...kay." I inspected the item he had handed me. It was a black dress and seemed to be my size, almost. I guessed he didn't date a lot of short girls. The sleeves were a bit on the long side as well, and the dress came down to my ankles, but otherwise, it was okay. It was made of a thick-but-stretchy woolen material that fit my new body shape, and I anticipated I wouldn't feel cold in it. I didn't like the splits on the sides, but they came high enough for me to be able to walk normally in the otherwise body-hugging dress. I could picture the Asian woman he had brought to Harry's birthday party wearing it. It would look a lot better on her, for sure.

I emerged from the bathroom a new woman. I felt

as strong as an ox, ready to take on the world. The jaw and muscle pain were still there, but my desire to kick Sasha's butt put it in the background.

"Now what do we do?"

"I don't know," Tom said. "You were going to give Sasha further instructions. Have you thought about it at all?"

I dropped into the seat next to him on the couch.

"To be honest, no, I haven't. I'm afraid I've had other things on my mind."

"Yeah, me too."

We looked at each other and then both looked away. We sat in silence for a while.

"Tom, I need to get to the hospital. I need to know how Charlie's doing."

"Of course, I'll take you there."

We decided to bring Kostya's phone with us this time.

A Hospital Visit

At the hospital, I learned that Charlie was out of surgery. The station nurse directed us to his room. Before I went in, Tom caught me by my elbow.

"I'll just be out here, okay?"

I nodded, thankful he gave me some privacy.

I opened the door and found Charlie hooked up to tubes and wires, asleep. Sue and Marlon sat at Charlie's bed. Sue's eyes were red and swollen from crying.

"Oh, Little Smudge," I said as I embraced her. "What are you doing here?" Over Sue's shoulder, I silently demanded an answer from Marlon. He scratched his cheek and looked away.

"I'm so sorry, Mom," Sue said. "I couldn't do anything. They put a cloth with chloroform over my mouth, and they took Sonny. I didn't protect him."

"It's okay, honey. It's not your fault." I kissed her cheek and put my hand under her chin. "It's not your fault."

"I know," she said, her eyes tearing up, "but still. I should have been paying more attention. I was the one taking care of him."

I squeezed Sue's arm as I realized I shouldn't have delegated my responsibility. Not to my daughter.

"Sue, listen to me. It is not your fault. These people are ruthless, and there was nothing you could have done. They would have taken Sonny one way or another. I'm so glad you're okay." I hugged her again.

When we parted, Sue lowered her eyes and nodded.

"I've stopped taking the medication, Mom. They make me drowsy. I don't want to feel that way anymore."

"That's good to hear, Little Smudge. I'm glad you're not as long as you're feeling okay without it. Now, tell me how your father's doing. What did the doctors say?" I took Charlie's limp hand in mine.

Sue wiped her eyes and took a deep breath before she spoke.

"They said he's doing fine. He was very lucky that the bullet missed his heart. His lung had collapsed, but the position you'd put him in minimized the bleeding and the air coming in."

Charlie lay so still. His bruises were darker now, the contrast with his pale skin more obvious. There was a square bandage covering his ear and his left hand had a clean bandage as well. I noted he had a middle finger again.

"How...? I thought it couldn't be attached anymore?"

"He was lucky, Mom," Sue said. "It's because he's still turning. The virus makes his body heal faster, and they're giving it a go. It isn't certain it'll work, so they're going to vaccinate as soon as they know it doesn't. Otherwise, they're going to wait as long as they can with the vaccination."

Relief washed over me and not just because Charlie was going to be okay. I also didn't have to keep things from my daughter anymore. Sue now knew that Charlie had been turned as wasn't accusing me for not telling her. I smiled a quick smile at Marlon. I had no doubt he had a hand in explaining to Sue why I hadn't told her.

I wiped some hair from Charlie's forehead and kissed him.

"Why are his arms bandaged?" I asked as my fingers touched the white cotton.

"Mom, the bullet wound wasn't the only injury he had."

I closed my eyes, dreading what Sue was about to tell me.

"Go on."

"The doctor said that apart from missing his ear and finger, he had multiple bruises, bite marks, and cigarette burns all over his body. They have treated him horribly."

Only now did I remember the holes in his shirt and pants when I found him. I stroked Charlie's face. Anger fueled the fire that fed my hatred for Sasha.

"They're going to pay for what they've done to you, Smudge. I swear."

"I want to help," Sue said.

I looked at her with my stern, motherly look.

"You can't stop me, Mom. Sonny's my brother, and I need to get him back. If you're going after Sasha, I'm coming with you. I feel responsible, and I won't be able to live with myself if anything happened to Sonny."

A fear washed over me. I didn't want what they had done to Charlie to happen to my daughter.

"Sue," I said, "these people are dangerous. I wouldn't be able to live with myself if they hurt you."

"Goddammit, Mom! I don't care what happens to me. I need to get Sonny back!"

Her pupils were large, so I guessed she was speaking the truth about the medication. I caught Marlon's eyes.

"I already tried," he said as he hitched up his shoulders.

It was clear Sue wasn't going to change her mind. Maybe she was right. Maybe this was something she needed to do. If I didn't involve her in Sonny's rescue, what would happen to her? I dreaded her condition becoming even worse. If I let Sue come with me and get Sonny back, this might boost her confidence and fight off this PTSD once and for all. What was there to lose? I inspected the ceiling as I made up my mind.

"Okay, but you do exactly what we tell you. No buts."

While I talked to her, Sue frowned.

Now what?

"Mom, you've got fangs..."

"Um, yeah. Tom and I have turned."

Both Marlon and Sue gasped in shock.

"Don't worry. It's only temporary. Tom's got antidotes, so we can turn back after we have Sonny back."

"But, how...?" Marlon said.

"Long story, which I'll tell you some other time."

Or not.

"Okay. So, how are we getting Sonny back?" Sue asked.

For the first time in years, her eyes sparkled.

Getting Pumped Up

We left Charlie asleep as we joined Tom and went to find a quiet place in the hospital where we could sit together.

"By the way, what in heaven's name are you wearing?" Sue asked.

"Good question." My eyes went to Tom as I answered.

Sue stumbled over her own feet as she tried to look at Tom as well.

"Are you okay?" I asked.

"Yeah, it's just that going cold turkey with the medication makes me a bit shaky."

I frowned, but Sue assured me she was fine. Tom asked Sue how Charlie was doing, and she was glad to change the subject.

We found an area where visitors could meet patients and they all took a seat. Before I did, I kept my distance and called Julie.

"Hi Jules," I said as soon as she picked up the call. "I'm at the hospital. Charlie's out of surgery but is going to be okay. I'm assuming you know about Sonny?"

"I do. Can I do anything to help?" I could hear genuine concern in her voice.

"Tom and I are going to get him back. Sue and Marlon are coming with us. I need someone to stay with Charlie, for when he wakes up. I don't want him to be alone when he does. Will you come and sit with him?"

The moment before Julie answered took forever in my mind. I tried to find a piece of nail to bite off in anticipation of her answer. Grayson had said she was sorry, but those were his words. I hadn't heard them from Julie herself yet. If she wanted our relationship to mend, she would say yes. If she said no... Well, that was it then.

"Of course, sis. I'll be there as soon as I can."

"Thanks, I knew I could count on you." I hung up, instantly questioning myself on the words I had used. She had wanted me to let go of Charlie before, so why did I think I could count on her?

Because she's family, you moron.

The others indicated they were waiting for me, and I hurried to them. I explained to Sue and Marlon that we were going to call Sasha with more information on swapping Kostya with Sonny.

"But we don't have Kostya," Sue said.

"No, but they don't know that." This had bugged me ever since the phone call with Sasha, and I had spoken without thinking. However, as soon as I saw Marlon in Charlie's room, I hoped the issue was solved. "We're going to dress up Marlon as Kostya." I dreaded

Marlon's reaction, but I needn't worry.

"Cool," he said as if he had just landed a lead role in a movie.

"It's going to be dangerous, Marlon, and if I had any other option, I'd do it in a flash."

"I understand," he said more seriously.

I pulled out Kostya's cell and called Sasha, putting the phone in speaker mode. We all held our breath, waiting for her to answer it.

"I'm listening," she said. Her voice was devoid of any emotion this time.

"Come to the school where we first met. One hour."

"Okay, let's end this now and forever." She hung up before I could say anything back.

"What did she mean by that, Mom? End it now and forever?"

I squeezed Sue's hand.

"Well, I guess we all can imagine what she meant with it, but we're not going to let that happen. We're going to end it though. I've had enough of that woman and her sons."

"Spoken like a real trouper," Tom said.

I threw him a quick glance before rolling my eyes.

"She sounded pretty confident," I said, "but she's forgetting we know that place inside out. That's why I chose it."

Tom sat upright, and Marlon cleared his throat.

"Um, Mom, maybe you do, but we don't," Sue said.

I realized she was right. I wasn't talking to Charlie here.

"Yeah, um, I'll just have to fill you in on the way there." I checked the time. It was a quarter to nine. "Let's quickly go and get Marlon outfitted like Kostya."

"I always wanted to dress up like a psychopath," Marlon said as he stood up.

"We don't know if the boys have joined in on the torture, Marlon. We must assume they're innocent until we hear what happened from Charlie. Until then, we'll have to do our utmost best not to hurt Arkady."

The three of them looked at me strangely. I filled them in on Kostya's interrogation as we walked to Tom's car. They deserved to know the whole truth, not just my side of the story.

"Jeez, that sounds awful," Marlon said when I finished.

"I can imagine what they're thinking of you now," Sue said. "It's wrong, but knowing what they know now, I can see their point of view."

***

We all were rather quiet while we were shopping. We bought Marlon light-gray jogging pants and a dark-gray hoodie; the clothes Kostya had worn when he was taken into custody. We made sure the hoodie was large enough, so it could hide Marlon's face in darkness. I thought he was a perfect stand-in for Kostya as he was about the same size and build.

After we got back into the car, Tom spoke.

"Now, we need to discuss involving the police."

"What do you mean? Why?" I asked.

"We can't leave the police out of this, Kate. You didn't involve them in getting Charlie back, and he was shot. If something happens again when we're trying to get Sonny back... I don't know. You may get yourself into deep shit."

"I don't care about getting into deep shit. I care about getting Sonny back."

Sue leaned forward.

"I know what he means, Mom. If anybody gets injured, people may start to think you're only acting out of your best interest, and that your intentions aren't as true as you say they are. We need witnesses."

I turned around to her, eyebrows raised. "You guys are my witnesses."

"Yes, but we're biased, Kate," Marlon pitched in. "A jury might choose not to believe us."

I guessed they were right. Things may not be interpreted the way we wanted to if Sasha and Arkady gave another account of what happened.

"Okay, I can see your point. But I don't want the police to be visible when we do the swap. Sasha may not let Sonny go if she sees them hanging about." I didn't mention my fear about what she might possibly do to

Sonny in that situation.

"How about you just call Grayson?" Tom said. "He represents the police but isn't dressed as one."

I glanced at him. So far, Tom had made it clear he wasn't friends with Grayson. For him to recommend getting Grayson involved showed me how good at heart he really was.

"Okay, I'll give him a call."

When Grayson picked up the phone, he immediately went into a defensive mode.

"We did everything we could, Kate, but we haven't been able to get anything out of the boy. I wished you hadn't left. We may have been able to pressure him a bit more with you there."

Grayson sounded tired. I guessed he had orders from his boss to end this case.

"Never mind Kostya. We got in contact with Sasha via Kostya's cell phone. I have agreed to meet her. That's what we're going to do now."

"What in heaven's name, Kate!" Grayson blew a fuse. "I told you to not to obstruct justice. You should have handed in the phone. You should have told me you had it!"

"I forgot, and I'm telling you now. We want you to be there. Just you, though. I don't want to risk Sasha hurting Sonny when we show up with the whole force."

"Who the hell is 'we' this time?"

"Me, Tom, Sue, and Marlon. I'm assuming you're

still at the Portland police station?"

"No, I'm already in Bullsbrook."

"Okay. We'll pick you up on our way there."

I hung up before he could object.

"Oops. He doesn't sound too happy," I said as I put my cell away.

"It's always better to ask forgiveness than to ask permission," Tom said.

"Ain't that the truth," Marlon said. I threw an angry stare at Tom before turning around to Marlon. "In this case," the boy added cheekily and grinned.

Marlon was a good guy. Sue was very lucky to have him. When this was all over, I needed to spend more time with the both of them.

Better still, let them have a holiday together from everything.

Confrontation

We picked up Grayson from the Bullsbrook police station and squeezed him into the back between Sue and Marlon. He immediately began grilling me.

"What arrangement did you make? Where are you going to meet? Does Sasha have anybody else there?"

"We're going to swap Sonny for Kostya, at the school, and Arkady will most likely be there. Anything else you want to know?"

"Yes, how are you going to swap Sonny for Kostya when he's in a cell at the Portland police station?" Grayson said testily.

"I'm going to be Kostya," Marlon said.

I couldn't see Marlon as he was sitting behind me, but his voice sounded like he did the ta-da thing with his arms. Grayson didn't seem to appreciate it as he abruptly pulled himself forward, almost occupying the passenger seat with me.

"Are you out of your mind?" he said. "This is way too dangerous. You can't let them get involved like this."

"Look, if you have a better idea, I'm all ears. If you haven't, this is the way the monkey's going to swing. We'll get them to hand over Sonny, and when he's safe, we'll get Sasha and Arkady. It's five against two. We should be able to overpower them."

"And what if they have guns? Then what, Kate? Have you thought about that?" Grayson spat.

"She lost the gun she had when Charlie got shot, so I'm not sure if she still has one. I'm assuming you're packing?" I asked.

Great use of slang, kiddo.

"I am, but the more guns, the higher the risk something goes wrong. Are you willing to take that risk?" he asked.

I knew I was. I looked around at the others. One after the other they nodded. Realizing there was no point in arguing, Grayson threw his body back into the seat.

"I'd prefer it if you let me get a SWAT team together."

"Can't, Grayson. I already told her we'd meet in about fifteen minutes. I'm not going to wait and have my son be abused as an ash tray and a private blood supply while you get your paperwork in order."

"Fine. But I want to make it absolutely clear that I don't take any responsibility for your actions."

"Understood," I said.

I wondered if his statement would hold in court as his presence sort of indicated that he agreed with what we had planned.

I actually don't know whether anybody can ever be

held responsible for someone else's actions.

"We're here," Tom said.

He parked in the parking lot and killed the engine. There was another car but no sign of Sasha. I checked the time.

"We've got an hour before people show up for night school," I said. "Let's get this over and done with. Marlon, I'll get out first and take you out of the car. Pretend to be my prisoner."

"I'll keep my hands behind my back," he said cheerfully as he pulled his hoodie over his head.

"Great thinking," Tom said. "Do you want me to come?"

"Yeah, I think I do. She's got Arkady, so I can bring you to even the odds. Sue, Grayson, you two to follow us as soon as possible. Try to prevent anybody seeing you, though. I want you as a backup only."

Sue winced but didn't dispute my orders. I caught Grayson's eye and hoped he got my subtle request of keeping Sue safe. He didn't know about Sue's current instability, but he gave me a nod. I returned it with a quick smile.

Tom, Marlon, and I got out of the car. I took in the school's playground. This was the place where it all began so many years ago. This was where I had first bumped into Caleb, where I had fallen in love with him, and the first time I had met Sasha. I automatically looked up in the direction of my former classroom on the top floor of the main building. My heart skipped a beat when I saw Sasha standing at the window of the hallway there. Had she been in the group taking Mr. Finkle? I always thought I had met her for the first time in the schoolyard. I couldn't shake away the shivers that crisscrossed my body, making my muscles move stiffly. Maybe I should've asked Tom to get me something else to wear.

Regardless of the distance, I knew Sasha had seen me. She moved away, into my classroom by the look of it. Why did she pick that location? What a stupid thing to do. I had expected Sasha to be in the open, on the schoolyard behind the toilet block, with multiple escape routes. My classroom had only one way in or out. If she was there, she was trapped. Then I remembered there was another door. This was leading to the storeroom, though, also a dead end.

"We need to go to the top floor," I said to Tom and Marlon. "Sasha's in my old classroom."

We moved toward the school entrance when Tom suddenly stopped me.

"Wait," he said. "We need to think about this carefully. It may be a trap. Why would she pick that room? Could there possibly be more suckers up there?"

"Of course there could be, but there's only one way to find out. The room has only one exit, apart from the door to the storeroom, but that doesn't lead anywhere else. Marlon, keep your eyes peeled. If you see any danger, I want you to back away."

"I will," he said.

"And don't try to speak. She'll immediately know you're not Kostya when you do."

Marlon nodded.

We climbed the stairs to the top floor. More memories of times gone by flashed in front of my eyes. In the hall, I had attacked soldiers for taking Charlie away from me. On the stairs, I had held a gun to Dr. Haley's head. In the hallway upstairs, Mr. Finkle had been taken by suckers. There were so many memories I'd rather forgot. Why in heaven's name did I pick this location?

When we reached my classroom, I held Marlon and Tom back. I peeked into the room through the corner of a window and only saw Sasha.

"Tom, you stay behind with Marlon until we know Sonny's there," I whispered. "Keep an eye out for Arkady, I don't know where he is."

They did as I asked. I saw Grayson and Sue come up the stairs and huddle there. I took a deep breath and entered the room.

Sasha stood near the window, her tall, slim silhouette like a cartoonish nightmare. I still didn't see anybody else in the room. I looked left and right, but there really was no one there.

"Where's my son?" I said.

"He's here," Sasha said. "Give me my son, and you'll

have yours."

She said it in a triumphant sort of way. As if she knew something I didn't. I didn't like it.

"No, I want to know you haven't hurt him first."

"No. You show me you have Kostya, and I'll show you your son."

I called out to Tom to bring Kostya into the room. When Sasha saw what she thought was her son, she called out to Arkady, who apparently was in the storeroom.

"Show him," she said, her eyes never leaving mine.

The door to the storeroom opened a little. Sonny was pushed into the opening. He seemed okay, happy even. Tension left my body for a moment.

Sonny smiled at us. "Mommy, Marlon!" he said elated.

Fuck!

Family Ties

Sasha's head snapped to Marlon, her eyes ablaze. Russian cursing, I assumed, came out of her mouth. Sonny disappeared out of view, and the door was slammed shut. I wasted no time and sprinted across the room. My initial fear was for Sonny's safety, so I made for the storeroom door. Sasha jumped at me, trying to prevent me getting there. From the corner of my eye, I saw Marlon throw himself at her. He blocked Sasha full-bodied, and I heard them crash to the floor behind me.

I ran for the storeroom door. Not stopping to open it the conventional way, I put all of my weight into it. It gave way like cardboard under my new sucker strength. I fell with the door into the room. Arkady stood in between the shelves in the first aisle. He held Sonny in front of him with one hand and had a glass beaker containing a clear liquid in his other hand. I didn't have to guess what the liquid was as the rotten egg smell in the room already told me it was sulfuric acid.

Sonny bumped into Arkady due to the shock of my entrance, and a little acid spilled from the beaker onto the floor. It ate itself into the linoleum, releasing more foul-smelling fumes. A band around my heart squeezed tight when, with an unsure movement, Arkady moved the beaker above Sonny's head. Sonny yelped as Arkady tightened his grip on him. I stretched out my arm toward them, my eyes locked on the beaker.

"Arkady, please, no!"

"Don't get any closer, or I'll do it!" the tall boy yelled at me, an edge to his voice.

Slowly, I stood up. All my muscles tensed, ready to jump at the slightest movement of Arkady's arm. When I was fully upright, and Arkady didn't appear to move, my stare left the beaker, seeking Arkady's eyes to plead with him. When they found them, blood instantly drained from my head. Oxygen deprived, I fought to stay conscious, holding on to the shelving, trying my best not to faint.

No, it can't be!

What I saw was impossible. Caleb was dead. I had burned his body. Yet, right in front of me stood the living version of him. I was looking into the eyes of the man I had loved so many years ago. The man I had shot. The man who had taken a bullet for me and died. The man whose eyes still haunted me almost every night.

"How can this be?" I said under my breath.

"What? What are you talking about? Don't get any closer," Arkady said when I took a step forward.

Hearing his voice made me realize I wasn't seeing a ghost. This wasn't Caleb. This was his son. I shook my head. How could this be? Kostya was the spitting image of Duncan. Yes, Sasha had loved both Duncan and Caleb, but on the same night?

Fuck, this changes everything.

I looked again at the two boys in front of me, struggling to figure out what to do. What was right and what was wrong? They were still fighting in the classroom. Sasha wasn't giving up just like that, but I wasn't worried about her. Marlon and Tom should be able to overpower her soon.

"Arkady, please listen to me," I began. "Sonny's my son."

Arkady only reacted by moving the bottle even closer to Sonny, who looked up at the bottle and tried to move away from it.

"Kady, why are you doing this?" he said. "It stinks, Kady, and you're hurting me."

Arkady threw a glance at Sonny. I could see the pain on his face. It appeared he didn't really want to do this.

"Arkady, listen," I said. "Sonny's father isn't Charlie. Caleb's his father. Your father is Sonny's father, Arkady. Sonny's your half-brother." I inched closer to them while I let the words sink in. Sonny was almost within my reach.

"That's... that's not possible," Arkady said. He pulled Sonny closer to him. "You killed Caleb, during Black October. You shot him. And he's not my father!" The boy was in tears now. He moved to the back of the storeroom, pulling Sonny with him.

I had to tell Arkady the truth which had been denied from him for so long.

"No, Arkady. Caleb didn't die that night. Yes, I shot him, but it was only a warning shot, nothing fatal. The second bullet was an accident as we fell. He was injured badly, but they saved him. He lived in a sucker internment camp for years. A few years ago, we met again. He loved me, Arkady. Your father loved me. And I loved him. I never wanted to kill him."

Liar.

"When we escaped the camp, he took a bullet for me. He saved my life. That's how he died, Arkady. Loving me." I pressed my hands to my chest. The pain of losing Caleb still hurt. "I spent one night with Caleb. Sonny's his son. And I know you're Caleb's son too. You both have his eyes." The words drove home the realization, and my eyes filled with tears.

Sonny put his tiny hand on Arkady's, the one holding the beaker, and looked up at him.

"Kady, you can't kill me now. We're brothers. You don't kill family," he said.

I put my hand over my mouth. Tears I was trying to hold back blurred my sight.

Slowly, Arkady moved the beaker away from Sonny.

"No, I guess not. We don't kill family," he said with a smile. He put the beaker on a shelf behind him.

I let my tears fall. Sonny gave Arkady a big hug. I

rushed forward, plucked my son off Arkady, and gave him the biggest hug ever. On a whim, I pulled Arkady into the hug as well. He hesitated at first but then put his arms around us. Relief washed over me. It was finally over. Sasha was no longer a threat, and Sonny was safe. To top it all, we had gained a new family member.

After I got my emotions under control, I realized there was no more fighting going on next door.

"There's so much I need to tell you, but that can wait. Let's go," I said. I put Sonny down, and he grabbed Arkady's hand, both of them having huge grins on their faces. They followed me into the classroom.

As we entered the room, everyone turned to us. I took in the scene in front of me. Sue was inspecting Marlon's wounds. Tom held Sasha by her upper arms. Grayson had his handcuffs out and was about to put them on her.

"There's a first aid kit in the front desk," I said.

Marlon moved to get it.

I followed Sasha's gaze which fell upon Arkady and Sonny holding hands. Hatred oozed out of her aura. In a sudden upwelling of fury, she kicked Tom to the side of his leg where she had shot him before. While Tom screamed in pain and let go of her to grab his leg, Sasha dove for Sonny. Arkady was faster than I was and flung Sonny into my arms. In the meantime, Sue had seen Sasha's reaction and dove after her. She pushed Sasha with all her might away from where Sonny had been. Sasha couldn't stop her momentum. She fell on Arkady, and the two of them crashed through the window.

I let Sonny slip to the floor. With dread, headed over to the window and carefully looked out over the broken glass and down. Arkady hung with one hand from the window sill, blood and glass on his face. Sasha clung to his leg.

"Hold on," I said to Arkady as I threw my arm at him.

He swung his free arm up, and I pulled him by his sleeve, so he could grab the window sill with two hands. I tried to hoist the rest of him up, but the glass was in the way. Tom had joined me and started pulling the broken glass from the window frame. I glanced beyond at Sasha, checking if she was in dire need of help. When my gaze found hers, it found the same hatred she had always had for me.

"Sasha, hold on. Let me help you." I pulled a piece of glass out of the way, leaned over, and stretched my hand out to her.

"Why would I want your help?" she said. "You'll just throw me back into jail for killing Charlie."

"No, I won't. Charlie isn't dead. The bullet missed his heart. He's had surgery, but he'll live. Besides, you and I both know it was an accident." I hoped she'd take my peace offer.

Her gaze held me for a moment before resting back on my other hand holding onto her son.

"You may take my sons, but you'll never take me."

She let go.

A New Direction

Sasha fell to the ground and bounced up with the ease of an alley cat. Without looking up, she sped off.

We carefully hoisted Arkady back inside.

"Are you okay?" I asked once he had both his feet on the floor.

"Yes, thanks. I'm fine," Arkady said. He leaned out of the window as he shook the glass from him. I noticed him checking left and right, but his mother was already gone.

"I'm sorry, Arkady. I don't want to come between you and your mother. I would have helped her if she'd let me."

"I know. I don't think she wants to be helped, though. Not by you, anyway."

"No, I don't think so either."

Sonny dragged Sue over to Arkady.

"Sue, this is Kady. He's my half-brother," he said to her. His whole face beamed with the message.

"Nice to meet you," Sue said, uncertain of how to react.

"Likewise," Arkady said. "And you are?"

"Sue's my half-sister," Sonny said before Sue could answer. Suddenly, he frowned. "Mommy, if Kady's my half-brother and Sue's my half-sister, does that mean that they are whole brother and sister?"

"No, Little Man, Arkady's mommy and daddy are not Sue's."

Sonny had to think about that one.

"Please, call me Kady," the tall boy said. "Everybody else does."

"I hate to break up the happy family reunion, but I must take this man into custody," Grayson said. "He's a suspect of two kidnaps." He turned Kady around and handcuffed him. Kady let him without a struggle. I thought the cuffing was unnecessary but wasn't going to oppose Grayson.

"We'll come and see you tomorrow," I said as I put my hand on Kady's arm.

He nodded. "I'd like that."

Sonny gave Kady another big hug, his little arms around the tall boy's legs.

"See you soon, big half-brother," he said as he looked up.

"I'll be looking forward to that, little half-brother," Kady replied and winked at Sonny.

The boy didn't look as bad as his twin brother had seemed. Something told me that the two of them not only resembled their fathers physically but also psychologically.

I went to Marlon, and he winced when I touched his bruised face.

"I'll live," he said, and Sue kissed him. He was lucky he didn't have a split lip.

"I'll make sure of that," she whispered to him.

"Well, in the meantime, let me do what I can," I said as I retrieved the first aid kit.

I took my time taking care of Marlon's wounds. When I finished, I took care of Tom's wounds as good as I could. The ones from yesterday had already begun to heal, and his face now sported a kaleidoscope of colors. I also checked if there were any glass splinters in Kady's face and cleaned up his cuts as well as I could.

When I was done, Grayson guided Kady out of the classroom. We all followed them down the hallway.

"Are you okay?" I asked Tom. My fingers traced the scratches Sasha's nails had left on his face. I had covered them with iodine, making the skin around them orange, and the wounds look twice as bad.

"Yes, I'll live, but boy, can that woman fight." He moved his lower jaw from left to right. "Throws a mean punch too."

I chuckled. "Don't tell me you thought women couldn't fight."

Tom dipped his head toward me.

"I know from experience they can."

"Let's not get behind," I said, smiling, and together we caught up with the rest.

As we walked downstairs, Tom dipped his mouth to my ear again.

"Houston, we have a problem," he whispered.

A pang of alarm shot through me. Was he injured more than he had initially told me? Would his leg wound be bleeding again?

"What is it?" I said, dreading his reply.

"Don't tell anyone, but we won't all fit in my car," he said.

My eyes met his, and I began to giggle. Sue and Marlon glanced back at us, clearly wondering what had gotten into me. Seeing their faces made me laugh even harder. When we arrived at the car, Grayson looked at it and scratched the top of his head. I was roaring now, having trouble keeping myself on my feet, tears of laughter streaming down my face. Tom, who was also laughing, helped keeping me upright while trying to explain to Sue and Marlon what was happening.

Sue's cell phone rang, and she answered it. The conversation was short. Her face turned ashen.

"What is it?" I asked as I wiped the tears from my face.

"That was Alex. She said she was leaving for school when she noticed an unknown car speeding out of our driveway, and that our door was open. She decided to check it out. The door appeared to have been kicked in and our home trashed."

"That must have been Sasha," Marlon said. "She's pissed off because I beat her up. This is her way to get back to us."

"That's not all," Sue said. "Sasha wrote on the wall with red sauce. It says, 'The dwarf is next.'"

Killing A Vampire

The news made my giggle fit disappear instantaneously. I had to get to Charlie as soon as possible. Sasha now knew he was at the hospital and he was in no state to defend himself.

"I'm sorry, guys. I need to go," I said as I put my hand on the car door handle.

"I'm coming with you," Sue said and moved to get into the car as well.

"No, Little Smudge," I said and put my hand on her arm. "I need you to keep Sonny safe for me." I couldn't risk her coming with me and giving Sasha another opportunity to do my family harm.

"I'll walk them to the police station," Grayson said before Sue could utter an objection. "That's the safest place for them at the moment."

"Thanks. Please let the police in Portland know they need to get to the hospital."

"I will," Grayson said.

Without a word, I got into the car and slammed the door shut. Tom had already taken his place behind the wheel, and with squealing tires, we left the school ground.

After I managed to put my seatbelt on, I called Julie.

"Hi sis," she said when she answered. "He's not awake yet but doing fine."

"Jules, she's on her way! We got Sonny back, unharmed, but Sasha escaped and went to the farm. She trashed Sue and Marlon's place. Now she's out to get Charlie!"

"Damn," Julie said. "I'll tell the staff here and see what we can do."

"Grayson is warning the police, so you may get some help. Tom and I are on our way, but I don't think we'll make it in time." I took a breath to say something, hesitated, then said it anyway. "Please, Jules. Keep Charlie safe for me." I knew it was obvious, but I had to say it.

"Of course, you know I will," she said.

"Love you. You take care of yourself."

"You know me. Love you too."

I smiled, knowing she couldn't see it. "See you soon, sis."

"See you soon. Gotta go now," she said and ended our conversation.

As I put my cell phone away, my acid reflux hurt. If I didn't know any better, I felt like I was having a heart attack. It wouldn't be unexpected, considering the stress of the situation. Sasha, who had turned, was on a mission of destruction, and I wouldn't be there to protect Julie or Charlie. I hoped with all my heart that the police would stop Sasha in time.

Tom didn't keep to the speed limit, testing the car's abilities to the max. He had to slow down once we crossed Portland's city limits. The closer we came to Maine Medical Center, the more obvious it became Sasha didn't seem worried anymore about doing her evil work without leaving a trace. It was as if she had plowed her way through traffic. There were damaged cars on the side of the road everywhere. Tom weaved through the wreckage and made it to the entrance of the hospital where we found her wrecked and abandoned car. There were also four police cars. All of their lights were flashing, making the wall of the hospital a maniacal vision.

Tom and I ran into the building. Inside, there was chaos and carnage. People screamed and ran around, some of them covered in blood. I couldn't imagine Sasha hurting all these innocent people, not after she shot Tom in the leg instead of killing him. Tom grabbed the first police officer we came across. He pulled out his FBI ID from his back pocket.

"Special Agent Moore. Where's the woman from the car outside?" he asked.

"I'm not sure," the officer said.

"Come with us," I said. "We know where she's going."

Tom and I ran to the elevators, the police officer followed us. We took the first elevator available.

"What's happened so far?" I asked after the doors

closed, and I pressed the button to the fourth floor, to Charlie's room, about twenty times.

"We were called in for a revenge-type situation," he said. "We expected a sucker woman to come in to try to get to a particular patient. The staff was alerted and refused to hand out the information. We hadn't expected the woman going crazy. She just started ripping out throats. The first victims were the two officers who tried to stop her. She kept on going until she got the information she wanted. We had sent two officers earlier, to guard this patient. They moved him to another room, just in case. They have been notified and have now been ordered to shoot on sight. In the meantime, we're waiting for a SWAT team, you know, the fully armed and protected guys. Hey, aren't you that SAMM woman?"

"Yes, I am. And that sucker woman you're talking about is on her way to kill my partner."

"Oh," he said, "bummer."

The understatement of the year.

The elevator doors opened. I stormed out and ran in the direction of Charlie's room. Just before we arrived at the last corner, we heard shots fired and a man screaming. Tom held us back. He did a quick peek around the corner. The screaming stopped.

"Clear," he said. We ran toward Charlie's room. One of the police officers lay on the floor, his throat ripped out. The other officer sat leaning against the wall, still alive but clutching his neck, struggling for breath. Tom kneeled down next to the man, putting pressure on the wound to stop the blood gushing out. I noticed the holster of the man was empty. We heard fighting going on in Charlie's room.

The officer who had come with us took his gun out, aiming it at the door.

"Let's go," I said to him.

Suddenly, a shot was fired in the room and the fighting stopped. Was I too late? I wanted to run into the room, but the officer held me back. With his gun out in front of him, he went in before me. As soon as he entered the room, more shots were fired. The officer fell back against me, his body going down like a bag of potatoes. I caught him and saw multiple blood stains grow on his uniform. I shook my head in Tom's direction. He let his head fall. I prized the gun from the hand of the dead man and lifted his body in front of me as a shield. Tom tried to stop me but couldn't let go of the injured man's throat if he wanted him to stay alive. I ignored his shouts and entered the room.

My eyes had to adjust to the low light level. Sasha fired more shots, the corpse jolting with the hits until I heard only clicks. I peeked around the body. When I saw Sasha dive away, I pointed the gun in her direction and pulled the trigger. Sasha screamed. Had I hit her?

Keeping the officer's body upright, I made my way further into the room. I now had a clear shot of Sasha, who crouched in a corner, and I pulled the trigger. It, too, clicked empty. I let the body of the police officer slide to the floor and threw the gun away. My eyes had now adjusted to the glow of the minimal bedhead light. A flighty scan around the room made my fears real. It was Julie's body on the floor. She was lying face down in the middle of the room, blood pooling around her. I ducked down and checked her pulse. I had trouble finding one, but it was there, rapid and weak.

Sasha jumped onto the bed. I didn't know if Charlie was still alive, but if he was, it wouldn't be for long if I didn't do something fast. As I moved to jump, my foot slipped on the blood-covered floor. I hit my knee cap on the ground, and pain shot through my leg, immobilizing me for a second. By the time I looked up, Sasha bared her fangs at me, then at Charlie. She pulled away the sheets, driving her fangs into Charlie's throat. Or so she thought. She got a mouthful of pillows instead.

Sasha's roar of anger was the most frightening sound I had ever heard. I lunged again, this time making sure I didn't slip, and I pulled her off the bed. We fell to the ground. I jumped up immediately, ready to take her on. Sasha also sprung to her feet. Her wig had come off in the fall, and her face could have come straight out of hell. Her black eyes shot fire as she directed all her anger toward me. Finally, she was going to deal with the root of her problem. Finally, the fight was going to be between her and me.

Come and get it!

She lunged at me. I was able to move sideways and fend off her attack, but she soon recovered and came at me again. It took quite some effort not to step onto the two bodies or slip on the blood covering the floor. I used all the defense moves Marlon had taught me, keeping myself out of her reach. I managed to throw in some counter moves, but I had to come up with a more permanent solution as I wouldn't be able to keep this up for long.

At some point, I pushed Sasha off, and she slid away from me through the blood. This was my moment. I grabbed the end of the bed and swung my legs at her. I caught her around her neck, and with the momentum of my body, I threw her onto the floor. Unfortunately, I landed badly with Sasha's weight on my already sore knee. I screamed out in pain. Did I tear a tendon? It felt like I did.

We both struggled to get up again. Before I knew it, Sasha reached out and grabbed me by my throat. I could only just slip my hand in between. No doubt she would have ripped out my voice box if I hadn't. With my free hand, I tried to claw at her eyes. She pulled back her face, but instead of grabbing my wrist, her other arm hung limp next to her body. I began to feel lightheaded as her grip on my throat was still powerful. Why didn't she use her other arm?

It was then that the dim light reflected off the blood staining her shirt. Apparently, someone had put a bullet into her shoulder. I stretched and jammed my index finger into the bullet wound. Sasha screamed in agony and let go of me. We both pulled back into safety.

We stood there, catching our breath.

"Let it go, Sasha," I panted. "I don't want to hurt you."

Are you sure?

"Never! You took everything from me. All I had, all I worked for. You took my lover, my looks, and now my sons. I have nothing to live for. Only to kill you."

Joanne's words came back to me. Despite of what the woman had tried to tell me, I had to convince Sasha to stop. The only other option was that one of us would die tonight. An option that had a too uncertain outcome for my liking.

We circled each other as we spoke, Sasha clutching her limp arm, me limping on my injured leg.

"Look, you think I killed Caleb, but I didn't. He lived. He died three years ago when he took a bullet for me while I was escaping the sucker internment camp. I never wanted to kill him, Sasha. I loved him. Sonny's his son."

Sasha gasped at my words.

"We all make mistakes," I continued. "But there's time to change things. We can work this out. Kady's Caleb's son. You know this. Heaven knows why you never told him, but there's no denying it. He's got Caleb's eyes. Sonny's Caleb's son too, so they're half-brothers. That sort of makes you family. You don't kill family. Kady said so himself. You'll never see Kady again if you kill me." I hoped Sasha could be persuaded to stop fighting if I mentioned her son in the conversation. It was clutching at straws, but I couldn't think of anything else at the moment.

Before she could say something, Sasha's attention was drawn to something behind me. I threw a glance over my shoulder and saw a SWAT team officer, completely dressed in bullet-proof vest and helmet, enter the room. His arms were outstretched, pointing a gun.

Sasha roared. I turned back to her, only to see her move from a crouch into a jump. She came straight at me, her claws reaching for my face. As she flew through the air, I had less than a split second to react. I threw my body at the SWAT team guy, put my hands over the man's hands, and pulled the trigger several times. Sasha's body twitched in the air as the bullets hit her. The three of us collided and fell to the floor.

When the sounds had died, another tactical team member peeked into the room. His mate on the floor signed that all was okay. The guy at the door gave the message to the people in the hallway. Immediately, Tom pushed his way into the room. He pulled Sasha off me and onto her back. Multiple bullet wounds in her head and torso oozed blood. She would not be getting up again.

"Julie," I panted. "Check Julie."

Tom moved away from Sasha's body, and I, too, scrambled over the floor toward my sister. Tom helped me turn her around. Her face was as white as a sheet. I feared she was dead, and I was about to start wailing when Julie suddenly opened her eyes. I couldn't believe she made it.

"Julie! Jules, you silly girl. What did you do?" I cried. I inspected her body, but it was unclear what the problem was. It was too dark in the room.

"Can somebody put the fucking light on!" I yelled.

Someone flicked the switch. I could now see that Julie's entire shirt was covered in blood.

Tom got up and yelled for a doctor. He disappeared into the corridor.

I cradled Julie's head in my lap and stroked her hair.

"I thought I could stop her," Julie said.

"Oh, stupid cow. I didn't want you to do that. Don't you die on me now, you hear. Don't you die." Tears poured down my cheeks.

"Kate, I can't feel my legs."

My whole body felt numb as I regarded Julie's unmoving legs.

A doctor kneeled next to us and ripped open Julie's shirt. A tiny hole in Julie's abdomen oozed blood. The doctor immediately put pressure on Julie's wound and called for a rapid response team. Tom helped me up as a team of nurses and doctors came into the room to tend to Julie. She was heaved onto a gurney and rushed out.

Both the dead officer's body and Sasha's body were checked but left for the forensic team to deal with.

A bit lost and forlorn with all that was happening, Tom and I went into the corridor. A man walked up to us. I recognized him as the Portland detective that had interrogated me earlier. He interrogated us and took notes. When he was done, he told us not to leave town and left. We were alone again.

A nurse hurried past.

"Please," I said as I stopped him. "Can you tell me where Charlie is? The man who was supposed to be in this room? I'm his partner."

"Sure," he said. "He's two rooms up."

I let go of him, and he hurried along on his way to save more lives. Tom and I walked over to the indicated room. I stopped before entering and looked up at Tom.

"I'll be here if you need me," he said.

His face was still swollen, scratched, and bloodied. I owed him so much and had no idea how to thank him. I moved onto my tippy-toes, pulled him closer by his neck, and kissed him on his least injured cheek.

"Thank you. For everything."

"Anytime, Kate. Anytime." The corners of his mouth curled up again, and we held each other's stare for a moment.

I let go, pulled my dress down, and opened the door to Charlie's room.

Reunion

The room was dark except for that ridiculous, little light above the hospital bed, which cast a warm glow over Charlie. There were all sorts of wires and tubes attached to him. The one thing that piqued my interest for a moment was the blood bag feeding his vein. A wave of saliva washed through my mouth. I swallowed and focused on Charlie. I closed the door behind me, and Charlie's head moved toward the sound.

"Hey, you're awake," I said and walked over. I took his hand in mine and kissed him. It was a light kiss as Charlie's breathing was very shallow. "How are you feeling?"

"Much better... now I know... you're safe," he managed to say. His words were interspersed with his deliberate breathing. His gaze fell on the blood covering my face and he reached out. "Are you hurt?"

"No, don't worry. It's not my blood."

His breathing became more labored.

"Does it hurt? Do you want me to call a nurse?"

Charlie lifted his free arm and made a vague wave gesture.

"I'm fine," he said.

I sat down and kissed his hand. It hurt me so much

to see him like this.

We didn't say anything for a while.

"I'm so sorry, Charlie. I shouldn't have said what I said. You're the best daddy ever. Sonny loves you. I love you." I held his hand to my cheek, my tears wetting it.

Charlie frowned at me at first, and then smiled.

"I'd already... forgotten," he said. "I shouldn't... have nagged you... about Sonny."

I grinned. Usually, I was the nagger.

"I know you meant well, Smudge. You were right." I sighed. "I think I should rethink my involvement with SAMM."

Charlie squeezed my hand as he tried to sit up.

"Don't you dare... stop doing... what you're doing," he managed to say. The heart rate monitor began beeping faster, and I got half out of my seat.

"Don't. Lay down. Don't you stress about it." I worried he would tear stitches and open wounds if he moved. "I won't quit completely, never completely."

There were serious doubts flying through my mind right now about what was right for Sonny, Sue, and Charlie, though. I had never calculated myself into the equation when working for SAMM, doing all I could for the suckers, but I had forgotten it affected them as well.

Charlie held his intense stare.

"We'll talk about it when you feel better, okay?"

Charlie relaxed a little. Then he tensed again.

"Is... is Sasha...?"

I nodded.

"She's gone. She got to your room, but fortunately, you had been moved. When she realized she couldn't get to you, she wanted to kill me. I tried to convince her otherwise, but she wouldn't listen. I had no other choice but to shoot her. It was self-defense."

Charlie looked away for a moment.

"What about... her sons?"

"Both in custody. Did you realize Kostya is Duncan's son while Arkady's Caleb's son?"

Charlie nodded.

"Kady's... a nice boy," he said. "He gave me food... and water."

"Yes, we figured that out too. Sonny's over the moon he has a half-brother."

Charlie pulled a face that told me he wasn't quite sure if he was happy about that statement.

"We'll go and see him when you get out of here, and you're ready to face him again."

Charlie sighed and lifted his free arm a little before letting it flop onto the bed in a sign of frustration. I wanted to console him so badly, make him feel better. Was it a good idea to tell him about Julie now or was it better to wait? I guessed now was a good a time as any, better to get it over and done with.

"You won't be the only one staying here, Smudge."

He looked at me in alarm.

"Julie got shot. The silly cow thought she could stop Sasha. She's in surgery now. Just before she passed out, she said she couldn't feel her legs. I have no idea what the extent of her injury is yet."

Charlie's breathing became erratic. Tears streamed from the sides of his eyes.

"She'll be okay. They're doing the best they can." I stroked his face and kissed his hand until he had calmed down a little.

"She told me...She told me what... she'd said... to you... She felt bad... She wanted... to make it right... I didn't want... her to. Couldn't do... anything." His body cramped up in frustration and pain, causing various machines next to him to start beeping in alarm.

"Shhh. There was nothing you could have done, Smudge. It was her choice."

Deep down, I felt responsible for Julie's predicament. I was the one who'd asked her to keep Charlie safe. I could've let the police deal with it. If anyone was to blame, it was me.

"It's not your fault," I said again to Charlie.

A nurse came in and checked Charlie's monitors. She adjusted a drip.

"He needs to rest now," she said to me.

I nodded, and she left.

"I've got to go. I'm going to check up on Julie. Sue and Sonny are at the police station in Bullsbrook. I'll bring them for a visit tomorrow. You go and rest now."

Charlie nodded, and I got up.

There was one thing still on my mind I didn't have an answer to. It would bug me forever if I didn't ask.

"Smudge... why did you say 'let me die' when I was trying to get you out of the house?"

Charlie looked at me as he squeezed my hand.

"I wanted you... to go... to be safe. Didn't want... you to get... caught." His face was as apologetic as it could get.

You've got to be kidding me.

"So you didn't want to die?"

He didn't move immediately and then tipped his head ever so slightly to the side. Had he really contemplated dying? Had I really driven him so far? Had they tortured him so much he didn't see a way out?

"I'm glad... you saved... me... I love you."

I pursed my lips and squeezed his hand.

"You, my man, are the worst person to express himself."

"Says who?" he said, a quick smile on his lips.

"Touché." I gave him a flighty kiss. "Go and sleep now. I'll be back as soon as I can."

Charlie closed his eyes and nodded. His skin was still very pale. Reluctant to leave him, I kissed his hand one more time before I left.

***

I found Tom sitting a little further in the corridor. The hospital was quiet once again, and there was no one else around.

"Hey, Sunshine. How's he doing?" he asked.

"He's doing okay. He's very tired, but it seems he's going to be alright. Have you heard anything yet about Julie?"

Tom shook his head. I sat down next to him. I called Sue and let her know what had happened. She had already heard from Grayson through the Portland detective but was so relieved that we were okay. She was sad to hear about Julie. I told her I'd let her know as soon as I had news from the surgeon. For now, I wanted her to go home to our place and take Sonny with her, so he could sleep in his own bed again. I told her she and Marlon could sleep in my bed as I planned to stay at the hospital overnight, and that tomorrow morning, they could come and visit Charlie and Julie. Sue agreed, and we said our goodbyes.

"Do you want me to stay?" Tom asked.

I put my hand on his.

"No, I'll be fine. But thank you for offering. I don't know what I would've done without you."

"I'm sure you'd have managed just fine without me, Kate. That's the kind of person you are," he said.

"Right." I looked away.

Let's agree to disagree.

Tom put his hand in his pocket and pulled out a

syringe. He handed it to me.

"It's not as bad as going in," he said, "but do take some aspirin. Those fangs going back up again are a killer, or so I've heard."

"They go back up?" That was something the original vaccine didn't do. I was rather disappointed about this new development.

"Yeah, they do. They're still working on getting rid of the whole fang and blood-thirst issue, but it's already progress you don't need any surgery."

"You've got that right. Thanks." I pocketed the syringe.

Tom got up, and I followed suit.

"I'll be seeing you around," he said and turned to leave.

I grabbed him by his sleeve and pulled him back. I threw my arms around his body and hugged him. He put his arms around me and kissed my head. I kept him close, breathing in his scent once more, until it became awkward. When I finally let him go, he took both my hands and kissed them. He walked away without looking back.

I stood staring in the direction he left until I heard a familiar nasal sound behind me calling my name. I turned around and found Rhona and Harry hurrying up the hallway. We sat down, and I told them all that had happened.

Epilogue

It appeared that the bullet that had taken Julie down had lodged itself in her spine. The surgeon was able to take it out, but substantial damage was done, and Julie became wheelchair bound. She was still able to do her job as she did most from her office, anyway. Her apartment had to be adjusted, but that was no issue at all. I did a public call for help, and we received a seriously generous gift from an unknown donor which made the transition for Julie easy, financially and time-wise. The works were all done before she was dismissed by her doctors.

Grayson insisted on picking Julie up from the hospital and bringing her home. He had been visiting her on a daily basis and the fact that she was now wheelchair-bound didn't shy him away from the relationship. He never moved in with her, claiming his job was too demanding for that, but they were happy when they were together. I warmed up to him once I saw how much he cared for her. He wasn't a bad person, just not someone who ticked my boxes. He ticked Julie's, though, and she his. I was happy for them.

When I went to pick up Sue, Marlon, and Sonny the day after the shooting, I found my lawn filled with paparazzi again. As I worked my way through the mayhem to my front door, I realized they were interviewing Sue. She was answering their questions like a veteran. I had always tried to keep her away from the media, but maybe I had done the wrong thing. She seemed to be thriving on all the attention. On our way toward the hospital, I mentioned my decision to take a step back from SAMM, and Sue didn't hesitate to say she wouldn't mind taking over my role. She told me she loved talking to the press, and I knew she would beat this PTSD soon. After the event, she frequented Dr. Strang less and less and slept better without any drugs. It was like a miracle.

Charlie's finger was accepted by his body and he regained full function of his hand again with only a tingling and the scars remaining as evidence of what had happened. When the doctors were certain the finger 'took,' they vaccinated him. As soon as Charlie was able, he told the police about his kidnap experience. Sasha had tortured him, cutting off his finger and ear while Kostya had held him down. Kostya had been the one to put the cigarette marks on him and biting him repeatedly, using him as his personal blood supply. Arkady had refused to be part of any of the torture. He had been the one that had taken care of Charlie, feeding him, giving him water, and providing him with the bucket after Sasha had refused to let Charlie use the toilet. As a result, Kostya was sentenced to a lifetime in prison.

Arkady only had to sit out a relatively short sentence for the kidnapping of Charlie and Sonny, which he insisted he had been forced to do by his mother and brother. Sonny had wanted to visit his half-brother every day but agreed to twice a week after I explained to him how far away the sucker prison was. They became very good friends when Kady was finally released. Marlon arranged for Kady to get a job on the farm, and he was happy there. He more or less became part of our family. Even Charlie overcame his initial aversion to having him around.

John Smith, in another twist of Sasha's schemes, appeared to be the owner of the house where we found Charlie. He was charged with a five-year imprisonment for knowingly harboring a fugitive who committed serious crimes. He finally had his comeuppance.

As expected, there was an outcry over the slaughter Sasha had left in her wake at the hospital. There hadn't been violence like this in Maine for a long time. When it was explained to the public that it had been a revenge spree, the whole fuss about it died down quickly, the sucker crime forgotten by most people like any other violent crime in the country. It was evidence that suckers were well and truly accepted as part of our society.

I made sure I didn't work for SAMM for a few weeks when Charlie was dismissed from the hospital, and I cherished our time together while he was off work as well. Charlie was adamant to go back to work as soon as possible, though, and who was I to stop him?

The whole of last week made it clear to me I needed to spend more time with my family. Before Charlie was back home, Sue and I worked together for a while to let her get the hang of being a spokesperson for SAMM. I spent more time together with her, which I loved, and I took more time to spend with Sonny. Charlie had still been disappointed when I told him I was laying down my role for SAMM and tried to persuade me not to, but I kept my ground. He accepted my decision when I told him I was going to keep working behind the scenes. It meant shorter hours and less being away from home, which meant a more stable situation for Sonny. He couldn't agree more with that.

The only thing I was pretty active about, before handing over my job to Sue, was getting all the malls to be open twenty-four/seven. I hadn't forgotten my experience while in 'Bat Beats,' and through pulling a few Council strings and promising the shop owners a better turnover, the malls were soon open day and night for the public. It was another win for suckers through SAMM.

I convinced Charlie to move to a new house. I couldn't stand being reminded of the anxious times I spent in our old one. We soon found a house close to the school that had a lovelier garden and a larger shed that Charlie loved. The house also had more bedrooms which were a bonus when we had Kady or Sue and Marlon come over for a sleepover.

I didn't see Tom for months after the shooting. One day, I saw him again at Rhona and Harry's place. I gave him a big hug that I held a bit longer than was necessary, inhaling in his oceanic scent that brought up fond memories. He told me that his falling-out with the Bratva Boss had been settled when Sasha had died. It appeared the Boss had agreed to Sasha's request, to let her have her revenge, only out of pity for his former lover. She had been emotionally blackmailing him since she had been released from prison, and he was glad to be rid of her.

The reason Tom had disappeared for a couple of months was because his FBI cover had been blown during the broadcast. His bosses had thought it better for him to lie low for a while. I was able to convince Tom to tell Harry and Rhona what he did for a living. They were very surprised, and Rhona, over time, changed her attitude toward him which made his visits less unpleasant and more frequent.

I had dreaded Tom's reaction toward Charlie the first time the three of us were in the same room. It was a surprise Tom seemed to be happy seeing Charlie and me together, and there was no jealousy on Tom's part. Charlie had been very thankful Tom had helped saving him and Sonny. He became a good friend of ours.

Sometimes, though, I would catch Tom sitting all alone in a corner, his eyes on me but glazed over. When he would suddenly notice me looking at him, his cheeky grin would appear. I would have to look away blushing. Never again did we talk about what happened that night.

Charlie and I, after years and years, finally tied the knot. We got married in a little chapel and had a huge wedding party afterward. Charlie accepted Sonny officially as his son, letting him call him 'Dad,' and I cried once I had the papers in my hands. I was so happy. I loved Charlie, I loved my family, and I loved finally living my suburban dream life.

THE END

Releasing A Vampire

Prequel

Settle into a cozy corner with this novelette and find out about the events that lead up to the action-packed, suspenseful urban fantasy yet funny Suckers Trilogy.

Who created the deadly *Succedaneum* virus? What was it meant to do? How did it escape into the world?

What relationship did Kate have with Charlie before the virus broke out? What was her life like when Black October began? How did Kate deal with her world falling apart?

Living Like a Vampire

Book 1

Kate is trying very hard to stay alive in a world thrown into chaos. Charlie is trying very hard to get Kate to notice him. When Caleb comes to the scene, things change, but is it for the better?

Kate had just begun her new job as a high school science teacher and was looking forward to living a suburban dream life. All her hopes and dreams turn into smoke as a virus turns people into vampires roaming the world in packs and killing everybody they can get their hands on. Together with her friends Sue and Charlie, she hides at a campground. They think they are safe there. They are wrong.

They are attacked by a pack of suckers and Kate has to flee again. She gets separated from her friends, accidentally bumps into a handsome sucker who then mysteriously disappears, after which she has to pretend to be a sucker to stay alive. Having met Caleb, surviving is no longer the only thing on Kate's mind.

Will Kate stay alive and human while pursuing this mysterious stranger?

Pick up this action-packed, fast-paced, suspenseful novel and explore the depths of Kate's emotions as she struggles to make sense of it all.

Raising A Vampire

Book 2

Kate and her little family have lead a quiet life. An unfortunate event sees Kate following her daughter into prison. Events drive the happy family apart.

One day, Kate makes the mistake to invite a colleague into her home. He betrays her trust and commits an act of violence. When Kate's daughter comes to the rescue, she exposes herself for what she really is; a sucker. Kate accompanies her daughter when she is sent to a sucker internment camp. The situation quickly spirals downhill when an old flame from the past turns up and rekindles Kate's love for him.

Once more, Kate is thrown into turmoil and heartache.

Join Kate as she struggles with the loss of a good friend, as she pushes her daughter away from her instead of keeping her on the right path, and as she tries to stay faithful to her partner.

Can Kate keep her family and her wits together?

Review

Dear Reader,

If you liked reading my novel, please write a review on your favorite book retailer's website. Every review helps me forward as an author (and I love reading them!).

If you really, really like my writing, why not sign up for my newsletter in online magazine form? It contains author interviews, short stories, promos, and freebies. You can sign up for it on the home page of my website (jackydahlhaus.com), and when you do, you'll receive the Prequel novelette to the Suckers trilogy, Releasing A Vampire, for FREE!

With kind regards,

Jacky Dahlhaus

Connect

You can connect with me via:

Email:
jackydahlhaus@gmail.com

Twitter:
https://twitter.com/JackyDahlhaus

Instagram:
https://www.instagram.com/jackydahlhaus/

Facebook:
https://www.facebook.com/Jacky-Dahlhaus-Author-166614624053352/

My Website:
https://jackydahlhaus.com

Thank you so much for reading, and I hope to read your review soon, see your name on my mailing list, and be able to send you updates on my next book!

Jacky Dahlhaus

Acknowledgements

The Suckers trilogy is finished, and I'm extremely proud I did it. I wouldn't have been able to create these awesome stories without the help of my dear Canadian friend Stephanie, my American/Egyptian friend Kathleen, my Russian friend Ekaterina, and my all my friends from the Suckers Launch Team. I appreciate you giving up your precious time to read my books and make me learn yet new things about the English language. I thank you from the bottom of my heart!

Thanks go out to my dear children, who have helped me when I was stuck with my plot, and who let me know when I needed to improve a sentence structure. Your input was much appreciated.

As always, I wouldn't have been able to do all this work if it hadn't been for the love and support of my dear husband. I love you with all my heart.

Jacky Dahlhaus

About the Author

Jacky Dahlhaus has worked many jobs and tried many hobbies before she realized writing gave her such pleasure. She loves to write paranormal fantasy stories while delving into the human psyche with all its faults and mysteries.

Next to writing novels, Jacky helps indie authors by promoting them on her blog, writes an online newsletter/magazine, runs writing clubs (for adults and children) at the local library, and is a writer and director for Aberdeenshire Film Productions.

When not busy with the above (which is rare nowadays), Jacky works on renovating her Scottish Victorian home, watches movies with her family, and tries to stop her two Jack Russells from barking for no good reason.

Killing A Vampire is her third novel and the last book in the Suckers trilogy.

jackydahlhaus.com